# KISS

'At the heart of KISS . . . is an emotional truthfulness, courage and comedy'
*The Times*

♥

'A sensitive tale of sexuality and love'
*Independent*

♥

'A beautiful and touching story about love and whom it's directed to'
*First News*

♥

'KISS is a must-read for teens and parents alike'
*Irish Independent*

♥

'Wilson, renowned for tackling issues other children's writers don't, writes beautifully about first love, lost love and gay love. It's a great read for both boys and girls'
*Sunday Tribune*

Join the official Jacqueline Wilson fan club at
www.jacquelinewilson.co.uk

# KISS

## Jacqueline Wilson

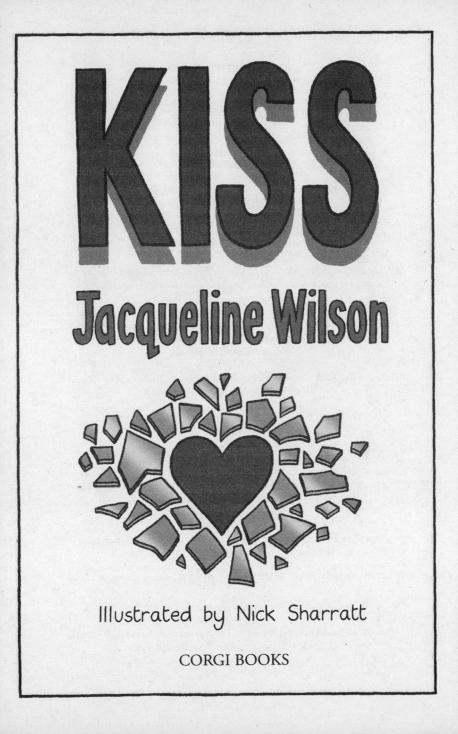

Illustrated by Nick Sharratt

CORGI BOOKS

KISS

A CORGI BOOK 978 0 552 55441 1

First published in Great Britain by Doubleday,
an imprint of Random House Children's Books
A Random House Group Company

Doubleday edition published 2007
Corgi edition published 2008

3 5 7 9 10 8 6 4 2

Corgi Books are published by Random House Children's Books,
61–63 Uxbridge Road, London W5 5SA

www.**kids**at**randomhouse**.co.uk
www.**rbooks**.co.uk

The Random House Group Limited supports The Forest Stewardship
Council (FSC), the leading international forest certification organisation. All our
titles that are printed on Greenpeace approved FSC certified paper carry the FSC logo.
Our paper procurement policy can be found at
www.rbooks.co.uk/environment

Addresses for companies within The Random House Group Limited can
be found at: www.randomhouse.co.uk/offices.htm

THE RANDOM HOUSE GROUP Limited Reg. No. 954009

A CIP catalogue record for this book is available from the British Library.

Printed and bound in Great Britain by CPI Bookmarque, Croydon, CR0 4TD

*To Vicky Ireland*

I hated lunch times. I always missed Carl so much.

When we were in middle school we spent all our time together. We'd rush off the moment the bell went, shovel down our school dinners in ten minutes flat, and then we'd have a whole hour just being *us*. We'd sneak off to one of our special favourite places. When it was sunny we'd sprawl by the sandpit or sit kicking our legs on the wall near the bike sheds. We'd lurk in the library most of the winter. It didn't really matter where we were, just so long as we were together.

Some days we didn't talk much; we just read our books, chuckling or commenting every now and then. Sometimes we drew together or played silly paper games. But *most* days we'd invent another episode of Glassworld. We'd act it out, though we couldn't do it properly at school the way we could inside the Glass Hut. The other kids thought us weird enough as it was. If they came across us declaring undying love as King Carlo and Queen Sylviana they'd fall about laughing. We'd mutter under our breath and make minute gestures and the magic would start working and we'd be whirled off to the glitter of Glassworld.

It was always a shock when the bell rang for afternoon school, shattering our crystal crowns and glass boots. We trudged back along the pizza-smelling corridors in our shabby trainers, wishing we could stay in Glassworld for ever.

I still kept the Glassworld Chronicles up to date in our huge manuscript book, and Carl occasionally added notes or an illustration, but we didn't often act it out nowadays. Carl always had so much boring homework. Sometimes he didn't come to the Glass Hut for days and I'd have to go calling for him.

It didn't always work then. He'd follow me down through the garden and sit in the hut with me, but he'd be all quiet and moody and not contribute anything, or he'd be silly and mess around and say his speeches in stupid voices, sending it all up. I could generally get him to play properly eventually, but it was very hard work.

'Maybe you shouldn't keep pestering Carl to play with you,' said Mum.

'But he's my best friend in all the world.

2

We always play together,' I said.

'Oh, Sylvie,' said Mum. She sighed. Nowadays she often sighed when she talked to me. 'You're too old for this playing lark now, making up all these secret imaginary games. It's not normal. You're thirteen, for God's sake. When are you going to start acting like a teenager?'

'You don't know anything about it,' I said loftily. 'They're not little kids' games. We're writing our own series of books. You wait. They'll be published one day and Carl and I will make millions, what with all the royalties and the foreign rights and the film deals.'

'Oh well, you can maybe pay off the mortgage then,' said Mum. She sighed again. 'Who do you think you are, eh? J. K. Rowling? Anyway, Carl doesn't seem quite so keen on this playing – sorry, *writing* lark nowadays. You're both growing up. Maybe it's time to make a few new friends. Isn't there anyone you can make friends with at school?'

'I've got heaps of friends,' I lied. 'I've got Lucy. She's my friend.'

That was true enough. Lucy and I had made friends that worrying first day in Milstead High School. I'd known her in first school and middle school, but I hadn't ever needed to make a proper best friend of any of the girls because I'd always had Carl.

It was hard trying to make friends now in Year Nine. Nearly everyone had been at our middle school so they just carried on in the

3

same twosomes or little gangs. There were several new girls in our form, but they palled up together. There was also Miranda Holbein in the other Year Nine form, but she was way out of my league.

It was a great relief when Lucy asked if I'd sit next to her and acted friendly. She was a giggly girl with very pink cheeks, as if she was permanently embarrassed. She sang in the choir and was always very *good*. She had pageboy hair and always had a shining white school shirt and never hitched up her knee-length skirt and wore polished brown lace-up shoes. She looked almost as babyish as I did. So we sat next to each other in every lesson and shared chocolates and crisps at break. We chatted about ordinary humdrum things like television programmes (she liked anything to do with hospitals and wanted to be a nurse when she grew up) and pop stars (she loved several members of boy bands in a devoted little-sisterly fashion, knowing off by heart their birth signs and favourite food and every single number one on their albums, in order).

Lucy was fine for an everyday friend. I would never ever count her as my *best* friend, of course. She lived just round the corner from school so she went home at lunch time. I lived too far away. Anyway, my mum was busy working at the building society, not home to cook me egg and chips like Lucy's mum. I was stuck for company each lunch time. We weren't

4

allowed mobile phones at school but I mentally sent Carl text messages: I MISS U. TALK 2 ME. C U IN G H 2NITE?

We used to pretend we were so in tune with each other we were telepathic. Maybe our psychic brainwaves weren't wired up for new technology. Nothing went *ching-ching* in Carl's head. If he ever tried to send me similar messages I didn't pick them up, though I waited tensely enough, eager and alert.

I asked Carl over and over what he did during his lunch times at Kingsmere Grammar but he was unusually uncommunicative. He ate. He read.

'Oh, come on, Carl. Tell me everything,' I said. '*Elaborate*. I want detail.'

'OK. You want me to describe my visit to the boys' toilet in elaborate detail?'

'Stop being so irritating. You know what I mean. Who do you talk to? What do you do? What do you think about?'

'Maybe you'd like to follow me around with a webcam,' said Carl. He suddenly grinned, and switched to manic TV-presenter mode. '*Here is our unwitting suspect, Carl Johnson. Let's hone in on him. Ah! What is he up to now? He's lifting a finger. Has he spotted us? Is he about to remonstrate? No, he's picking his nose. Let's have a close-up of the bogey, guys.*'

'Yuck!'

'*Oh, Carl's close friend Sylvie is making a pithy comment. Let's focus on little Sylvie. Smile at the camera, babe,'* he said, sticking his squared fingers right in front of my face.

I stuck my tongue out.

*'Keep it out, keep it out, that's the girl! We're now switching to our all-time favourite Live Op Channel. Ms Sylvie West has suffered all her childhood from Sharp Tongue Syndrome but the eminent ear, nose and throat specialist, Mr Carl Johnson, is about to operate. Scissors please, nurse!'*

'Yes, here are the scissors,' I said, snip-snapping my fingers. *'But we've switched to the Mystery Channel now and I'm playing a scary girl driven bonkers by her mad best friend so she decides to – stab – him – to – death!'*

I made my scissor fingers strike Carl's chest while he shrieked and staggered and fell flat at my feet, miming a bloody death. He did it so well that I could almost *see* a pool of scarlet blood.

I bent over him. He lay very still, eyes half open but staring past me, unblinking.

'Carl? Carl!' I said, giving his shoulder a little shake.

He didn't stir. My heart started beating faster. I crept closer, hanging my head down until my long hair tickled his cheeks. He didn't flinch. I listened. He didn't seem to be breathing.

'Stop it, Carl, you're frightening me!' I said.

He suddenly sat bolt upright so that our heads bumped together. I screamed.

*'Ah, I'm glad I'm frightening you because*

*we've switched to the Horror Channel now and I am a ghost come back to haunt you. Be very afraid, Sylvie West, because I am going to get you!'*

His hands clutched my neck but I wrestled with him. I was small and skinny but I could fight like a wildcat when I wanted. We tussled a bit but then Carl's fingers started tickling my neck. I creased up laughing and then tickled him in turn. We lay flat on our backs for a long time, giggling feebly. Then Carl reached out and held my hand in the special best-friendship clasp we'd invented way back when we were seven. I held his hand tight and knew that we were best friends for ever. More than best friends. We'd played weddings together when we were little. Carl used to make me rings out of sweet wrappers. Maybe he'd give me a real ring one day.

How could I ever compare my bland little conversations with Lucy to the glorious fun I always had with Carl?

There weren't really any other girls to go round with at lunch time. I got on with nearly everyone, but I didn't want to foist myself upon them. One time when I was sitting in the library Miranda Holbein sauntered in and waved her fingers at me. I was so startled I looked round, convinced she must be waving to someone behind me.

'I'm waving at you, silly!' said Miranda.

I waggled my fingers back foolishly and then gathered up my books and rushed for the door. I didn't want to annoy Miranda. We'd only been at the school a few weeks but she already had a serious reputation. She could make mincemeat of you if she didn't like your looks.

*I* didn't like my looks. I was so tiny people couldn't believe I was in Year Nine at high school. I looked the youngest of all the girls in my class. They all called me Little Titch. I didn't exactly get teased. I was looked on as the class mascot – quite cute, but not to be taken seriously.

Everyone was in total awe of Miranda. She looked much older than me, much older than any of us. She seemed at least sixteen, even in her bottle-green school uniform. She had bright magenta-red hair, obviously dyed, though this was strictly against school rules. She cheerily lied to Miss Michaels, swearing that every startling strand of hair was natural. It swung down past her pointed chin but she often plaited it in little rows, fastening each end with tiny beads and ribbons.

When her form teacher complained about their gaudiness she came to school the next day with green beads and ribbons to match our uniform. This was preposterous, but Miss Michaels let her get away with it!

Miranda seemed born to break every rule going. She was the girl everyone longed to look like but she wasn't really *pretty* and she wasn't even ultra-slim. She didn't seem to mind a bit that she was a little too curvy. In fact she seemed particularly pleased with herself, often standing with her hands on her hips, showing off her figure. The girls in her form said she never hid under her towel after showers. Apparently she stood there boldly, totally bare, not caring who stared at her.

She was clever and could come top in class if she bothered to work hard, but she generally messed around and forgot to do her homework. She knew all sorts of stuff and apparently chatted away to the teachers about painting or opera or architecture, but no one ever teased her for being a swot. She didn't even get teased for being posh, though she spoke in this deep fruity voice that would normally have been cruelly mimicked. It helped that she swore a great deal, not always totally out of earshot of the teachers. She told extraordinary anecdotes about the things she did with her boyfriends. She was nearly always surrounded by squealing girls going 'Oh, Miranda!'

I wandered into the girls' toilets this lunch time and there was a huddle of girls goggling at Miranda. She was perched precariously on one of the wash basins, swinging her legs, her feet in extraordinary buckled boots with long pointy toes.

She was in the middle of a very graphic description of what she had done with her boyfriend last night. I stopped, blushing furiously. The other girls giggled and nudged Miranda, who hadn't paused.

'Shut *up*, Miranda. Look, there's the Titch.'

'Hi, Titch,' said Miranda, giving me a wave again. Her fingernails were bitten but she'd painted each sliver of nail black, and inked artistic black roses inside each wrist. Then she carried on with her detailed account.

'Miranda! Stop it! The Titch has gone scarlet.'

Miranda smiled. 'Perhaps it's time she learned the facts of life,' she said. 'OK, Titch? Shall I enlighten you?'

'I *know* the facts of life, thanks,' I said.

I was starting to want to go to the loo rather badly now but I didn't want to go into a cubicle with them all listening to me.

'Ah, you might have a sketchy knowledge of the basic *facts*, but I doubt you've put them into practice,' said Miranda.

'Stop teasing the Titch, Miranda!'

'As if the Titch would ever have a boyfriend,' said Miranda, rolling her eyes at them.

'I do so have a boyfriend,' I said, stung. 'You shouldn't jump to conclusions. You don't know anything about me.'

The girls tensed excitedly. People didn't usually snap back at Miranda. I was astonished I'd done it myself.

Miranda didn't seem at all annoyed. 'I *want* to know all about you,' she said. '*And* your boyfriend. Tell me all about him.'

'He's called Carl,' I said.

'And?' said Miranda. 'Come on, Titch. What does he look like?'

'He's very good looking. Everyone says so, not just me. He's fair. His hair's lovely, very blond and straight. It flops over his forehead when it needs cutting. He's got brown eyes and he's got lovely skin, very clear – he never gets spots. He's not very tall but he's still quite a bit taller than me, obviously. He doesn't bother much with his clothes and yet he always looks just right, kind of cool and relaxed.'

'Wow!' said Miranda. She was sort of sending me up, and yet she seemed interested too. 'So what's he like as a person? I find all the really fit-looking guys are either terribly vain or they've got this total personality bypass.'

'No, Carl's not a bit like that. He's ever so funny and great at making stuff up and inventing things. He's very clever, much brainier than me. He knows just about everything. He'll go on and on about some subject he's truly interested in but he's never really boring.'

'So how long have you known this boy wonder?' Miranda asked. 'Or *do* you really know him? You're the girl who reads a lot. Maybe you're making up your own story now.'

'Yeah, like, as if a boy like that would want to hang out with the Titch!' said Alison, another new girl.

'She *does* know him,' said Patty Price. 'We were all in the same class in middle school.'

'So he's only our age,' said Miranda. 'Just a little boy. I *never* go out with boys my own age, they're so stupid and immature.'

11

'Carl isn't stupid,' I said.

'No, he's, like, ultra-brainy,' said Patty. 'He goes to Kingsmere Grammar now, doesn't he, Titch? He got a special scholarship. He's great at art too. He painted one wall back in middle school – this Venice scene with glass-blowers, and it was just like a real artist had done it.'

'He sounds interesting,' said Miranda. 'I want to meet him. Hey, Titch, bring him round to my place tonight.'

I stared at her. She was surely joking! All the other girls seemed equally amazed.

'Yeah, right,' I said.

'No, really. We'll have a party, it'll be great,' said Miranda.

'Oh, can I come, Miranda?'

'Can I?'

'I'm coming too!'

'Hey, hey, I'm asking the Titch, not you lot. Sylvie and her boyfriend Carl.' Miranda reached out with her pointy boot and gently prodded me with it. 'Will you come, Sylvie?'

No one ever called me Sylvie at school apart from the teachers. I was so surprised I didn't know what to say.

I had to say *no*, of course. The very idea of Carl and me going to one of Miranda's parties was preposterous. But you didn't just say *No thanks* to a girl like Miranda.

'Well, that would be lovely,' I mumbled, ready to start in on some excuse.

Miranda didn't give me a chance.

'Great,' she said, jumping down from the wash basin. 'See you around eight. It's ninety-four Lark Drive.'

She was off with a flounce of her short skirt before I could say another word. The others all ran after her, still begging to come too.

I was left with my heart thudding, wondering what on earth I was going to do now.

'Miranda Holbein's invited me to a party at her house tonight,' I told Lucy at the start of afternoon school.

'Oh yeah, like, really!' said Lucy, breaking off a finger of her Kit-Kat and giving it to me. 'I know it's mean to bad-mouth people but I truly can't stand that Miranda. She's so posey, such a show-off.'

'I know. But she really *has* invited me. And she's asked Carl too.'

'But she doesn't know Carl. She doesn't even know *you*, Titch.'

'I know. I don't get it.'

'Is it a big party? Do you think she'll invite me?' said Lucy, sounding hopeful.

'I thought you couldn't stick her.'

'I can't. And you wouldn't ever catch me going

to one of her parties. Honestly, the things that go on!'

'What?'

'Well, this girl in Year Ten knows her, and her cousin went to a party in the summer, and *apparently* . . .' Lucy started whispering stuff in my ear.

'Rubbish!' I said uneasily. 'You're making it up. No one does that anyway, not in real life.'

'You wouldn't know. You're so innocent, Titch,' said Lucy.

I wanted to hit her even though she was my friend. I could put up with Miranda and her pals patronizing me but not *Lucy*. Her mum and dad called her Lucy Locket and she had three Bear Factory bears, Billy, Bobby and Bernie, and she still liked watching her old Disney videos.

'Well, if I go to Miranda's party I won't be innocent much longer,' I said.

'You're not really going to go, are you?' said Lucy.

'Of course I am,' I said, though I had no intention whatsoever of doing so.

'And *Carl*'s going?'

'Yep,' I said, wondering why toads weren't tumbling out of my lips, I was telling so many lies.

'But you're always saying Carl's so anti-social,' said Lucy.

This has been a kind lie. When I first made friends with Lucy I wanted to show Carl that I'd managed to make a good friend even though I felt so lonely and half a person without him. I also wanted to show Lucy just how close Carl and I still were. I suppose I wanted to show off. I was mad enough to invite them both round to tea one Saturday. It was *awful*.

Lucy arrived in a dreadful silly-frilly dress and shoes with heels. They seemed too big for her. Maybe they belonged to her mother. She wore thick make-up, though she forgot she was wearing it and kept rubbing her eyes so it smeared all over the place and made her look like a panda. She spoke in a silly self-conscious way in front of Carl, and whenever he said anything at all, even 'Can you pass me the cakes?' she giggled. She practically *wet* herself she giggled so much. I wanted to die.

Carl made a bolt for home the moment he'd finished his tea. He barely paused to say goodbye. I didn't want Lucy's feelings to be hurt so I pretended he was going through a very shy withdrawn stage and couldn't really cope with company.

Carl was incredulous that I had become so friendly with Lucy. For a long time he used poor Lucy's name whenever he thought anything especially twee, silly or naff.

'Oh, dear God, switch that programme off, it's too Lucy for words,' or 'What have you got that skirt on for, it's a bit Lucy, isn't it?' or 'You don't look *right* with lipstick, Sylvie, it makes you look Lucyfied.'

It wasn't fair. I didn't really like Lucy very much either, but I needed *someone* to go round with at school.

'I can't see Carl wanting to go to a party with a whole lot of strangers,' Lucy said now.

'You're probably right,' I said.

I went home in a daze. I was sure I wasn't *really* going to Miranda's. I *wanted* Carl to refuse, and then I could use him as a convenient excuse.

When I got home to our semi-detached houses I went down Carl's crazy-paving path instead of my own. I knocked at the front door and Carl's brother Jake opened it. He just grunted when he saw me and ambled off up the stairs again, leaving the door open so I could come inside.

He was sixteen, in Year Eleven at my school. He wasn't as brainy as his brother and hadn't sat for any special scholarships. He didn't look a bit like Carl. He had dark untidy hair and very dark eyes so you could barely see his pupils. He'd been quite small for his age once but now he was this great lanky guy of at least six foot. He was bright enough but he rarely bothered with much homework. The only thing he worked hard at was playing his guitar.

I wondered what Miranda would make of Jake. I thought he was far more her cup of tea, can of lager, whatever. He'd probably go for her too, even though she was only in Year Nine. I had a feeling Miranda was already famous throughout the school.

17

'Miranda Holbein has invited Carl and me to a party tonight!' I called up the stairs after him.

He paused on the top step. 'Cool!' he said, trying not to sound too impressed. He peered down at me. 'She's invited *Carl?*' He shook his head. 'He won't go.'

'I know,' I said. 'Where is he? In his bedroom doing his homework?'

'Like the nerdy little swot he is,' said Jake, pushing Carl's door open. 'Oh. Not here. His bike was round the back so he must be somewhere.'

'Don't worry, I'll look for him,' I said.

I was pleased. Jake hadn't said more than two consecutive words to me for years. Just one mention of Miranda Holbein and I seemed to have become cool by association.

I went looking for Carl. I tried the living room first, the looking-glass twin of my own. I liked the Johnsons' so much more. I loved their crimson velvet sofa and bright embroidered throws and big saggy cushions and the large red and blue and purple paintings on the wall.

Carl's mum was an amateur artist and the house was like her own gallery. She'd always nurtured Jake and Carl's artistic abilities too, encouraging them to crayon on the kitchen walls when they were little. There were a few of my own scribbles too. I'd crayoned a crazy wedding all along one wall, with me in a white meringue and Carl in a white suit so that we looked like an advert for washing powder. There

18

was a long colourful row of wedding guests: my mum and dad and Jake, and I'd added lots of children from school and our cat Flossie and my rabbit Lily Loppy (both long deceased) and Jake's dog Wild Thing (so wild he'd run away and never come back). They were all wearing big pink carnations, even the cat and the dog, and the rabbit had *two*, one on each ear.

Carl's mum Jules was washing lettuce at the kitchen sink.

'Hi, Sylvie sweetheart,' she said.

'Hi, Jules,' I said.

She wouldn't let me call her Aunty Julia, let alone Mrs Johnson. She was Jules to everyone, even the little kids at the nursery school where she worked part time. She'd obviously been doing finger painting with them today. There were little red and yellow fingerprints all over her big flowery trousers.

'I think Carl's down in his hut,' she said.

'Oh, great.'

'Sylvie?' said Jules. She paused, shaking the lettuce. 'Is Carl OK?'

'OK in what way?'

'I don't know.' She picked a little slug out of the lettuce, shuddering. 'Yuck! *Any* kind of way. He just seems a bit . . . quiet. You two haven't had a row, have you?'

'We never have rows,' I said.

We *did*, but I generally gave in quickly because I couldn't bear Carl being cross with me.

'Maybe it's something at school then,' said Jules. 'I keep wondering whether it was a good idea to uproot him and send him there.'

'No it wasn't!' I said.

'Oh, darling. I know it must have been very hard for you. For *both* of you. But you know what an old brainybox Carl is, and the grammar gets lots of boys into Oxbridge. He's keeping up with the work all right, I know that, though he's had a lot of catching up to do. Maybe he's just tired from working so much. I don't know though. He just sort of mooches about when he's at home, like he's got stuff on his mind.'

'He's always been a bit dreamy,' I said uneasily.

I felt flattered to be asked about Carl, as if I was the one who had the key to all his secrets, but I knew how he'd hate to think I was discussing him with his mum.

'Are you two still working on this book of yours?' said Jules.

'Oh yes,' I said, though we hadn't made up anything new since September, when I'd gone to the high school and Carl started at the grammar. I'd tried working on the book on my own but it wasn't the same without Carl. I'd only written two pages and then decided they were so silly and sentimental I ripped them right out of the book.

'When are we going to get to read it then?' said Jules.

'Oh, goodness! It's kind of private,' I said.

20

Jules shrieked as she found a truly gigantic slug. She dropped the lettuce in the sink, letting the cold water rinse it.

'I feel I really should buy organic veg but, oh God, I hate these slimy slugs.'

'Carl hates them too. He hates all creepy-crawlies.'

I had to be chief spider-catcher in the Glass Hut. Carl wanted to be a Buddhist and not kill anything but he wouldn't have minded a holocaust of the insect world.

'Tell me about it,' said Jules. '*Last* time we had salad he found some little buggy thing on his plate and squealed a bit, just out of shock, I think, but Jake and Mick were merciless. He got teased for being a wimp the entire week, poor boy.'

Mick was Jules's husband. He was a big broad man with a bit of a beer gut. He looked like a labourer in his scruffy T-shirts and sagging jeans but he was actually a lecturer in Politics at the university. He was always very kind to me but he teased me too. He called me Silent Sylvie because I barely said two words in his presence, and when I had my hair in plaits he could never pass me without pulling on a pigtail and going *Ding-ding*.

Carl said he sometimes couldn't stick his dad.

I said Carl was lucky to still *have* his dad. That shut him up.

My dad isn't dead. He just cleared off two years ago. I used to see him every weekend for the first few months, but when his girlfriend had their baby he stopped bothering.

Carl and I had great fun making up two warrior kings in Glassworld, one a jokey buffoon and one an untrustworthy philanderer. They donned heavy metal armour and fought in time to heavy-metal music, sweating inside their visors as they hacked and whacked frantically with their silver swords. They fought all day and half the night without managing to inflict a single wound, and then died within a minute of each other of exhaustion and apoplexy.

Jules gingerly batted the lettuce from one side of the sink to the other. 'Horrid little sluggery sluggers,' she said. She paused. 'Sylvie, you don't think Carl's being teased at school, do you?'

I stared at her. 'Everyone looks *up* to Carl,' I said. 'Everyone was just desperate to be his friend.'

'Yes, I know they made a big fuss of him at Milstead. But maybe it's different at the grammar? All those boys . . . He says he's got friends but he never really talks about them properly. I've tried asking him about it but he just clams up with me. You know, "I'm fine, Mum, just leave it."'

'I know,' I said. He clammed up with me too.

'Thank God he's got you for his friend, Sylvie. But I wish he'd make *more* friends. He just holes up in his room or down in the hut. I wish he'd get *out* more.'

'Well, I've come to invite him to a party,' I said.

22

'Really! Oh wow, great,' said Jules, suddenly so happy she threw the soaking lettuce up in the air, showering herself with water drops.

'I don't think he'll *go* though,' I said. 'I don't think *I'm* going. It's this girl at school and she's so grown up and scary – goodness knows what they'll get up to at her party.'

I wanted Jules to come the heavy mother and forbid Carl and me to go now, but she still looked eager.

'You and Carl are sensible kids. You won't do anything too silly. And if it's at this girl's house I suppose her parents will be there keeping an eye on things.'

Miranda seemed to come from such an alien world I couldn't even imagine her *having* parents.

'Don't get too excited, Jules,' I said. 'You know Carl isn't really a party kind of boy.'

'Go and ask him!'

'OK, OK!'

I went out of the Johnsons' kitchen door into their back garden. It was the twin of ours, but Jules had been imaginative with all sorts of colourful plants and weird painted statues and shrubs. Wind chimes tinkled from every tree as I walked down the garden, right to the bottom behind the yew hedge, where the Glass Hut was.

It looked like an ordinary large garden hut at first glance. It was made of planks of pale wood with a latched door and two small windows. They each had a stained-glass roundel of white-robed angels with gold wings gliding across a ruby glass carpet. I stroked them gently, my finger following the black lead outline, our little ritual ever since Carl bought them with his Christmas money last year.

I knocked at the door, our special knock, Morse code for *glass*. Carl was supposed to knock right back. I waited. The Glass Hut was silent.

'Carl?' I called.

I heard a sigh.

'Is that you, Carl?'

'Not just now, Sylvie. Sorry. I'm doing my homework.'

'I need to talk to you,' I said, and I opened the door and went inside.

Carl wasn't doing his homework. He didn't even have his books out of his school bag. He was lying back on the old velvet sofa, hands behind his head, staring up at the chandelier.

It was a real cut-glass Victorian chandelier, a little one with twelve droplets, though three were broken, and the chandelier itself didn't actually work. Mick wouldn't let Carl have the hut properly wired for it, so the only light was from the naked bulb sticking out of the wall. Carl had painted it with rainbow swirls so that it looked slightly more decorative.

There were five shelves running round two of the walls, originally meant to hold flowerpots and seed trays. Carl kept his glass collection here, in glowing colour-co-ordinated rows: little glass animals on the top shelf, then drinking glasses, then vases, then ashtrays and paper-weights, and then his precious pieces. The Glass Boy stood in the middle of the special shelf, tranquil, dreamy, his thick hair brushed forward over his forehead in strands of glass. He didn't wear any clothes but he didn't look remotely self-conscious. He stood staring at some distant horizon, his arms loosely hanging, his legs braced. Maybe he was watching for something, waiting for someone.

Carl's Great-aunt Esther had called him her Cupid, but he wasn't a baby and he didn't have little wings or even a bow and arrow. Carl had fallen in love with the Glass Boy on a visit to his great-aunt when he was five. She had fallen in love with this serious, angelic little nephew, so different from his harum-scarum brother. At the end of the visit she presented Carl with her 'Cupid'.

Carl's parents thought this a bizarre gesture. Even Jules was sure Carl would play with the Glass Boy and smash him into glass splinters. But Carl kept him on a shelf and simply treasured him. When he was six he asked for a glass animal for a birthday present. He started looking for glass vases and ashtrays and ornaments in jumble sales and summer fairs as he got older. His collection grew too big for his small bedroom so one summer he quietly started converting the garden hut.

I helped too, and went on all his glass-hunting expeditions. I couldn't get properly interested on my own behalf. I liked dangling crystals with their rainbow sparkles, but I couldn't see why all the other glass stuff meant so much to Carl. Still, I was very happy to be included in his glass world. I knew all about Murano glass and planned for us to go on a special trip to Venice one day – maybe for our honeymoon!

I looked everywhere for a glass *girl*, but so far hadn't found one. I invented the Glassworld Chronicles instead. They started off as a fairy story about a boy and a girl cast out into such a wintry world that they froze and turned into glass. We elaborated and expanded until together we'd invented an entire glass world and a cast of hundreds. My glass boy and girl became the King and Queen of Glassworld. They had family, friends and bitter enemies. There were a host of servants, some treasures, some treacherous. They had a menagerie of exotic pets: penguins and polar bears, a pair of hairy mammoths, and a stable of white unicorns with glass horns and hooves.

They were all so real to me that I actually shivered inside the hot little hut, living it all so vividly. Nowadays I was on tenterhooks with Carl, wondering if he'd play properly. I didn't know what tenterhooks *were*, but whenever he made fun of me I felt little stabs in my stomach as if I'd been caught like a fish on a hook.

'Sylvie, I'm not in the *mood*,' said Carl, his eyes closed.

He was stretched out like a marble effigy on a tomb, not moving. I looked at his beautiful face, his long lashes, his slim nose, his soft lips. I wondered what would happen if I subverted the traditional fairy tale and woke Carl with a kiss.

I giggled nervously. Carl opened one eye.

'*What?*' he said. 'Just run away and play, little girl.'

'Don't you *little girl* me. I'm only two months younger than you. And I don't want to play. I'm here to pass on a party invitation.'

'Oh God,' said Carl, closing his eye again. 'Please don't make me go to Lucy's party.'

'It's not Lucy's party. It's Miranda Holbein's party.'

'Who?' said Carl. 'Miranda? I don't know any Mirandas.'

'Neither do I, not properly, but everyone knows about her. I told Jake she'd asked us to her party and he was dead impressed, you could tell. I'm sure I've told you about her, Carl. She's just amazing. She's the girl everyone wants to be but wouldn't dare. Goodness knows why she's invited us.'

Carl lay still as a statue but both his eyes were open now.

'I don't get this *us* bit,' he said.

'Well, I was going on about you a bit in the girls' toilets. Miranda and the others thought I was making it up but Patty Price was there and she started on about you too.'

'So I'm the chief topic of conversation in your girls' toilets?' said Carl.

I was scared he might get cross. It was a huge relief when he started chuckling.

'So there they all are, the fresh young damsels of Milstead High School, each locked in her lavatory cubicle, seated in splendour, calling to each other like demented doves: *Carl, Carl, Carl, Carl, Carl, Carl!*'

I started giggling. I sat on the edge of the sofa, by his feet.

'Scrunch up a bit, Carl. OK, Milstead Pin-Up Boy. What shall I say to Miranda?'

'When is this party of hers?'

'Like, *tonight*. She decided just like that.' I snapped my fingers. 'Imagine us suddenly announcing to our mums, "Right, I'm having a party tonight. Provide all the food and drink and music and stuff and make yourselves scarce." *Do* they have food at proper teenage parties? And will they have real drink, do you think – wine and beer and vodka or whatever?'

'Well, we'll find out,' said Carl, sitting up.

I stared at him. 'We're not really going to *go* are we? I mean, it's such short notice we could easily get out of it.'

'Why don't we go if she's such an amazing girl?'

'Well. Because . . . I'll feel so shy and stupid.'

'I'll be there, silly.'

'And I don't have the right sort of things to wear. I know they all wear the most incredible stuff out of school. Miranda looks at least eighteen. I *wish* I didn't look such a total baby.' I tugged at my plaits. 'Look at my hair, for God's sake!'

'You can brush it out and wear it loose. It looks great like that,' Carl said encouragingly.

'I could wear my black skirt and hitch it right up. Do you think that would look . . . sexy?'

'Not if it's all bunched up at the waist. You don't want to look as if you've tried too hard. Just wear your jeans and a T-shirt and you'll look fine.' Carl gave my hand a quick squeeze. I clung to his fingers.

'Are you teasing me, Carl? Are we really going?'

29

'Yep, why not? Everyone's telling us to grow up and socialize and party like everyone else, so we'll try it out, eh? Don't worry. If it's a total bore or dead scary or whatever we'll just stay for one drink and then come straight home again.'

'Carl . . . I hope you don't mind, but I kind of told Miranda you're my boyfriend.'

'Well, I am, aren't I?' said Carl.

His blond hair fell forward over his brow like the Glass Boy's on the shelf. He smiled at me, his brown eyes shining. All the dangling crystals glittered in the late sunlight, casting rainbow reflections across the hut. I felt dazzled with happiness.

I ran home to try on all my clothes and experiment with hairstyles for the party. I met up with Miss Miles on the stairs. Miss Miles is our lodger. She's an old lady who will never wear purple like the poem. She has several beige knitted suits and cardigans, and thick beige stockings which always loop around her ankles, Nora Batty-style. She has her hair dyed a blondy beige colour and rubs beige foundation over her wrinkly face. Her spare beige bra and big knickers drip on the towel rail once a week, evidence that she is totally colour co-ordinated.

'You look full of the joys of spring today, Sylvie,' she said.

'I'm going to a party,' I said.

'Ooh, lovely! I hope you get lots of ice cream and jelly and birthday cake.'

'Er – yes,' I said, dodging round her. She seems to think I'm about six years old.

'What colour is your party frock?' she called after me.

'I haven't really got one,' I said, going into my little bedroom.

Mum used to sleep in Miss Miles's room when Dad was around. She's moved into the little bedroom now. I got the box room. It wasn't much bigger than a cupboard. I had a mirror, but I had to stand on my bed to see what I looked like all over.

I didn't think much of myself in any of my clothes. I was still experimenting when Mum came home from work.

'What are you up to, Sylvie?' she said, putting her head round the door. 'Hey, I hope you're not thinking of going out like that – that skirt's much too short.'

'I know. And it bunches up at the waist, just like Carl said. And I don't look sexy, I look *stupid*,' I said, pulling it off in despair.

'I don't think I want you looking sexy,' said Mum.

'Carl says just wear jeans but you can't wear jeans to a party. It would be different if they were *designer*.'

'Don't start. They're Tesco's finest – what more could a girl wish for? And what party? You haven't said anything about a party.'

'Because I've only just got asked. It's tonight,

at Miranda's. She this girl in Year Nine, the other class.'

'What sort of party is it? And how are you going to get home? I'm knackered, Sylvie. I don't want to stay up late to come and pick you up. I just want to have a bath and go to bed straight after supper.'

'Carl's going too, so his mum or dad will pick us up, no problem,' I said.

'*Carl's* going? What is this party, then? Why didn't you tell me about it earlier?'

'I told you, I didn't *know* about it earlier. Oh, Mum, don't fuss. Look, you were the one who said it was time I grew up. Miranda and her friends are *ever* so grown up.'

'Yes, that's what I'm worried about. There's a happy medium. This party – Miranda's parents will be there, won't they?'

'Of course.'

'And there won't be any alcohol?'

'As if!' I said firmly. 'Mum, I'll be fine. And I'll have Carl to look after me. I *can* go, can't I? It's just that Miranda isn't the sort of girl who asks you twice.'

'Whereabouts does she live?'

'Lark Drive.'

Mum raised her eyebrows. 'Then she's dead posh,' she said. 'Those houses cost a fortune. Maybe you shouldn't wear your jeans.'

'Well, what *should* I wear?' I said, standing there, still in my bra and knickers. I didn't really need a bra at all yet but I wasn't going to be the only girl in my class who didn't wear one.

'God knows,' said Mum. She giggled. 'A tiara and evening frock?'

'Oh, ha-ha.'

I had a best dress, a terrible velvety pinafore thing, but it was old now, and I looked about five in it anyway.

In the end I took Carl's advice and wore my jeans and a v-necked black sweater of Mum's. The wool made my skin itch and it was going to be too hot for a party but it looked more sophisticated than my own T-shirts. I privately stuffed paper tissues in my bra to give me a little shape.

I brushed my hair out but I still looked lamentably little-girly. I tried copying Miranda's elaborate hairstyle, experimenting with beads and bits of thread. I wasn't sure it looked any better.

'Is that the latest style for long hair?' Mum said doubtfully. 'I could twirl it up in a bun thing for you if you like.'

'No thanks,' I said. 'Miranda has her hair like this. Sort of.'

'You seem very keen on this Miranda all of a sudden,' Mum said. 'Write down her full address then. Oh God, I don't know whether I should let you go, not when we don't even know them. Maybe I'd better ring Miranda's mother and just check up on this party situation.'

'Don't, Mum! I'll die of embarrassment. They

all think I'm a total baby already. They laugh at me and call me the Titch.'

'That's not very nice of them,' said Mum. 'Do they tease you a lot?'

'Well, a bit. But it's OK. I'm kind of used to it.'

Mum sighed. 'I don't know. It used to be so lovely when you were back in first school and everyone was so friendly and all the mums knew each other. I suppose middle school was OK, but now the high seems so big and scary. They've lost that special atmosphere. I'm not happy with it as a school. And yet there's Carl at the grammar and Jules doesn't think he's happy there either. She thinks *he*'s maybe being teased now.'

'She said. But he's fine, Mum. We're both fine.'

Mum suddenly gave me a hug. 'I know you are,' she said, nuzzling her head against mine.

'Mind my hair, Mum!'

'OK, OK. Sorry! Oh, Sylvie, fancy you going off to a proper party. You will be sensible, won't you?'

'*Yes*, Mum.'

'Yes, I know you will. Take no notice. I'm just being daft.' Mum rubbed her forehead the way she always does when she's tired.

'Jules or Mick will come and collect us, right, so you can go to bed early,' I said.

'Yeah, like I'm going to be able to sleep before you're back!' said Mum.

It was weird saying goodbye to her. She was eating her supper on a tray, watching *Coronation Street*.

'You have fun, darling,' she said. She looked at her microwaved pasta and the television, shaking her head. 'I seem to have turned into a sad old woman,' she said. She lowered her voice. 'I'll turn into Miss Miles if I don't watch out. Oh dear, I wish *I* had a party to go to.'

'Oh, Mum,' I said, suddenly feeling awful.

'Forget I said that. I'm just feeling stupidly sorry for myself. Go on, off you go. You look lovely, darling. Enjoy yourself.'

Jules drove us to Lark Drive, positively burbling with excitement.

'It's no big deal, Mum,' said Carl. 'You're acting like we've been invited to hang out with the Geldof girls. It's just a little suburban party. Relax!'

Carl certainly looked relaxed in his white T-shirt and blue jeans, totally cool and understated, but he was jiggling his leg up and down, always a sign he was tense. I felt a wave of love for him because he was going to Miranda's party for my sake. I reached out and gave his hand a grateful squeeze. Both our palms were clammy and damp.

Even Jules looked nervous when she turned into Lark Drive. It was well-lit with lampposts, all in a fancy repro-Victorian design. Each house was set back from the road in its own grounds. Some were big red-brick villas with gables and turrets and towers.

'Cor, lummy,' said Jules in mock-cockney. 'You're partying with the posh nobs tonight.'

'Miranda can't live in one of these houses!' I said.

My heart started thudding. Maybe she was playing a joke on me. Yes, of course. She didn't really want to invite me to her party and meet my boyfriend. She just wanted to make a fool of me, pretending she lived in one of these extra-ordinary mansions. She was probably killing herself laughing now, imagining me trailing up and down Lark Drive looking for a non-existent party.

'I've made a mistake, Jules,' I said, nearly in tears. 'Let's go back home.'

Carl edged closer to me. 'Hey, it's OK. Don't worry, I'm here.'

'No, I've just realized, Miranda's playing a joke on me. I bet there isn't even a number ninety-four. I'm such an *idiot*,' I wailed.

'The houses aren't quite so grand this end,' said Jules as we drove past several square modern houses with mock Regency pillars. 'There's certainly a hotch-potch of styles! That's ninety, ninety-two – oh look! It's the white house at the end!'

It wasn't Victorian, it wasn't new, it wasn't mock anything, it was utterly different from all the other houses in the road, a large white

1920s house with a flat roof and stained-glass windows. It was gently floodlit so it glowed like a great moon.

'Oh, wow, look at the Art Deco glass!' said Carl.

'Look at the Art Deco *everything*!' said Jules. 'It's so beautiful. I'm sure I've seen it featured in one of those glossy home magazines. So can your Miranda really live here?'

'No way,' I said. 'I've led us all on a wild-goose chase. I'm sorry.'

'We'll go and knock on the door and see,' said Carl.

'No!' I said. 'Well, OK, but they won't even have heard of her, I'll bet.'

Carl and I got out of the car. Jules got out too, tucking her wild hair behind her ears. She rubbed at a paint stain on her trousers and sighed.

'Oh, well. Pretend I'm simply your chauffeur, kids,' she said.

We went through the white gate and walked up the York-stone path, looking up at the house as reverently as if it was a cathedral. Carl gazed at the stained glass, transfixed by the pink flowers, the blue butterflies, the glowing sun with spreading rays.

Jules pressed the doorbell timidly. 'Did that work? Did you hear it ring?'

We waited. Nothing happened. Jules tried again, pressing firmly this time. The bell rang immediately, making us all jump. Then the door opened and there was Miranda herself.

'Hi,' she said casually.

She didn't *look* casual. She was wearing a black lace long-sleeved top, a tight skirt and her pointy boots. She had a black velvet ribbon round her white neck, heavy black eye make-up and dark red lipstick. She looked fantastic.

'Hello,' I said, my voice quavery. 'Er, this is Carl and Jules, his mum. Um. Is the party still on?'

'Sure,' said Miranda. 'Come in, all of you.'

'Well, I'm just delivering them,' said Jules.

'Are you sure you don't want to stop for a drink?' said Miranda.

'No, no,' said Jules. 'So, when should I come and collect Sylvie and Carl?'

Miranda shrugged. 'Whenever.'

'About . . . eleven?' Jules suggested tentatively.

'Fine,' said Miranda. 'Or later.'

We nodded at Jules and then followed Miranda indoors. Well, *I* followed Miranda. Carl was looking at the windows close up, very gently fingering the lead and stroking the glossy glass.

'Carl!' I hissed.

Miranda stopped, her head on one side. Her eyes were screwed up, looking at Carl. 'You like the windows? Come and see the ones in the conservatory.'

We walked along the hall, through a huge quarry-tiled kitchen with a dresser full of matching china, all stylized orange flowers, and

39

then into a glass room of green palms and great fans of fern, with pink and purple orchids everywhere. The conservatory had a frieze of stained glass running right round it, wonderful flowers and plants in rich crimsons and chrome yellows and jade green. The French windows were stained glass too, with birds in each panel – bluebirds, canaries, finches, magpies, parrots.

Carl stood on tiptoe, as if he was going to fly like a bird himself. I worried that he looked a little *too* enchanted. I didn't want Miranda to think him totally weird. But it was OK. She was smiling at him.

'Great, isn't it?' she said.

'The flowers are original nineteen twenties,' said Carl. 'But the birds?'

'They're new. Ish. There used to be flowers in the door panes but there was a little accident. I slammed straight through them. I was riding this go-cart, you see, and I didn't quite get to grips with the steering. So there I was, spouting blood like a scarlet fountain and my dad was just going "Oh God, my stained-glass window!"'

'Quite right too,' said Carl. 'It's much easier to mend you than a beautiful original window.'

Miranda laughed. 'Yeah. So he was going to get the door glass replaced at great expense and I was losing my allowance for the rest of my life, but then he saw these modern birds in the stained-glass guy's studio and that was it, he had to have them – at even greater expense.'

'How much is that?' said Carl. I knew he was thinking of the Glass Hut.

'Thousands,' said Miranda.

'Oh,' said Carl.

'When we get the film deal for the book,' I said softly.

'The book?' said Miranda.

'Yes. Well. We're writing this book together,' I said.

I looked at Carl, wondering if he was cross with me. The book wasn't exactly a secret but it wasn't the sort of thing we talked about to other people.

'What's it about?' said Miranda curiously.

'It's just kind of fantasy,' I said vaguely.

'Can I read it?'

'Well—'

'Certainly not,' said Carl.

'Why, are you worried it's silly baby stuff?' said Miranda. 'Dragons and princesses and precious rings?'

'On the contrary,' said Carl. 'It's highly original and we're not letting anyone read it in case they steal our ideas.'

Miranda sighed. I was so impressed by the way Carl talked back at her. She made me feel incredibly tongue-tied, whereas Carl didn't seem remotely in awe of her.

'So where's this party then?' he said. He looked round. 'Are we it?'

'Wait and see,' said Miranda. 'Come along.'

She beckoned with her finger, her black nail

polish gleaming. We followed her back through the kitchen to the hall. Someone switched on some music in one of the front rooms so I walked towards it.

'No, no,' said Miranda. 'That's Parentland. We're downstairs.' She opened another door with steps leading downwards.

'You're having a party in your cellar?' said Carl.

'Such larks,' said Miranda. 'We'll take turns to lock each other up in the dark. My pet rats like to play this game too.'

I blinked. She had to be joking, although with Miranda you could never quite tell.

It wasn't a cellar at all, thank goodness. It had been converted into a comfortable den with a large television set, two sofas and several huge cushions, and books spilling off the shelves and crowding every corner of the carpet.

'Here's our party,' said Miranda. 'Small but ultra-select.'

There were three people sitting in a neat row on one of the sofas. They weren't from our school. The girl was very fair, very thin, very white. Her long waist-length hair was white-blonde, the colour of cream, and her skin was eerily pale. The boy on her left was Asian, very good looking, with beautiful big brown eyes and long eyelashes. The boy on her right was black, very tall and fit looking, with a cool hairstyle and a nose stud. It was as if Miranda had chosen her friends like ornaments, to look as decorative as possible.

'Alice, Raj and Andy,' said Miranda, gesturing to them. 'This is Sylvie and Carl.'

I was so glad she didn't call me the Titch.

'What would you like to drink?' said Miranda, going to a fridge in the corner.

I glanced quickly at the three on the sofa. I was enormously relieved. Alice had a bottle of fizzy water and Raj and Andy had Coca-Cola.

'Coke, please,' said Carl.

'Me too,' I said.

Raj was looking Carl up and down. 'You go to Kingsmere Grammar, don't you?' he said. 'I'm in Year Ten.'

'Oh. Right. Cool,' said Carl. He seemed flustered.

'You're friends with the football guy, Paul the Ball,' said Raj.

'Well. Kind of,' said Carl.

I stared at him. He hadn't told me he was friends with anyone at Kingsmere, especially not some footballer. Carl hated sports.

'Who's this Paul?' I asked.

Carl ignored me. He was looking at Andy. 'Are you at Kingsmere too?'

'No, Alice and I go to Southfield,' he said. 'Miranda's old school. Until they chucked her out.'

'Did you really get expelled, Miranda? What did you do?'

'It was mostly what I *didn't* do, like go to

lessons, do my homework, wear my school uniform, all that dull dreary stuff,' said Miranda, giving us our drinks.

Carl sat on the empty sofa. Miranda sat beside him. I lowered myself cautiously onto one of the squashy cushions, very glad I hadn't decided to wear the short skirt.

'I don't call running right round the gym stark naked dull and dreary,' said Alice.

'If only I'd been there,' said Andy, sighing.

Miranda took a crisp from a bowl and flicked it at him. 'It was just a silly dare,' she said. 'No big deal. I don't know why it caused such a fuss.'

'Let's play Dares now,' said Andy.

'Boring,' said Miranda. 'And infantile. We'll watch a movie instead.'

I liked this idea. It was a lot less stressful than trying to think of things to say. I wondered what sort of film Miranda might choose. I thought it might be a grossly explicit sex film. It was a relief when it turned out to be a horror movie about a gang of teenagers at someone's party. They're all lolling around drinking and nibbling stuff and teasing each other, just like us. They think their parents are upstairs, but when the main girl goes to ask her dad for some more beer she can't find him. She can't find her mum either. Then she hears this awful heavy breathing right behind her and she charges back to her room and slams the door shut, and there she is, stuck with her friends, with this Thing thumping against the door, trying to get in.

44

I'd have been scared to watch it on my own, or even snuggled up with Carl, but it was different watching with Miranda. She held the remote on her lap and kept rewinding the good parts so that we could all chant along with the cast, and then sometimes we fast-forwarded so we had to gabble like mad, and then we all had to do the sound effects in unison. It was especially good fun doing the heavy breathing.

'Your parents will wonder what in the world's going on, Miranda,' said Raj.

'Oh, my parents are too involved in getting stoned with their boring buddies upstairs,' said Miranda.

I couldn't tell if she was joking or not. She pretended to be scared when the Thing started walking right through the door, and clutched hold of Carl. She'd turned the light off but the television screen gave a little glow. I could see she was gripping Carl's elbow. Her shoulder was nudging against his armpit, as if she was hoping he'd put his arm round her.

I watched Miranda, my heart hammering under the hot black sweater. What was she playing at? She knew Carl was my boyfriend.

I couldn't make out if Raj or Andy was Miranda's boyfriend or whether they were all simply friends. Maybe in their circles friends casually cuddled up together without it meaning anything? She couldn't be deliberately making a play for my boyfriend right in front of all of us.

I waited to see what Carl would do. He didn't push her away but he didn't put his arm round her either. He stayed very still, as if he was part of the sofa, while Miranda fidgeted around beside him.

'I'm going for a real drink,' she said. 'It must be all this talk of beer. Anyone fancy a can?'

'Do you need to ask, babe?' said Andy.

'Don't *babe* me!' said Miranda, pretending to punch his nose.

He played at punching her back, and then he started tickling her, while she squealed and doubled up. They ended up wrestling on the carpet, Miranda showing a lot of her shapely plump legs. She was being very physical with Andy, boyfriend or not. This was obviously the way they carried on.

I thought about Carl and me. We had wrestling matches too, but it was different. Childish and silly, not a bit sexual. Perhaps it was because we'd known each other so long. Jules used to tuck us into the same bed together when I was staying over at their house. When we got covered in mud or paint she'd pop us both in the same bath.

I imagined sharing a bed or a bath with Carl now.

'You look like you need a beer, Sylvie – you're bright red in the face,' said Miranda, peering up at me from the floor. 'Hey, you're *blushing!*'

'No wonder! Look at you, sprawling all over the floor with your skirt rucked up,' said Raj, pulling Miranda's skirt straight, tutting at her like an old grandma. 'Go on, girl, get me a beer too.'

'Who else wants beer?' said Miranda.

I glanced at Carl. I'd never drunk beer in my life and I was pretty sure he hadn't either. We'd always agreed it smelled pretty revolting.

'Carl?' said Miranda, leaning up on one elbow. 'Would you like a beer?'

'Sure,' said Carl, like it was no big deal at all. So of course I said sure too.

'Alice?' Miranda asked.

'Beer? Too many calories,' said Alice. 'Just water for me.'

'You'll be on a drip-feed down Anorexic Alley if you don't watch out, girl,' said Miranda. 'Come on, Sylvie, come and help me carry all the stuff.'

I felt absurdly proud that she'd singled me out to help. I followed her up the stairs.

'You're right about Carl,' Miranda said. 'He's seriously cute. I'd like him for *my* boyfriend.'

'But . . . he's *mine*,' I said.

'I know, I know, only kidding,' said Miranda, linking arms with me.

'What about Andy and Raj? Are either of them your boyfriend?'

'They're just mates,' said Miranda. 'Well, I'm sure they'd *like* to be more, seeing as I'm so drop-dead gorgeous.' She fluttered her eyelashes and posed with one hand on her hip. I *think* she was joking.

'So who *is* your boyfriend then?' I asked as we went into the kitchen.

'I haven't got one at this current moment in time.'

'Yes you have! You were telling Patty and the others about him in the toilets today!'

'Oh, I was just winding them up,' said Miranda, laughing.

She opened the fridge and took out four cans of beer and a large bottle of fizzy water. She threw all four of the cans at me, as if we were part of a complicated juggling act. I dropped one and it thumped on the quarry tiles with a tremendous clatter, but thank goodness didn't explode. Miranda delved further into the fridge and found cheese and grapes and pâté, and then foraged in a cupboard for salty biscuits and crisps and a huge slab of Swiss chocolate. She reached into another cupboard and found a nearly full bottle of single malt whisky. She shoved them all carelessly in a shopping bag, threw the fizzy water way up in the air, caught it expertly as it spiralled down again, and grinned at me.

'Feast time,' she said.

The living-room door opened as we walked towards the cellar steps. Miranda grabbed my cans of beer and chucked them quickly into the carrier out of sight. A bearded man put his head round the door.

'That wasn't beer, was it?' he said.

'Blame Sylvie, Dad. She's an eight-pints-a-night girl,' said Miranda.

I gave a little squeak. Miranda's dad smiled at me.

'Don't let my daughter lead you astray,' he said. 'So you're Sylvie. Do you go to Miranda's school? No, hang on, you're not old enough.'

I took a deep breath. I so hated it when people thought I was a baby.

'Honestly, Dad!' said Miranda, rolling her eyes. 'She's in Year Nine like me. Take no notice, Sylvie. Come on, let's get back to the others.'

'Sorry, sorry! I'm blind as a bat without my glasses, Sylvie,' said Mr Holbein. 'I'm glad Miranda's making friends at her new school. Come back again soon!' He gave me a little wave and went back into the living room.

'Doesn't your dad realize that everyone's desperate to be your friend, Miranda!' I said.

'Are they?' said Miranda. 'You didn't seem at *all* desperate to be friends, Sylvie. You looked appalled when I asked you round. I never thought you'd turn up.'

'What about Patty and all the rest of your gang? Why didn't you ask them too?'

'They're OK, but only for school. They're all a bit samey and boring. You're different.'

'Yeah, I look about six years old.'

'My dad is so silly. And anyway, what does it matter if you look a bit young for your age? You don't *act* young. I really really envy your relationship with Carl – the way you guys have been friends for so long and do seriously cool things like writing books together. He's so good looking too, it's not fair! Tell you what, I'll swap you Carl for Raj *and* Andy, how about that?'

'No thanks.'

'Meanie. Hey, let's get back. Carl could be making out with Alice – I'm sure she fancies him too.'

50

'Was Alice your best friend from your old school?'

'Yep. Hey, you can be my best friend from my *new* school.'

'Cool,' I said, trying to sound casual.

I was immensely flattered but also worried. I wasn't sure I could handle being Miranda's friend. And what was I going to do about Lucy? I almost started wishing I was *with* Lucy. When we were together I could just relax and feel cosy and say the first thing I thought of. Lucy liked Carl but she didn't try to cuddle up to him and entice him away from me.

I wondered what might happen when we'd all drunk our beers. Alice didn't seem particularly interested in Carl, thank goodness. When we got back she was chatting to Andy about some school thing. Raj and Carl were talking school stuff too. I went and sat next to Carl quickly, before Miranda could get there.

'Who's this Paul?' I said again.

'He's just this guy in my class,' said Carl.

'And he's really into football?'

'He's only like a junior David Beckham,' said Raj. 'Isn't he going to be signed up to one of the top clubs, Carl?'

'Maybe,' said Carl. 'I don't know him *that* well. I mean, everyone knows him, don't they, Raj?'

'Like me!' said Miranda. She cosied up to both boys. 'I'm into football too. I was captain of the girls' team at Southfield, wasn't I, Alice?'

'Until you stuck the two footballs up your

shirt for the demonstration match on Open Day,' said Alice, giggling.

Everyone cheered when Miranda tipped the carrier bag upside down and the bottle of whisky spun on the floor.

'Laphroaig – good taste!' said Carl, as if he was a whisky connoisseur. He had first swig, straight from the bottle. I couldn't help being impressed. He didn't shudder, he just swallowed appreciatively and then wiped his lips with the back of his hand as if it was a practised gesture. Miranda took the bottle from him and glugged several mouthfuls. Then Andy. Then Raj, though he tilted the bottle craftily and barely had one sip. I did the same, blocking the neck of the bottle with my tongue. I felt the whisky burning into it, hot and peaty and disgusting.

Alice shook her head at the whisky bottle and sipped her water demurely. We swigged our beer straight from the can. I didn't like that taste either. It was cooler, but sour and dirty. I had to swallow hard to stop myself spitting it straight out. I ate some grapes to take the taste away. I watched Carl carefully. He kept raising his can to his lips, and he had another swig when the whisky bottle was passed round.

'I thought you weren't meant to mix beer and whisky,' said Raj, with another very cautious mini-sip.

'Beer and whisky makes you frisky!' said Miranda, raising her eyebrows.

'No, no, whisky and beer makes you queer!'

said Andy. He waggled his own eyebrows camply, winking at Raj and Carl. 'Watch out, duckies.'

Miranda shared the food out. There were no knives or plates. People just bit off big chunks of cheese or chocolate as they fancied.

I started to wonder why I wasn't feeling drunk. I'd had hardly any whisky but I'd drunk half my beer, yet it didn't seem to be having any effect whatsoever. Maybe you had to drink can after can. If so, I wondered how anyone ever persevered. It would be like trying to down several bottles of cough medicine.

'Could I have a little bit of your water, Alice?' I asked.

She gave me some, but it was a big mistake. I started hiccupping.

'Hark at Sylvie! She's drunk already,' said Miranda.

'I'm not the slightest bit drunk! It was the fizzy water,' I said. I made two terrible hiccupy-burping noises and clamped my hand over my mouth.

'Maybe you shouldn't finish your can, Syl. Here, I'll drink it,' said Carl.

'I'm *not* drunk,' I said, taking another swig of my beer, nearly choking myself on another hiccup.

'We need to distract her,' said Miranda. 'Let's play a game. I know! How about Snog Spin?'

'Yay!' said Andy.

'Double yay with knobs on,' said Raj.

53

'God, you guys are so basic,' said Alice, sighing.

Carl and I said nothing. We didn't know what Snog Spin was but it was obvious it wasn't some Blind Man's Buff party game for little kids.

'OK, we need a bottle,' said Miranda.

She grabbed the whisky bottle, took another big swig, and then screwed the top on tightly.

'Sit round in a circle, my lovelies, and we'll let the Snog Spin begin,' she said.

I hiccupped, sighed, and sat down cross-legged on the floor. I felt a little shift inside my head as I moved, an odd unscrewing. Maybe I was starting to be a little bit drunk after all.

Carl came and sat beside me. Miranda sat next to him, then Andy, then Alice, then Raj on my other side. He started giggling. We all did, even Alice, though she couldn't possibly be drunk.

'OK,' said Miranda, and she spun the whisky bottle hard. It whizzed round and round, fast at first, and then more and more slowly. We watched, mesmerized. The cap of the bottle ended up pointing directly at Carl.

'Aha!' said Miranda. 'It's you, Carl.'

I saw him swallow, though he stayed looking totally cool.

'So?' he said.

'So we have to select your snogging victim,' said Miranda, and she set the bottle spinning again.

It spun round and round and round while we

all watched. I knew exactly when it would pause and point.

'Ooops! I guess it's me,' said Miranda, smiling and showing her little cat teeth.

'That's a fix!' said Andy, looking miffed because she hadn't chosen him.

'Fix fix fix!' Raj echoed.

'How could I possibly fix it?' said Miranda. 'I gave the bottle a tremendous twirl. Shut *up*, you lot. Right, Carl. You and me. Snog time.'

'In front of everyone?' said Carl.

'What's your problem?' said Miranda.

Carl swallowed again. 'It's a little . . . childish,' he said cleverly. He stood up and held out his hand to Miranda. 'We'll step outside a moment.'

Miranda stood up, grinning. She took his hand. I hiccupped and she looked at me. 'You're cool with this, aren't you, Sylvie? It's just a bit of silly fun,' she said.

'Yeah, yeah, fine,' I said.

What *else* could I say in front of them all! I watched Carl and Miranda walk hand in hand out of the door and into the darkness outside.

6

'She must have cheated,' said Andy, spinning the bottle experimentally.

'Ssh!' said Raj. 'Let's listen.'

We sat still, not moving. We heard nothing. I hiccupped miserably.

'For God's sake, you sound like a chicken,' said Andy, imitating me.

'I wonder what they're up to?' said Raj. He started kissing his own hand, making gross slurping noises. *'Oh, Carl, you're dead sexy,'* he said in a silly girly voice.

'Shut up,' I said. My heart was banging as if it might burst straight through my chest and spatter Mum's black sweater scarlet. I'd never kissed Carl.

I didn't know what to do. Should I storm outside and tear Carl and Miranda apart? Andy was right. I didn't just sound like a chicken. I was *behaving* like one, too scared to stop my boyfriend kissing my best friend. But no one was acting as if it was a big deal. Maybe this was a silly game played by cool kids everywhere? Lucy hadn't tried to kiss Carl but maybe she'd have liked to? Miranda was certainly liking it. She'd made it obvious she fancied Carl from the moment she set eyes on him.

How did Carl feel? I couldn't stop imagining him kissing Miranda, his soft lips on her lip-sticked pout, his hands playing with her intricate plaits. I suddenly stood up. The room swayed so I swayed with it, feeling as if I was on a boat in a storm. I put one foot doggedly in front of the other towards the door.

'Where are you going, Sylvie?' said Alice.

'She's going to play I Spy,' said Raj. 'Come on, let's all peek.'

But just then the door opened and Carl and Miranda walked back into the room. Andy and Raj applauded and wolf-whistled. Miranda was pink and beaming, tossing her head, hands on her hips. Carl strolled in with his thumbs in his front jeans pockets in a determined effort to look casual. He saw me staring and gave me a little smile. If it was meant to be reassuring, it didn't work.

'Sit down, Sylvie! Come on, maybe it's your turn next,' said Miranda, bending down to spin the bottle.

'How come you do all the spinning, Miranda? Let me have a go,' said Raj.

'It's my house, Raj. This is my den. This game is totally my invention. So guess what, *I* get to spin the bottle,' said Miranda.

'You're too skilled with that bottle! Let's use *my* bottle now,' said Alice, draining it of the last drop of fizzy water.

'What are you, a camel?' said Miranda. 'No, we don't want any of your plastic rubbish, we need a proper glass bottle. Right!' She set it spinning again.

The bottle moved slowly this time, round once, round twice, slowing down already, looking as if it might be stopping at me, but it edged past, crept past Raj too and pointed at Alice.

'There you are, darling!' said Miranda. 'Soooo, who are you going to snog, mmm?'

She spun the bottle again. Alice sighed and rolled her eyes, pretending not to care. I could see a little pulse beating in her pale forehead. Maybe she was hoping for Carl too?

'Raj!' said Miranda as the bottle stopped.

Raj smacked his lips and made silly kissy noises, lunging at her.

'Give over!' said Alice. 'Not *here*. Outside.'

She stalked off, with Raj trotting eagerly behind her. They were only outside the door two seconds and then Alice marched back in.

Their applause was paltry.

'Hey, call that a kiss? I've had better kisses from my great-aunties,' Raj complained.

'You should smarten up your sweet-talk then, little boy,' said Alice.

'Give me another go, Miranda,' said Raj as she set it spinning.

'*I* don't choose. I have no control over this bottle whatsoever,' said Miranda. 'It's psychic force, darling. Fate. Whatever. Isn't that right, Sylvie?'

She smiled at me. I couldn't help smiling back. She set the bottle off again. I knew what was coming next. The bottle spun. I felt I was spinning with it, whirled round and round so fast I grew giddy and could barely breathe. The bottle slowed and we all watched it edge towards me.

'Aha!' said Miranda. 'Sylvie's turn!'

I swallowed. 'I'm not sure I *want* a turn,' I said.

'What sort of total wimpy response is that?' said Miranda, snorting. 'Of course you want a turn!'

'No I don't. I'll give my turn to Raj as he wants another go.'

'You can't do that! Now, stop pontificating and we'll play. We have to see who your snog partner is.' She looked at me. 'Who do you *want* it to be, Sylvie? Use *your* psychic power to influence the bottle.'

I knew I didn't have much chance. Miranda had mastered the spinning so that with the right twist of her fingers and flick of her wrist she could make the bottle point wherever she wanted. Still, I stared at the bottle and tried willing it where I wanted. I wanted it to point to Carl, of course. I didn't want to kiss anyone else but him. I was scared though. I loved Carl. I hated it that he'd kissed Miranda. I wanted him to kiss me. I'd dreamed about it often enough. But we didn't do stuff like kissing. It would be so weird now, when we'd grown up together.

We'd have to get around to kissing some time, obviously. We were going to get married, for God's sake. Carl had given me a glass 'diamond' out of a Christmas cracker when we were seven years old. When we used to play weddings he'd fashion me a gold wedding band out of a yellow Quality Street toffee wrapper.

It seemed I couldn't concentrate hard enough on Carl, try as I might. The bottle slid past him, past Miranda, and stopped at Andy.

'Interesting choice, Sylvie,' said Miranda, eyebrows raised.

I couldn't say anything. I didn't want to hurt Andy's feelings. I didn't know what to do now.

I felt Carl's hand squeezing mine, encouraging me. I squeezed back gratefully and then stood up, trying to look Andy in the eye.

'OK?' I said.

'Sure,' said Andy, getting to his feet too.

We walked to the door, opened it and then walked into darkness. I blundered forward and bumped into a cupboard.

'Hey, careful. Come here,' said Andy. 'Where are you? You're such a little titch.'

'That's what they call me at school,' I said. 'I've always been small for my age and everyone says I'll suddenly spurt upwards and catch up with everyone else, but it hasn't happened yet, still, here's hoping, because it's horrible being so small and looking so stupid and babyish,' I burbled.

'Ssh,' Andy said gently. 'We're meant to be kissing.'

He reached out for me in the darkness, ducking his head down. Our noses bumped together in comical fashion. I giggled hysterically.

'Was that a hiccup?' said Andy. 'Hey, wait a second. You've stopped!'

He put his hands carefully on my cheeks, tilting my head, and then he kissed me on the corner of my mouth, so lightly I wasn't totally sure it had actually happened.

I felt weak with relief that it was such a sweet and simple kiss. We walked back into the den and sat down again. Carl was looking at me anxiously.

'Are you OK?' he whispered.

'Of course she's OK,' said Miranda.

I thought the Snog Spin would be over now we'd all had a turn, but Miranda started spinning the bottle again. Miranda and Raj. Alice and Andy. Then Miranda again. The bottle slowed and stopped at Alice.

Raj whistled. Andy grinned. I blinked at them both.

'Spin it again,' said Alice.

'No way!' said Raj. 'You've got to go with the bottle, that's the whole point.'

'But it's meant to be a girl-*boy*,' said Alice.

'Well, it's girl-*girl* this time,' said Raj. 'Go on, Alice, don't be a spoilsport.'

Alice sighed but stood up, tucking her white hair behind her pearly ears. She stuck her tongue out at Raj. It was surprisingly pink in her pale face.

'Come on, Alice,' said Miranda, holding out her hand.

'Don't go outside. Stay in here, girls, and give us guys a treat,' Raj begged.

'Calm down, silly boy,' said Miranda.

They disappeared outside.

'Oh, man!' said Andy.

Carl raised his eyebrows at me.

We all waited. We heard a lot of giggling going on, then slurpy sounds and moaning.

'Listen!' said Raj.

'They're just winding you up,' said Carl.

'And succeeding,' said Raj.

Miranda and Alice came back into the den arm in arm, still giggling.

Miranda knelt to spin the bottle again. '*Now* whose turn will it be?' she said.

'Can't we move on to some other game?' said Carl. 'Isn't this getting a bit boring?'

'I think it's just starting to get really interesting,' said Miranda, spinning away. The bottle stopped, pointing at Carl.

'Aha! Your go again, Carl. So let's see . . .'

She spun it again. Carl sighed, leaning back, hands behind his head, as if he couldn't care less. I stared at the bottle for him, wondering if it would be me this time.

It wasn't me. It wasn't Miranda. It wasn't Alice.

It was Raj.

'Oh, no!' said Raj.

'Oh yes,' said Miranda.

'You're cheating, Miranda. You're doing it deliberately,' said Raj.

'Now who's being a spoilsport?' said Alice.

'*I* am,' said Carl, getting up. He held out his hand to me. 'Come on, Sylvie. I think it's time we went home.'

'Oh don't be so stuffy, Carl,' said Miranda.

'Loosen up, boys, it's only a bit of fun. *We* did it,' said Alice.

'Well, just a quick peck, darling,' said Raj in a silly camp voice, waving a limp wrist around.

'It's not fun, it's childish,' said Carl. He looked at me. 'Are you coming, Sylvie?'

'Yes,' I said, knowing it was no use arguing with him once his mind was made up.

Miranda didn't give up easily. She stood beside Carl, gazing up at him with her big brown eyes.

'Don't go, Carl. OK, you don't have to kiss Raj. I agree, he's not the most inviting prospect.'

'Thanks a bunch!' said Raj. 'I have my followers, you know. Maybe I'm just not Carl's type.'

'We'll play something else,' said Miranda.

'I'm tired of playing games,' said Carl. 'Night, Miranda. Thank you for inviting us. Night, everyone.'

He gave a quick wave and went out of the door. I shrugged helplessly and followed him.

Miranda didn't come to see us out. We stumbled around in the dark, having to feel our way up the stairs because we couldn't find the light switch. We emerged blinking in the brightly lit hall. The starburst clock hanging on the wall said it was only twenty to eleven.

'Jules is not coming till eleven, Carl.'

'Well, we'll wait outside,' said Carl. He fingered the stained glass on the front door one more time and then opened it.

It was cold outside and neither of us had jackets. I started shivering.

'Jump up and down a bit,' said Carl.

'I can't jump, I feel too dizzy. Do you think I'm drunk?'

'I shouldn't think so.'

'Carl, what's the matter?' I said, tucking my hand into his arm.

'Nothing. I'm fine.'

'Why did you walk out like that?'

'You know why. It was getting boring.'

'You didn't seem to mind when you kissed Miranda. Carl . . . did you kiss her properly?'

'As opposed to *im*properly?'

'I mean, did you give her a proper kiss on the

lips? You know, a real smoochy film-star-type kiss.'

'Wasn't that what we were supposed to do? Didn't Andy kiss you then?'

'Well, sort of. But no one was expecting you and Raj to have a proper *snog*.'

'Look, he goes to my school. I'm not having him saying stuff. Do you understand now?'

'Well. Not really,' I said. 'Hey, who's this new friend of yours?'

'What friend?' said Carl.

'Raj said you had this friend who plays football. You never told me about him.'

'There's nothing to tell,' said Carl, and stalked off down the road.

I went running after him. 'Don't walk off and leave me!'

'I'm not. I'm just stamping around a bit to get warm,' said Carl. He reached out and took my hand. 'God, your hand feels like ice. I'm sorry. Here, let me try and warm you up.' He put my hands between his and rubbed them up and down.

'Why are you so cross, Carl?'

'I'm not cross with you, just your silly friends.'

'You like Miranda.'

'No, I don't. She's so needy, desperate to be the centre of attention all the time. She thinks she's so outrageous when really she's just pathetic.'

'Is she pathetic at kissing?'

'I don't know. I haven't had that much experience of kissing.'

'Yes, but did you *like* kissing her?'

'It was OK. Ish. It didn't really do much for me if I'm honest.'

'Well, maybe you should try kissing someone else as a comparison,' I mumbled.

'What? Someone like *Raj*?'

'No!' I took a deep breath. I didn't feel quite drunk enough but I decided to go for it anyway. 'Someone like me.'

Carl relaxed. He held onto my hands, leaned forward – and kissed my *nose*. 'There! Happy now?'

'Not my nose!'

'You've got a nice nose, little and snubby and cute.'

'Kiss me on my lips.'

'Can't risk it, Syl. We might get all inflamed and risk our beautiful friendship,' Carl said, messing about.

I wriggled away from him, my feelings hurt. I didn't want to joke about it. I couldn't understand why he didn't want to kiss me properly.

'Sylvie? Don't look such a saddo. Listen, I'm sorry I broke up the party. They were all just getting on my nerves. I don't want to hang out with them. I want to be with you. Tell you what, let's play Glassworld tomorrow.'

'Really?' I said. 'You haven't wanted to play for ages.'

'Tomorrow afternoon, in the Glass Hut. Is it a date?'

'You bet,' I said.

Jules was surprised to find us standing hand in hand by the kerb, ready and waiting for her at eleven.

'I was rather hoping I could knock at the door and get asked in,' she said. 'What's it like inside?'

'Fabulous stained glass, an Eileen Gray red lacquer table in the hall, Clarice Cliff china in the cabinet . . . You'd love it, Mum,' said Carl.

'So what about this Miranda and her friends?' Jules asked.

'They don't live up to the décor,' said Carl.

'What are they like?' Jules asked anxiously.

'Oh, Mum. You know. Spoiled. Silly. Rich.'

'Sylvie, *you* tell me,' said Jules.

I did my best. I described Miranda and Alice and Raj and Andy in detail. I gave Jules a censored account of our evening, leaving out the beer and the whisky drinking and the Snog Spin session.

I had to recite it all over again when I got home to *my* mum. She was in her nightie sitting at her computer in the living room, sipping a glass of supermarket wine. She was playing one of her old eighties compilations, Blondie and Yazz and Annie Lennox – all the girls she used to dance to in the long-ago days when she went clubbing.

I approached her warily, because she sometimes got all tearful. She gave me a surprisingly cheerful smile and asked me all about my night out. She switched off her computer but kept the CD spinning, her toes tapping.

'You sound as if you had a great time, Syl. I'm so pleased,' she said, getting up and giving me a hug.

Perhaps she'd had more than one glass of wine because she hung onto me, swaying a little, and then she started spinning me round, dancing with me. We pranced around foolishly, and then started up our own little dance routine, forwards, back, hip twitch, twirl, faster and faster till we lost our balance and fell about laughing. We were mucking around just like sisters. I felt like confiding in her.

'I wish I was more like Miranda,' I said.

'Is she very pretty?'

'No, not really, but she acts like she is,' I said.

'Ah,' said Mum.

'And she's very keen on Carl,' I said.

'*Uh-oh!*' said Mum. 'What about Carl? What does he think of her?'

'Well, he *says* he's not very keen. In fact he said she irritated him. He called her a poor little rich girl.'

'Then you've not got anything to worry about, silly.'

'Well . . .' I couldn't tell Mum that Carl had kissed Miranda when he still wouldn't kiss me.

'Never mind Carl,' said Mum. 'What about the other boys? Did you fancy any of them?'

I stared at her. 'Mum! I just want Carl, you know that.'

'I know you two have been joined at the hip since you were tiny but you're both growing up now. It might be time to move on to other friendships.'

'Carl's my best friend and my boyfriend and we're going to get married – you *know* that, Mum.'

'That was just a baby game. You don't want to think about marrying Carl. You don't want to think about marrying *anyone*. Where does marriage get you?' said Mum, rubbing her bare finger where she used to wear her wedding ring. But then she smiled at me. 'Well, getting married got me *you*, and that makes it all worth while,' she said, giving me a hug. 'Come on, let's go to bed. It's OK for you, you can have a lie-in on Saturday. I've got blooming work.'

She gave me a goodnight kiss and then

peered at me suspiciously. 'Have you been drinking beer?'

'Have you been drinking *wine*?'

'I'm not thirteen years old, Cheekyface.'

'I'm very nearly fourteen.'

'Will you want a party?'

'No! Just a birthday tea with Carl.'

It was his birthday next. I had his present all ready, carefully wrapped and hidden in the back of my wardrobe. It was an old crystal champagne glass, decorated around the stem with green grape vines. I'd found it in a Cancer Research shop. I wasn't sure how old it was or whether it had any real value. I simply thought it was beautiful. I wished I had a pair so that Carl and I could drink pink champagne from them on our wedding day.

I dreamed about Carl when I went to sleep, but Miranda was in the dream too, and Raj and Andy and Alice. The bottle kept spinning and then I seemed to be spinning too, round and round until I was totally dizzy. I was in pitch darkness and I couldn't grab hold of anyone to steady myself. I kept feeling for Carl but I couldn't find him. He wasn't there any more. He'd somehow crept out of the room.

I woke up and the phone was ringing and ringing. It was gone ten. Mum had left a cup of tea on my bedside table but it was stone cold now. I ran downstairs in my pyjamas, wondering if it was Carl, hoping he wasn't going to back out of our Glassworld date.

It was only Lucy, desperate to know how I'd got on at Miranda's party.

I told her exactly what had happened, needing to see what she made of it all. She kept giving little squeals.

'That Miranda! What a C-O-W!' she said, spelling it out. It was the nearest she got to swearing. 'Fancy kissing Carl. And he seriously *let* her?'

'Well, it was just a game. It wasn't serious,' I said anxiously.

'Don't be silly, Titchy, she's trying to take him away from you. She makes me so sick. I wouldn't have any more to do with her if I were you.'

I was pretty sure Miranda wouldn't want any more to do with me now I'd walked out of her party. I decided not to tell Lucy that she'd asked me to be her best friend. It would make her even more vitriolic. She suggested we go shopping together in the afternoon but I said I was going to go round to Carl's.

'Oh, OK,' she said. Then, 'Can I come too?'

I took a deep breath. 'Well, we're going to be working on our book together.'

'I could work on it too. I'm good at English, you know I am. In fact I'm thinking of being a writer when I grow up. I've written lots of stories about my teddies.'

I shut my eyes. I knew exactly how Carl would react if I brought Lucy along and suggested we introduce Billy and Bobby and Bernie to Glassworld.

71

'Our story's kind of private, Lucy. It's just for Carl and me. We write it in Carl's hut.'

Lucy sniffed at the other end of the phone. 'It's not a *dirty* story, is it?' she said.

'No it's not!' I said crossly.

'It sounds a bit weird though. What's this hut like?'

'It's where Carl keeps his glass collection.'

'Yeah, that's a bit weird too, a boy collecting glasses!'

'It's not just glasses. It's all different kinds of glass – he's got the most fantastic collection.'

'Then show me, go on. Please. Ask me over this afternoon and take me round to Carl's.'

'I can't, Lucy. Carl doesn't ever let anyone in the Glass Hut apart from me.'

Lucy rang off, sounding very huffy. I worried that I'd hurt her feelings, but I couldn't really help it.

I spent the rest of the morning working out new episodes of Glassworld to impress Carl. I invented a new character, a Princess Mirandarette, who lived in a glittering white snow palace. I drew her dressed in black velvet with a white fur hat and collar and black boots with spiky steel heels. I gave her a white snow leopard and a black jaguar for pets, and drew a huge black crow perching on her shoulder. I drew Queen Sylviana beside her. She was Queen of all Glassworld and I drew her in her purple robes of state with her ruby crown and her regal ruby high-heels, but she looked pale and powerless standing next to

72

Princess Mirandarette. Her leopard and jaguar looked like they could eat Queen Sylviana's twin talking Siamese cats for breakfast.

I sighed. I drew King Carlo in the middle of the page, between the Princess and the Queen. I hadn't left much space for him so I had to draw a very slim, pared-down version of His Regal Majesty, leaving out his customary lengthy ermine train. I drew his crystal crown, each point studded with a round ruby; I drew the royal-blue sash over his shoulder; I drew his white silk suit, leaving most of it plain white page but carefully shading it with pale grey; I drew his ruby cuff links just peeping out from his sleeves; I drew his glass boots; I drew his dear face, big brown eyes, small neat nose, soft lips with a perfect cupid's bow. These lips were smiling but his eyes weren't looking left at me. They were turned to the right, towards the interloping Princess.

I suddenly scribbled all over her with my black felt pen, ruining my picture.

I made myself cheese on toast for lunch. I knew Jules wouldn't mind if I went next door and ate with them but Carl had specifically said afternoon and I didn't want him to feel I was being too pushy. I tried to work out in my head his definition of afternoon. I thought he probably meant three o'clock, but when it came to it I couldn't wait any longer than two.

I went out of the back door and walked down our garden. It wasn't a garden any more, it was

73

wilderness. Mum had long since stopped trying to mow the lawn or do any planting or weeding.

'I've got to prioritize,' she said defensively.

Carl's father mowed our lawn several times the first summer my dad left us, but then he slipped out of the habit and Mum was too proud to ask him. We had a couple of student lodgers for a while and they sometimes had a go, but they couldn't seem to work the lawnmower and go in a straight line. Then Mum caught them taking drugs and got rid of them in case I got corrupted and we all got prosecuted.

Miss Miles fiddled around planting a few pansies here and there, but she didn't have the strength to mow the lawn. Mum wanted to get rid of the grass altogether. She had a vision of a Japanese garden, all smooth grey pebbles and decorative green shrubs.

'One day, when I've got the time and cash,' she said. 'One day . . . when pigs start flapping their little wings and go flying through the air waving their trotters.'

I decided that when Carl and I published the Glassworld Chronicles and made our fortunes I'd treat Mum to her Japanese garden. I'd buy her an embroidered kimono to wear in it. She could lie on a little futon reading haikus and drinking green tea . . .

I waded through nettles and borage and dandelions to the door in the wooden fence at the bottom of our garden. I edged through it into the colourful flowery world of the Johnsons' garden and walked over to the Glass Hut. I rapped our special knock on the door but there was no answer.

I waited for a minute. I could walk up to the house and find Carl. Or I could go into the Glass Hut and wait for him there. Carl had never told me not to enter the Glass Hut without him. He hadn't needed to. It was far more private than his bedroom. I only went there at his invitation.

I knew I should wait. But my hand was itching. It reached out as if acting independently. It seized the handle and opened the door.

I stepped inside and closed the door after me. I didn't switch the light on. Red and blue and green glowed through the stained-glass windows, softening the gloom. I gazed at the neat glass rows. I reached out a finger and stroked the slippery hair of the Glass Boy. I lifted a glass goblet, pretending to take a sip. I took down the paperweights one by one and peered into each tiny world. My hand was trembling slightly, but I was very careful.

When I'd touched every single piece of glass for luck I took the big Glassworld book from the shelf and sat cross-legged on the sofa, flicking through the pages. We wrote it in an old marbled accounts book, so large you needed two hands to lift it. We'd stuck in so many paintings and drawings and general additions and amendments that the pages stuck out like stiff petticoats, making it even more unwieldy to handle.

The first few chapters were a weird mishmash. I'd written this very babyish beginning, with lots of bad drawings, rows of Glassworld characters all smiling the same banana-shaped smile, batting their long eyelashes and looking to the left because I'd only just learned how to draw a half-profile and was proud of my accomplishment. Their feet all pointed to the left too because I hadn't yet figured out how to draw a foot from the front. They looked like a mad chorus line about to start doing can-can kicks.

Carl had done drawings at the beginning too, but his were all very careful illustrations of Venetian glass-blowing. He'd constructed an entire Glassworld history from ancient GlassRoman times when the original Glass Palaces were erected. They were embellished wondrously by GlassVenetians, with brilliant chandeliers and mirrors and gigantic glass cabinets glittering with glass ewers, basins, bowls, pots, plates, candlesticks and every size and kind of drinking vessel.

I stipulated that there should be different Glassworld alcoholic beverages for each colour of glass: white wine for the clear glass, red wine for the ruby glass, blueberry wine for blue, cassis for purple, crème de menthe for green glass and whisky for amber glass. I spent ages concocting colour-co-ordinated meals for the glass plates. I had multi-coloured tiny fruit sweets in the millefiori bowls.

We only got into our stride with the story line when we were nine or ten. We started writing proper Glassworld Chronicles, developing the royal family saga. They coped with births, marriages and many deaths. They went to war, fought off foreign invaders and dealt with a revolution by the workers in the great Glassworks. They shivered in their ermine robes during the Great Glass Ice Age and shuddered when a violent tempest cracked the Glass Palace from top to bottom.

Carl and I made it up as we went along, acting it out, interrupting each other excitedly, scribbling stuff down until our hands ached. We stayed cooped up in the Glass Hut hour after hour, never noticing the time.

It began to change when Carl started at the grammar. He had so much homework he didn't have time to invent Glassworld – and when he did have the time he didn't have the inclination.

I wondered if Carl had been making any notes. I looked around the hut hopefully. There were two black notebooks on the shelf but they were Carl's proper glass books, one full of descriptions of glass in the Victoria and Albert, his favourite museum, and the other bright with paintings of stained-glass windows all over Britain. There was a square black sketchbook tucked behind them. I flicked through it, smiling. There were drawings of Pre-Raphaelite stained glass, bright felt-pen sketches of Chihuly glass at the V and A, delicate pencil sketches of Lalique glass at Brighton museum. There were a few blank pages, and then, right at the back, there were Carl's own designs, variations of the Glass Boy. He drew him standing on tiptoe, stretching, sitting, flying with swirled glass wings. As the sketches progressed the Glass Boy came to life. He was running, eyes narrowed against the wind, arms pumping, legs pounding. His leg was drawn back, aiming carefully, about to kick an invisible ball. He was leaping high in the air, arm punching in triumph.

I snapped the sketchbook shut and put it carefully behind the two glass notebooks at exactly the correct angle.

I thought about a glass *girl*. I tried out several self-conscious poses. Would Carl want to sketch me or would he laugh at me? He'd probably fob me off gently, the way he'd kissed me on the nose.

*Why* wouldn't he kiss me properly? I suddenly panicked, wondering if I had the most terrible bad breath. Andy hadn't backed away from me, groaning, but maybe he was heroically polite. I tried cupping my hand in front of my mouth and breathing out. I could detect nothing but I still worried.

Maybe I didn't smell repellent, maybe I *looked* repellent. I'd started to get a bit spotty, though I tried hard to disguise it. I still looked embarrassingly young for my age, but I was starting to get a *little* bit of a figure now, though little was the operative word. I looked a sad scrawny baby compared to Miranda.

Did he secretly fancy her? I was his girlfriend, wasn't I? Why didn't he fancy me? Maybe I should simply ask him. It needn't be such a big deal. He was my best friend, closer than a brother. Why did I feel so shy, so scared?

He came into the Glass Hut half an hour later.

'Hey, Sylvie,' he said, not sounding surprised, nor cross that I'd barged in by myself.

He was wearing a white T-shirt, blue jeans and white trainers, ordinary clothes I'd seen him wear a hundred times before, but he looked newly wonderful in them. I looked at the fair peachiness of his skin, the little hollow at his neck, the slight swell of the muscles on his arms, the tautness of his stomach emphasized by his plaited leather belt.

'Budge up a bit, Syl,' he said, gently nudging me with his trainers.

I sniffed his warm toast boy smell, but there was another sharp lemony scent, unfamiliar. I sniffed several times.

'Are you getting a cold?' said Carl, opening the huge Glassworld tome and flicking through the early pages.

'What's that smell?'

Carl sniffed too. 'Your shampoo?'

'No, it's not me, it's you.' I got closer. 'Definitely.'

'Are you saying I pong?' said Carl.

'No. Well, yes, but pleasantly. Like perfume.'

'I'm not wearing perfume! I was just trying out a tiny drop of Jake's aftershave, that's all,' said Carl.

I stared at his smooth skin. 'You don't shave!'

'That doesn't mean I don't want to smell OK,' Carl said. '*You* wear perfume sometimes.'

I'd once snaffled some of my mum's French perfume but it was old and stale, a long-ago birthday present from my dad. The bottle had been gathering dust on her dressing table ever since. I was simply trying to use up the perfume so that Carl could have the pretty cut-glass bottle for his collection, but Mum got cross and Carl moaned about the smell, saying it made his nose prickle and his eyes sting.

He seemed totally unaffected by his own aftershave. I wondered if he had put it on for my benefit. My heart started thudding.

'I love that smell,' I said hurriedly. 'It's much nicer on you than it is on Jake.'

Carl smiled at me, still flicking through the Glassworld Chronicles. 'Do you think King Carlo and Queen Sylviana wear perfume?' he said. 'Aha, they're forced to wear pungent oils and bury their regal noses in silken handkerchiefs during the Great Summer Stench when the Victorian Glassworld sewers collapse . . .'

'Oh *yes*, because an enemy spy slipped down a manhole and blew up the brick sewer, so that not only is half of Glassworld mired in filthy mud, the entire royal family having to be carried by sedan chair so that the royal feet aren't sullied, but also giant rats have now escaped from the depths of the stinky sewers and now there is a plague of them, over-running Glassworld, biting babies, getting in all the food cupboards, running over people's faces in bed at night. *So*, Queen Sylviana gives her splendid Siamese cats the task of killing all the rats—'

'But they are totally useless little lap-cats. They cower away from the rats and hide behind Queen Sylviana's velvet sofa, mewing piteously. No, no, we need a Pied Piper, fresh from Hamelin. King Carlo spots him strolling nonchalantly through the palace grounds. His pied cloak trails on the filthy floor but none of the mud sticks to it, and his feet in their natty mismatch boots stay surprisingly mud-free too. His red and yellow garb looks curiously like a football strip. Indeed, as he nears the palace he starts kicking one of the prize pumpkins in the royal vegetable gardens. He breaks into a run, dribbling it nimbly down the ruby gravel driveway, all the while piping away. Queen Sylviana peers round the royal velvet curtains at the Piper. She catches her breath at the sight of his sweet face, his broad shoulders, his well-muscled long legs in their pied tights—'

'No she doesn't! She wonders who this mad

fool is, dressed so bizarrely. Red and yellow look ridiculous worn together. How dare he pick any of the pumpkins! Queen Sylviana wants this impertinent interloper punished. He is banished to the dungeons—'

'OK, he shrugs his shoulders and does not struggle because he sees that Queen Sylviana is quite mad. Maybe she's so aware of his physical charm that she's temporarily unbalanced. Whatever. So the Piper lurks in his little dungeon. He's been put on bread-and-water rations but he's still got his pumpkin, so he passes his time gouging out the flesh with the end of his pipe, munching his monotonous vegetable meal. The rats gather in force, their yellow teeth glinting by the light of his one flickering candle, but if he plays just eight bars of his haunting melody they are hypnotized, utterly catatonic. Ha, *rat*atonic! They stay motionless, in aural ecstasy. King Carlo visits this strange new prisoner and sees for himself the extent of his powers. He sets him free and commands him to walk around the town playing his pipe, similarly enchanting every single rat. He succeeds in just one quick circuit, and then he leads them up up up to Mount Eruption, the terrifying Glassworld volcano, and all the rats scamper madly because the mount is red-hot and burning their paws. The Piper is far fleeter, his boots barely touching the ground, so that he isn't even slightly singed, and he strides unharmed to the very edge of the fiery inferno, still playing persuasively, and all the rats tumble down down down in a squealing squeaking flurry and are all burned to a crisp. So the general stench in Glassworld is given an even more rancid reek of roasted rat flesh, so the problem is even more dire, soooooo . . .'

Carl looked at me. 'Come on, come on. I've been talking for ages. It's your turn now, Sylvie.'

I sighed, trying to think. I didn't really want to carry on. I felt hypnotized like the poor rats. Carl hadn't been so inventive, so fired up, so totally involved in Glassworld for ages. I'd longed for him to play it properly, the way we did when we were little kids, but now I wasn't quite so sure. *I* was usually the one with the best ideas, the one who invented new characters and planned every aspect of the plot. I felt usurped, wrong-footed, left out. I couldn't get *into* the story. I was stuck in the hut, holding the paperweight in my hand, while Carl was inside Glassworld with his King and this new irritating Piper who seemed to have taken over, charming everyone with his ludicrous get-up and crude music. I wanted him out of Glassworld.

'Queen Sylviana had not been idle when she was rather unkindly closeted in her bedroom, erroneously deemed mad. She sensed right from the beginning that the Piper was a dangerous enchanter. He not only bewitched rats, he bewitched children, women, men – even kings. He was actually in league with the enemy spy who blew up the Glassworld sewers. It was all part of his dastardly plot to charm his way into the royal circle and eventually usurp the King himself.'

'Rubbish!' said Carl. 'You're spoiling it.'

'Look, it's my go now – you had ages and ages. I'm *not* spoiling it. I'll make it turn out right, you'll see. *So*, Queen Sylviana tossed and turned on her silk swansdown pillow, trying to think what to do for the best. Her own magical powers were in decline, as she always sank into a terrible depression when she felt she was out of favour with the King. She thought hard of all the women in the world strong enough to play the Piper at his own game. She looked into her Glassworld mirror, and every facet of the glass shone rainbow spectrums in her face. She closed her eyes, dazzled, and when she tried opening them again she did not see her own reflection, she saw a plump and comely raven-haired enchantress, Princess Mirandarette, playing with her potions in her Ice Palace in the Snowland Steppes. Queen Sylviana shivered, knowing Mirandarette's powers. She was the most ruthless of all the enchanters, showing no mercy, because she had a sliver of ice in her heart. She was her only chance.

'Queen Sylviana summoned up all her magical strength and sent a psychic message through the ether. Princess Mirandarette smiled. She donned her white fur robes, called for her reindeer sleigh, and set off across the night sky, travelling faster than the speed of light to Glassworld. As her sleigh hovered over the beleaguered city the reindeer threw back their heavy antlered heads at the stench and trod thin air, not wanting to land in such a polluted place. Princess Mirandarette waved her moonstone sceptre thrice above her head and snow started falling, such thick, rapid snow that Glassworld all but disappeared, just the very pinnacles and spires sticking out of the all-enveloping snow blanket. She circled above, her sceptre flashing through the air, lowering the temperature so suddenly that Mirandarette turned a ghostly shade of blue beneath her furs. Then her arm shot out and she summoned the sun itself, and the snow melted almost instantly, taking with it all the stench and mire, miraculously cleaning Glassworld until it sparkled in the glorious sunshine. Princess Mirandarette sparkled too, a radiance glowing around her like an all-encompassing heavenly halo. King Carlo stepped out of his palace, wondering who had performed this truly miraculous feat, and saw her standing there, and he was dazzled by her beauty—'

'No he wasn't,' said Carl.

'Yes, yes, he fell passionately in love at first sight, though he claimed indifference to her. He did not even thank her very graciously—'

'Utter bilge! Shut *up*, Sylvie!'

'Not not not bilge, it's beautiful storytelling. Now listen, I have a cunning plan, it's all part of the plot—'

'I'm not listening,' Carl said childishly, putting his hands over his ears.

'Listen to me!' I grabbed his hands and pulled them away. I wanted to spin out the story but now I could see I had to blurt it out. 'King Carlo fancies Princess Mirandarette *because* she's enchanted him, it's not his fault, but *then* she sees this Piper person and he plays his silly old fluty tune and suddenly *she's* the one who's helplessly enchanted. She follows him as blindly as all those awful rats and he charms her away to wherever he came from. So they're both gone for ever and King Carlo and Queen Sylviana breathe the cool cleansed air of Glassworld and gaze into each other's eyes, all enchantments over, and they renew their wedding vows and live happily ever after,' I gabbled, still holding onto Carl's hands.

Then I stopped. Carl stopped. We looked at each other. *We* were gazing into each other's eyes. It was the perfect moment. I waited. I waited and waited. Carl didn't move towards me and kiss my lips. He looked past me, over my shoulder, at the Glass Boy poised on the shelf.

Lucy was still sulking on Monday but Miranda was surprisingly friendly. She came rushing up to me at lunch time, giving me a hug, as if we'd been best friends for ever.

'Hey, Sylvie,' she said. 'Let's slope off somewhere by ourselves. You haven't had lunch yet, have you? Shall we slip out the back way and go and get chips?'

We were strictly forbidden to leave the school premises at lunch time. I was usually a timid little goody-goody – but I nodded yes. I tried to act as if it was no big deal but my heart started thumping as we walked round the back of the canteen, ducked behind a delivery van and then ran out through the trade entrance. We carried on running to the end of the road and then slowed to a stop, laughing.

'There! I knew it would be easy-peasy,' said Miranda. 'Come on, let's find the chip shop.'

'So you've never done this before?'

'Never.' She smiled. 'You're obviously a bad influence, Sylvie. You're leading me astray.'

'Yeah, like I'm the really bad naughty girl,' I said.

'You are, you are. Look at you on Friday night, snogging my boyfriend.'

'*What?*'

'Andy kept going on about you after you left. He really fancies you.'

'Rubbish! And Andy isn't your boyfriend. You were snogging *my* boyfriend.' I swallowed. 'Miranda, was it a *proper* snog?'

Miranda peered at me. 'Hey, you didn't really mind, did you? It was just a silly game. I didn't mean to upset anyone. I get crazy sometimes, I always push things too far. I could have kicked myself when Carl walked out like that. It was just meant to be a *laugh*.'

'Oh well,' I said lamely.

'Carl isn't still mad at me, is he?'

I shrugged.

'You're so *lucky* having a boyfriend like Carl. He's so interesting. Most boys are so incredibly *basic*. They just want to fool around all the time. Andy and Raj are OK, I suppose, but they get on my nerves. Would you believe they started up a farting competition after you left? I was glad you guys weren't there to witness it. It was so irritating. Alice and I left them to it.

We went up to my bedroom and played music. Alice danced around for a bit. She watches pop videos compulsively and she's perfected all these little routines. It's kind of pathetic. Although Alice is one of my totally-for-always best friends I often find her irritating too. Is that awful?'

'Well. I suppose I find my best friend irritating too sometimes,' I mumbled. I felt incredibly disloyal to Lucy but it was true.

'I frequently irritate *myself*,' said Miranda. 'Do I irritate you, Sylvie?'

'Not at all,' I said politely.

'I bet I irritate Carl,' said Miranda.

I hesitated.

'Yeah, right,' she said, sighing. 'I know, I know, I'm too full-on for most guys, especially someone as complex as Carl. I wish I had the knack of just *being*. I've always got to prance around and show off.'

'But it works, Miranda, you know it does.'

Miranda pulled a face. 'It only works with the people I'm not really bothered about.'

'It worked with me!' I said. 'So you're obviously not bothered with me, right?'

'Wrong wrong wrong,' said Miranda. 'You've always intrigued me. You hang out with silly old Lucylocks and yet you don't twitter and giggle like she does. You wander round at lunch time looking dead mysterious and you jump if someone talks to you, as if you're deep in thought, in another world entirely—'

90

'Glassworld,' I said, and then I put my hand over my mouth.

'Whichworld?'

'No. Nothing.'

'Come *on*. *What?* Did you say Glassworld? Is this the story you and Carl made up together?'

'You're too sharp, Miranda. Stop it!'

'Is it like Glasstown? You know, the stories the Brontës made up together when they were children?'

'The Brontës? Like, Charlotte and Emily? The ones who wrote great fat Victorian novels?'

'Yes, that's them. They weren't great fat *girls*, they were spindly little sisters, three of them and a brother who was a bit of a waste of space. Haven't you read *Jane Eyre*? Ha, that's who you remind me of, funny fierce dreamy little Jane. You must read it, Sylvie, and *Wuthering Heights*, it's got the most amazing beginning – *and* end, though it gets a bit muddly in the middle.'

'Aren't they rather long and difficult? They're classics.'

'Yeah, but they're fantastic dramatic love stories too. You'll love them. And then you'll get into reading about the Brontë family and how they lived in this bleak parsonage on the Yorkshire moors and they wrote these little books in minute handwriting when they were children about two imaginary worlds, Angria and Glasstown. I always thought how cool it would be to have a family like that so you could

91

all make up stuff together. I used to play all
kinds of pretend games when I was young and I
made the other kids play them too, but it was
definitely under sufferance. They all thought I
was totally weird. But now I've found you guys
we'll all be in the Weird Club together. So, tell
me all about Glassworld.'

'I can't. I really truly can't, Miranda, it's just
been our secret thing for years and years. Carl
would kill me if I breathed a word about it.'

I felt so worried she'd take offence but she
just shrugged and laughed.

'OK, OK, but you can't stop me making up *my*
world too. The Brontës had Glasstown and
Angria, remember. Yeah, I'll have *Sangria*,
that's like a Spanish drink – we drank heaps of
it in Madrid last year.'

'*You* drank it?'

'Well. A glass. My parents had great *jugs* of it.
Yes, Sangria will have red-wine fountains and
everyone will be very relaxed and there'll be lots
of dancing and it will be really really hot,
summer all the time, and it'll be like an island
so everyone can go swimming whenever they
fancy and the sea will be really warm and
there'll be dolphins – yeah, everyone will swim
with the dolphins and I shall speak dolphinese
like this!' She started squeaking and clicking,
flapping her hands like flippers. 'See, I'm good
at making it up, aren't I? You're going to get
bored holed up in Glassworld so you can come
and visit, right?'

'OK, I'd love to,' I said. 'So long as I have my own pet dolphin.'

'Absolutely. And your own pet piranha fish who will give you such a loving little nibble if you try to stroke it. I'll personally decorate your hair with pearls and coral beads and tie it with silky green seaweed. I'll give you a sea-green velvet dress to wear in the evenings buttoned with real pearls and you'll drink sangria out of green goblets—'

'Made in Glassworld,' I said. 'My gift to you.'

'You're a very polite girl so after you've stayed with me several weeks and I've thoroughly spoiled you you'll *have* to invite me to your . . . glass home?'

'Palace, if you please.' I hesitated. 'Actually, you've already visited Glassworld. I've written about it in the Chronicles.'

Miranda stopped in the middle of the pavement. 'Really? As me or as one of your made-up Glassworld people?'

'Sort of both.'

'What kind of an answer is that?'

'Look, it's *secret*, Miranda.'

'You can't just *appropriate* me and put me in your book and then refuse to tell me how you've portrayed me. *Why* won't you tell me? Have you made me a horrible character? Have you turned me into Miranda the Mad Hag, with a warty nose and black bristles on my chin? You *have*, haven't you? I'm psychic, I can tell.'

'Your psychic powers are rubbish because

you're not a bit mad or haggy, you're Princess Mirandarette, an enchantress.'

'Ah! So who do I enchant? Can I enchant Carl?'

'Absolutely not. He's the King and he's married to me,' I said.

'That's not fair! You can't bag him in real life *and* in Glassworld.'

'Yes I can!'

'Am I a brilliant enchantress?'

'The best.'

'Well then, I shall summon up all my powers and enchant old King Carl pronto to Sangria. I'll slip sleeping powder in his sangria and lie him down on my big velvet sofa and then I'll cuddle up beside him, and when he wakens in the morning the first person he'll see is me, and there we go, he'll be mine.'

'No, he *won't*,' I said, elbowing her.

'Ouch! You've got such bony little elbows. That *hurt*! It's OK, the charm only works when he's in Sangria. You can have him all to yourself in Glassworld. He'll just have an occasional holiday with me – now how fair is that? Hey, if I'm such a beautiful enchantress, how come I can't magic up a bog-standard chip shop, for heaven's sake. You'd think there'd be *one* in this manky parade of shops.'

'I thought you'd been to this chip shop before?'

'No, no, I've always been a good girl and stayed at school. It's just your bad influence. You're leading me astray!'

94

I nudged her again and she nudged me back. We staggered up the street, poking each other and giggling as a bus went past.

'Hey, look, it's going into town. Let's hop on it,' said Miranda.

'But we've got to be back by two!'

'We will. We'll just nip into McDonald's, OK? Come *on*.'

She caught hold of my hand and pulled me. I struggled for a few seconds, but then I let her tug me to the bus stop and haul me onto the bus.

# 10

'There!' Miranda said, laughing and panting as we flopped onto the front seat.

'I can't believe we're doing this,' I said. 'We'll be in *so* much trouble if someone sees us and reports us to the school.'

'Yeah, like, we're being totally wicked, nipping into town for a spot of lunch like thousands of other people,' said Miranda. 'That's what I hate about schools. They act like it's a total criminal offence and moral outrage if you're not wearing your school *tie*, for God's sake. It's all so trivial and stupid. And we've got years and years to go. I can't *wait* till I can just say stuff it.'

'What do you want to do when you leave? University?'

Miranda shrugged. 'I'd sooner art school.'

'Carl wants to go to art school too but he's so

brainy his parents want him to try for Oxford or Cambridge.'

'And is he going along with their plans?'

'I don't know,' I sighed. 'I don't know what Carl really thinks any more. It's so hard now he's at Kingsmere Grammar. He's sort of clammed up.'

'I thought you two had this totally magical relationship – true minds, imaginary worlds, big literary partnership, the whole caboodle.'

'Yes. Sort of. But when we were little we were so close we were like CarlandSylvie, one person. Even our families called us that. Now he's Carl and I'm Sylvie and I'm scared we're kind of losing it. I don't know why I'm telling you all this. I know you want Carl for yourself.'

'Maybe I want him because he's yours and not mine,' said Miranda. 'And if it's any consolation he doesn't seem remotely interested in me. Hey, maybe we're wasting our time sighing over him, Sylvie. I bet he's not agonizing over us right this minute.'

We got off the bus at the town centre. Miranda pulled me towards the big shopping centre.

'They've got a McDonald's downstairs. Or we could go to the food court. Do you fancy Thai food? Or a proper pizza, not like school muck?'

I fingered the five coins in my purse. 'I've only got enough for chips,' I said apologetically.

'Hey, it's my treat, naturally.'

'No. Why should you pay for me?'

'Because I'm the spoiled little rich girl. I always pay. It's why people put up with me,' said Miranda.

I looked at her. 'I never know when you're joking and when you're not.'

'Neither do I.'

'Well, I put up with you because I like you – and I want to pay for my own meal, OK?'

'OK! McDonald's then.'

It was crowded with mums and toddlers and clusters of teenagers. There were several boys in distinctive purple blazers.

'Look! Aren't they Kingsmere boys? Do you think Carl ever comes here?'

'He's never said. I wouldn't think so.'

'But he *could*. Suggest it, Sylvie! Then we could all meet up for lunch. It would be so cool. We could play Glassworld and Sangria together.'

'You mustn't tell him! Promise you won't. He'll be so mad at me,' I said as we collected our chips and went to sit down.

'You're not scared of him, are you?'

'No. I just don't want to upset him.'

'You are so sweet with him. Don't you believe in playing hard to get sometimes? Why don't you try acting up and being difficult? Maybe making out you're keen on someone else?'

'There wouldn't be any point. Carl knows me too well. I'm not the slightest bit interested in anyone else.'

'Oh, yawn! You're a hopeless case. Stuff your

chips in your gob before you come out with more sickening stuff. OK, it's obvious I can't try to get Carl off you. We'll have to get him to find a special pal for me. What about this footballer friend Raj mentioned? Have you met him?'

'No. I don't think he can be a *real* friend. Carl hates football.'

'Yes, but maybe he likes *him.*'

'He's never really mentioned him.'

'Well, *you* mention him. See if we can get together. You could come to my place. No silly kissing games, I promise. Well, unless we start serious snogging. You and Carl, me and football guy. I hope he's more David Beckham than Wayne Rooney in looks. Carl might come again even if it's just to admire my stained glass. Or we could go to your place if it would make him more comfortable.'

'My place *isn't* comfortable. Not any more.' I bit the end off a chip and then started arranging the others according to size.

Miranda waited, unusually tactful.

'My dad cleared off two years ago. He doesn't even bother to come to see me now, not that I care. He doesn't always send Mum money for me. She works, but we have to have lodgers too, to pay the mortgage. I had to move out of my proper bedroom. I just have this little cupboard room now. It's not big enough to have friends round.'

'I'm quite a small friend. Well, I'm ginormous compared to you, but everyone is. I can scrunch up small in your cupboard. And the two boys can lie on your bed – or even under it.'

Miranda used her own meal to demonstrate, turning her carton into a tiny room, her paper napkin into a bed, and then putting two chips on top and two underneath. Then she made one of the top chips lean over and kiss one of the bottom chips.

'Idiot. Have you got a watch on? What do you think the time is?'

'I don't know. Maybe half one? Let's just go and have a peer round TopShop, it's up on the first floor,' said Miranda, stuffing all four chips into her mouth and chomping enthusiastically.

'We'll be late back for school.'

'No we *won't*. God, you're such a worry-guts. Just the quickest of quick *peeps*, OK?'

I let her drag me out of McDonald's and up the escalator to TopShop. Inevitably, it wasn't a quick peep at all. Miranda spotted a black lace vest top she said she'd been looking for all her life.

'I've got enough cash on me. Heaps.'

'So buy it then. But do *hurry*.'

'I'll have to try it on. Maybe it won't stretch over my great big boobs.'

'Stop *boasting*.'

'I'm not, I'm not, I'm complaining like crazy – they get in the way so.'

'Well, lend them to me. I'm sick of being totally flat-chested. I look like a little *boy*, for God's sake.'

I wondered if that was why Carl didn't want

to kiss me. Maybe I simply didn't look grown up and girly enough.

I looked at the black silky vest with its slinky straps and pink lace edging. 'What do you think it would look like on me?' I asked wistfully.

'It would look great. You try one on too, come on.'

So I picked up one of the vests and we went to the changing rooms together. Miranda pulled her school sweater and blouse off unself-consciously. We were supposed to wear plain white underwear to school but she was wearing an amazing tangerine bra embroidered with little turquoise flowers.

'Wow,' I said. 'It's a good job you haven't got PE today.'

I turned away to shrug myself out of my own top. I was horribly embarrassed by my sad little girl's bra like a white bandage. I put the black vest on quickly. I peered hopefully into the mirror, expecting some kind of magical transformation. My reflection peered back. The vest just looked like a *vest*, the sort of garment you wore for warmth. The straps slid uselessly off my narrow shoulders, exposing the straps of my bra. The material drooped about me unattractively.

I looked at Miranda. The vest was transformed. It clung to her like a corset, the straps taut against her smooth white skin, the black lace stretched to the limit over her cleavage. The tangerine of her bra straps contrasted exotically. She looked incredible.

'It's not fair,' I said, tugging my vest off and hurriedly pulling on my school shirt.

'Hey, hang on, I didn't have a proper look.'

'You wouldn't want to. It looked *awful.*'

'I'm sure it didn't. Don't be like that. Maybe you need a smaller size.'

'They don't *come* in smaller sizes. None of the clothes in normal shops look right on me. I'm going to have to shop in bloody Mothercare.'

'Oh, Sylvie, you are funny.' Miranda gave me a sudden hug to cheer me up.

An assistant twitched the curtain to check on the cubicle and looked startled to see two girls embracing in their underwear.

'You're not meant to be in there together,' she said hastily, her cheeks pink. 'Come on, get dressed. I want you out of here.' She flounced off, rattling the rings of our cubicle curtain.

'Oh my God, she thinks we're getting it on together!' said Miranda, whooping with laughter.

'Oh, Miranda!' I said, going bright red. 'Quick, put your blouse on. Let's go!'

Miranda's laughter was terribly infectious. I started giggling too, and then I couldn't stop, even though I covered my mouth and bit my lips.

We staggered out of the changing room, snorting and squealing. I felt every sales girl was staring at us disapprovingly. I was ready to run right out of the shop, but Miranda made me wait.

'I want to buy the top, silly.'

'You can't buy it now!'

'Why not? It looks good on me, doesn't it?'

'But they're all looking at us, thinking we're
. . . you know.'

'Who cares? Anyway, so what if we were?
Grow *up*, Sylvie.'

I knew Miranda had the right attitude but I
couldn't help feeling horribly embarrassed as
we waited in the queue for her to pay. She made
it worse, playing to the crowd, putting her arm
round me and gazing at me fondly.

'Stop it!' I hissed.

'Oh come on, where's your sense of humour,
Coochie Face?' said Miranda, laughing at me.

I was even more upset when we got out of the
shop at last and saw the time on the big
ornamental clock.

'Oh no! It's nearly two! We'll be so *late*. We're
going to be in so much trouble! *Come on!*'

I started running. Miranda hung onto me.

'Don't, Sylvie. Slow down and start thinking.
You're right, we really will be in big trouble *if*
we go back to school now. If we waltz in halfway
through the afternoon then it'll be dead obvious
that we've been *out*. But if we don't go back at
all then they'll just think we're away ill or something. They don't take a register in the
afternoon, do they? The teachers won't even
notice.'

'But the other girls will know we were here
this morning.'

'No one will dare blab on me. Do you think old Lucylocks will tell?'

'She wouldn't tell to get me into trouble, but she might be worried about me, scared that something's happened.'

'Oh yeah, I suppose she might start flapping. Can't you text her? Look, borrow my mobile.'

'She hasn't got a mobile herself.'

'Oh, typical. What a bore that girl is. I don't know what you see in her, she's so smug and silly and lickle-girly.'

'No, she's not. Not really,' I said. 'Poor Lucy. Carl's always horrid about her too.'

'There! I knew Carl and I were soulmates. Anyway, let's hope Lickle Lucy holds her tongue because we've just got to stay out of school now, we've no serious option. So we might just as well enjoy ourselves, right? Let's go round *all* the shops. Hey, we could wind up all the shop girls pretending to have steamy sessions in the cubicles. Oh, Sylvie, your face! I'm just *joking*. Don't go all moody on me, there's a darling.'

'We're going to be in even more trouble if we miss the whole of afternoon school. And what will we do about our homework and stuff?'

'Oh, get a grip, girl. Copy off Lucy. Look, no one will notice at school, but if they *do* you can always say you were sick at lunch time or had a splitting headache or whatever and had to go home. Don't look so worried, it's easy to fob them off, believe me.'

'So easy you actually got expelled from your last school,' I said.

'I didn't get expelled for something as trivial as a teeny bit of truanting,' said Miranda. 'Come on, Sylvie, lighten up a little, let's have *fun*.'

I lightened, because there was no point darkening and spoiling everything.

'OK,' I said. 'Fun time.'

We *did* have fun going all round the shopping centre, in and out of every clothes shop, though I kept well away from the changing rooms whenever Miranda wanted to try anything on.

I did let her talk me into trying on shoes, and we paraded around in high heels and big boots and strappy sandals. Miranda adapted her gait according to her footwear, strutting and striding, even doing a Charleston step in diamanté twenties shoes. I was scared we'd get thrown out of the shoe shop too, but there was a young spotty guy serving us and he just sat back on his haunches, entranced. I watched Miranda admiringly too, though part of me wanted to kick her for being such a terrible show-off. But the thing was, she showed off so *brilliantly*. She was the Miranda Holbein Roadshow, rolling up and performing anywhere with cheeky charm.

I'd never had such fun going round the shops. Carl liked browsing in charity shops and antique centres but he hated the shopping centre and wouldn't set foot inside it. Mum was generally too intent on making a quick trip round Tesco.

She got depressed if we went window-shopping in the centre because we didn't have enough money to treat ourselves. I'd gone shopping with Lucy one Saturday afternoon but it hadn't been much fun. We'd had a staid cup of tea and a scone in a department store like a pair of pearl-strung old ladies, and then we'd wandered aimlessly around, Lucy only getting really animated in the Bear Factory.

I was surprised when Miranda wanted to go to the Bear Factory too. She entered into the spirit of the thing, playing with all the limp little bodies in the tub waiting to be filled with beans and turned into bouncing bears.

*'I want to be* yours, *Sylvie,'* she said, making empty little paws stroke me imploringly. *'Fill me up and set my little satin heart beating with love.'*

She was so good at making things seem real, just as good as Carl. I couldn't resist. I picked up the chosen bear and its head flopped wistfully, its eyes big and brown, its little mouth an imploring smile. There seemed something quaint and old-fashioned about him, so I called him Albert. He quivered approvingly.

Miranda took him to the machine to be filled up.

'No, don't. Stop it!' I said. 'We'll have to pay for him if we fill him up.'

'So? I'm not proposing we *steal* him. I've got heaps of money on me. More than enough for one small bear.'

'So you really want Albert?' I asked.

'No, you idiot, *you* do. So I'm buying him for you, OK?'

'You can't possibly—'

'I certainly can. Watch me!' said Miranda. She handed him over to be stuffed. 'Nice and portly, if you please. All bears should have proper plump tummies. Isn't that right, Albert?' She made him nod his head. The Bear Factory girl smiled, obviously used to people larking around.

Miranda chose Albert a little red satin heart to be sewn into his chest, and she recorded a message too. She put on a delightful growly voice and said, *'Grrr! I'm Albert Bear and I think Sylvie's grrreat!'*

We watched Albert being sewn up as proudly as two parents. When he was handed to me I felt that wonderful tight-chested surge of excitement that I used to feel long ago at Christmas when I was very little. I couldn't help hugging Albert, even though I worried that I looked ridiculous.

'Aah!' said Miranda. 'Now, let's kit him out in some clothes.'

'The clothes cost a fortune though. He doesn't need any, really,' I protested.

'Nonsense! He can't prance about stark naked if he's a middle-aged Victorian.'

Miranda picked him out a shirt, a canary-yellow waistcoat, a pair of trousers and some splendid scarlet boots.

'There! Very stylish, even if his costume is an *approximation* of Victoriana,' she said. 'Maybe we can make him a greatcoat and a top hat somehow. And wouldn't he look cute with an ebony cane? He's a bear with true style, Sylvie.' She complimented me as if I'd given birth to him myself.

She paid for him discreetly, not making a great show of her generosity, and then passed his carrier bag over to me when we were outside the shop.

'It's the best present I've ever had,' I said, hugging her.

'Well, you're the best friend I've ever had,' said Miranda, hugging me back.

I was delighted but unnerved. I badly wanted Miranda to be my best friend now – but what was I going to do about Lucy? And much more importantly, what about Carl? Would he mind? What did he really think about Miranda?

# 11

I went round to Carl's that evening. Jules said he was upstairs in his room doing his homework. I knocked on his door and went in. He wasn't doing his homework, he was lying on his bed with his hands behind his head, staring at the ceiling.

'Carl?'

He grunted at me, not sounding encouraging.

I stood in the middle of his room, peering around. It wasn't at all like the Glass Hut. It was like seeing lots of Carls reflecting right back to when he was a baby. There was his wooden Noah's Ark still sailing across the windowsill. An elderly plush giraffe grazed on the faded rug. *The Tale of Peter Rabbit* and *Where the Wild Things Are* and *Frog and Toad Are Friends* were tucked at one end of his bookshelf. String puppets dangled down from the ceiling. The walls were papered with his art – nursery school blue dogs and red horses, primary school ancient Romans lounging at the baths, Egyptian mummies glittering with gold paint.

There were his current possessions, of course – his computer, his glass reference books, his second-hand Penguin Modern Classics, his antique and collectors' fair magazines, neatly stacked.

His whole bedroom was always neat. There were never any clothes strewn across the floor, smelly socks screwed up under the bed, plates of food left mouldering on the carpet, all the usual boy things. There were no pin-ups either, no baby-faced girls with big breasts. I knew Carl wouldn't go for a Beyoncé or a Britney.

'Who do you fancy, Carl?' I asked.

He lifted his head, blinking at me. 'What?'

'You know, pin-ups. Women.'

'Oh. You sound like the guys at school. They're always on about that stuff.'

'*So*, who do you like the most?'

'I don't know. I'm not interested. I don't know any of these women so why should I get turned on by photos of them?'

'And the winner of the Male Political Correctness Award is Mr Carl Johnson,' I declared, pretending to hand him an imaginary trophy.

He didn't play along with me, still staring at

the ceiling, not moving a muscle. If his eyes hadn't been wide open I'd have sworn he was asleep.

'You're always lying prone now, Carl. You want to watch it. You'll get so used to horizontal life you'll keel over when you eventually stand up.' I paused. 'So who do you fancy out of the girls you know?'

Carl sighed. 'I don't know any girls.'

'Don't be ridiculous. You know heaps. Like . . .' I paused again, digging my nails into my palms. I decided to go for an easy option, though I felt mean. 'Lucy?'

'Oh yeah, I fancy Lucy like crazy,' said Carl. '*Not.*'

I felt mean using Lucy like this, even if she was totally unaware of it. But maybe I didn't have to be loyal to her any more.

She'd phoned up at five, asking what on earth had happened to me. When I told her I'd bunked off with Miranda she'd been appalled. She came over all righteous and goody-goody, going really over the top, saying I was jeopardizing my entire school career. I think she was mainly put out because I'd gone off with Miranda and not her. I let her lecture me for ten minutes. She went on and on about Miranda being a totally bad influence. She wasn't saying anything that was basically untrue, but I got so bored I said, 'Do shut up, Lucy. Miranda's my friend.'

Lucy put the phone down on me. It didn't look

as if *Lucy* was my friend any more. Still, did it really matter now I had Miranda?

'What about Miranda?' I said.

I'd paused too long. Carl had lost the thread of our conversation.

'What about her?' he said.

I swallowed. 'Do you fancy her?'

'No,' said Carl.

'Not one bit? She's ever so lively and attractive and dynamic. She's the sort of girl you can't help looking at.'

'I told you, I don't fancy her at all. She's not my type.'

I paced up and down his bedroom, trying to summon up the courage. I said it over and over in my head.

*Am I your type?*

*Do you fancy me?*

I couldn't quite manage it. I reverted to Miranda.

'She's not really a *type*. She's unique. I haven't ever met anyone else quite like her. I don't just mean the way she dresses, but the way she relates to people, and all the different things she knows. She can seem really outrageous, like she keeps pretending she's after you – well, I *think* it's pretending – but then she can be amazingly sweet to me. You'll never guess what Miranda bought me today, Carl.'

'Miranda Miranda Miranda. Hey, maybe she's *your* type, Sylvie,' said Carl. 'Do *you* fancy her?'

'Shut up!' I said. I felt my cheeks going scarlet as I remembered the girl in the shop.

'Syl? I didn't *mean* it. Anyway. Look. Do you think Miranda would like to come bowling some time?'

I stared at Carl. 'You want to go bowling with Miranda?' I repeated.

'Not just her. Us. We could go one Friday night.'

'The three of us?'

'Well. I could get one of the guys from school to come too. Maybe.'

'Which guy?'

'I don't know. Whoever wants to come.' Carl coughed and sat up. 'Paul was saying he likes going bowling. Maybe he could come.'

'Paul the football guy?'

'Yeah. Him.'

I went and sat down by Carl's giraffe, stroking her long soft droopy neck. It was so strange. It was all happening just as Miranda had suggested. Perhaps she really was an enchantress like her Glassworld counterpart? Why was Carl inviting her if he didn't like her? And why on earth was he suggesting *bowling*?

'You don't like bowling,' I said.

'I think it'll be fun.'

'You hated it that time you went with Jake.'

'Yeah, well, I hate anything I do with Jake,' said Carl. He stretched. 'So. This Friday? You and Miranda, Paul and me?'

'OK.'

'Great.' Carl smiled at me. It was a

113

devastatingly sweet smile, his brown eyes shining. I stopped puzzling over everything and smiled back.

'Now I really must get on with homework,' Carl said gently, getting his school bag and flipping through it for textbooks and jotters.

'You always have so much homework,' I said, sighing.

'You always have so little,' said Carl. 'And even then you don't always do it.'

'I haven't got any this evening. I don't even know what we got set, on account of the fact Miranda and I played truant this afternoon.'

I knew that would stop him in his tracks and divert him from his homework. I told him the whole story of our afternoon adventure. Carl looked reluctantly impressed. We'd often fantasized about playing truant when we were at school together. We'd even plotted the best way to do it and planned what we would do together on our snatched day of freedom. We'd never quite managed to *do* it.

'Miranda's got a lot of bottle,' said Carl. 'Still, better not get *too* carried away. You don't want to get into too much trouble.'

'Lucy thinks I'll get expelled.'

'Oh well, Lucy would.'

'I think we've broken friends, Lucy and me,' I said, nursing the giraffe.

'Well, that's cool, isn't it? Because you've got Miranda now.'

'Yes. She said she wants to be my best friend.

But you know what Miranda's like, Carl. You don't really know where you are with her. She could just as easily stop being your friend and become your worst enemy, and then where would I be?' I said, clutching the giraffe close to my chest.

'You'd be where you always are, best friends with me,' said Carl.

He reached out and we did our special best-friends clasp. I wanted to hang onto his hand but he gently disentangled his fingers and opened up his school books. I sat cross-legged watching him work for a few minutes and then I went home.

Mum was just coming down the road, struggling with shopping. I ran to help her, feeling guilty.

'I thought we were going to Tesco on Sunday morning when I can help,' I said, hauling flimsy plastic shopping bags indoors.

'Hey, hey, careful, there's eggs in that one. Don't try to carry them *all*, you'll hurt yourself.'

We struggled together down the hall into the kitchen and tumbled all the bags down on the floor. Mum switched on the kettle and started unpacking everything, putting food in the fridge and cupboards. I nicked a banana and then backed away towards the door.

'No, don't slope off, Sylvie. I want to talk to you,' said Mum ominously.

I froze, holding my banana in mid-air. I chewed my first mouthful but I seemed to have lost the ability to swallow. Had they noticed I wasn't at school and phoned Mum at the building society? Maybe some nosy neighbour had spotted me out with Miranda? Perhaps the shop where we'd tried on the vest tops had found out our names and reported us?

I stood still, clutching the stupid banana. 'Bananas are considered monkey food, but monkeys actually get severe tummy upsets if they eat lots of bananas,' I gabbled, trying to distract her. I launched into a ludicrous riff on bananas, from their excellent potassium content to their role in slapstick comedy, while Mum made us a cup of tea. Then she sat down at the table and beckoned me to join her. I still kept up the banana-gabble, picking off all the stringy bits and whittling it with a knife, turning it into a long white woman.

'Look, don't mess about with it, *eat* it! That bunch cost ninety-nine pee. It's meant to nourish you. It's not blooming playdough,' said Mum.

I put down the banana and knife. Mum didn't sound *cross*, exactly. She would be *extremely* cross if she knew I'd bunked off school. She couldn't know. So what was this all about? I took a quick peep at her. She was glancing at me equally furtively. We both giggled uneasily. Mum was bright-eyed and very pink, as if a fresh wind was blowing through the kitchen.

'I'm thinking of going out Sunday morning, Syl,' she said in a sudden blurt. 'I didn't think you'd mind. You can have a lie-in and then go round to Carl's. And I was wondering if it would be OK for you to have Sunday lunch there too.' Jules says it's fine with her. She's doing a roast so there'll be heaps for everyone.'

'So where are you going, Mum?' I asked, bewildered.

'I thought I might go swimming,' said Mum.

I stared at her. I'd never known Mum go swimming in her life before. I didn't even think she had a swimming costume. The whole world was going crazy. First Carl wanted to go bowling, now Mum wanted to go swimming. Was Lucy going to take up lap dancing? Would Miranda join the church choir?

'*Can* you swim, Mum?' I said.

'Yes. Well. I *used* to be able to. I can do breast stroke OK.'

Mum did little swimming movements with her hands. She looked nervous. I imagined her, pale and podgy, being splashed by a lot of screaming kids.

'I'll come with you, Mum. What's this swimming idea then? Do you want to get fit or something?'

'No, it's . . . "or something",' said Mum. 'I'm not going to the local baths, it's this club up in London. Well, I *think* I am. Maybe it's a totally ludicrous idea and I'll give up on it altogether.' She put her hands over her face, shaking her head. 'I think I've gone a bit mad. I know I'm acting crazy. I just can't help it though. I'm so sick of being sensible.' She made an odd little noise. I wasn't sure if she was laughing or crying.

'Mum?' I gently prised her hands away from her face.

She smiled at me, though her eyes were wet. 'The thing is, Sylvie, I'm seeing this man on Sunday.'

'Goodness!' I said. 'Why? Who is it? Some guy at work?'

'Do me a favour! They're all young enough to be my sons! No, this guy – look, swear not to tell anyone, not even Carl?'

'OK.'

'I haven't actually met him yet but I talk to him on the Internet.'

'*Mum!*'

'Don't look so shocked. It's not like one of those weird chat rooms. It's a website called "Not Waving But Drowning". I read about it somewhere and then I looked it up. It's a kind of humorous helpline thing.'

'About *drowning*? You're not going swimming!'

'No, no, silly! It's based on that Stevie Smith poem, "Not Waving But Drowning". It's always been one of my favourites – it's quietly desperate in a funny sort of way and I suppose there have been times when I've felt quietly desperate too. I'm fed up at work, I hate having to have lodgers in the house, even poor Miss Miles, I hate never going out, I just do the chores and slump in front of the television. I've felt like my whole life's over and I'm not yet forty.' Mum took a deep breath. 'Sooo, it was strangely comforting accessing this website and finding hundreds of other people just as desperate as me. *More* so. Some of their stories would break your heart.'

'If they're true,' I said.

Mum blinked. 'Well. Yes. I suppose there's always a risk some are making it all up. But some – well, you seriously couldn't imagine such situations!'

'What have you got yourself *into*, Mum?'

'Nothing! I've just made contact with a few people. We have a little chat on-line, that's all. Some can be a bit tedious but some are a real laugh. There's this one guy, Gerry, who's really sweet, and he's especially good at sending himself up. We sort of hit it off right from the start. You know the way you're immediately on the same wavelength?' Mum looked at me eagerly, eyes shining.

'Mum, you've never even met, you said.'

'Well, that's it. We're going to meet on Sunday and go swimming. I know it's a bit of a weird place for a first date.'

I couldn't help wincing.

'Don't be like that, Sylvie.'

'I'm not like anything, Mum. I'm just worried about you. I'm scared you might get hurt. He could *literally* hurt you. What if he's some raving nutter with a knife?'

'I don't think that's very likely.'

'He could drag you down a dark alley and rape you.'

'Oh, Sylvie, don't be silly. And that's especially not likely. I don't think he could drag me anywhere. You see, the thing is, Gerry's got this disability.'

'Oh God.' I knew it was awful of me but I immediately imagined two heads and no arms and legs.

Mum frowned at me. 'He had a stroke two years ago—'

'Is he *old*?'

'No, just a few years older than me. He was a builder, with a wife and two kids. He worked really hard, he did well, set up his own building company, bought the big house, posh car, had the fancy lifestyle. Then he got this pretty young girlfriend—'

'*Mum!*'

'I know, he's not proud of it at all. Anyway, he went off with the girlfriend and two months later he had a massive stroke. His whole life fell apart. The girlfriend left, the wife didn't want to take him back, he was in hospital and then spent three months in a stroke unit. He's OK now though. He's just left with a weakness down his right side, so he walks with a pronounced limp, but apart from that he's fine. Well, so he says. He's very into keeping as fit as possible and he goes swimming a lot at this private London club. He was describing it, all marble pillars, and I said it sounded fantastic so he's invited me to join him.'

'Oh, Mum! Are you sure you know what you're doing? What if he's seriously creepy?'

'Well, what's going to happen to me in a swimming pool? If I don't like him then we'll just call it a day. He's invited me for lunch too, but I can always say no. I want to give it a go though.'

'Aren't you scared, going to meet a total stranger?'

'Of course I am,' said Mum. 'Part of me doesn't believe I'm really doing this. But what the hell, Sylvie. It's better than being stuck at home feeling sorry for myself.'

'Well, good for you,' I said, though it was a struggle to get the words out.

I still thought Mum was mad. Or maybe I just felt unsettled. My mum was going out on a date before I'd ever gone on a date myself. No, wait. Was Friday night's bowling with Carl a date? Who was Carl really asking out anyway, me or Miranda?

I felt guilty about Lucy, so I bought her a bar of chocolate and a copy of *Heat* magazine. She thawed considerably. We had a long conversation about the Bear Factory and all the different furry variations and cute outfits on offer. I didn't tell her that Miranda had treated me to Albert Bear.

Meanwhile Miranda was busy telling everyone that she and I were going bowling with Carl and Football Paul. Lucy couldn't help overhearing.

'I've known you and Carl since first school! Why are you going bowling with Miranda and not me?'

I didn't know what to say. I couldn't possibly be truthful and tell her that Miranda was much more fun. I tried telling tactful fibs, pretending that I was sure Lucy would hate bowling, and that this football guy would probably be so boring it would be a penance to be in his company.

I didn't sound convincing. Lucy iced over like the Alps.

'Well, if you'd sooner go around with Miranda then that's fine with me,' she said.

It obviously wasn't fine at all. It was very uncomfortable sitting next to her in class when she was barely speaking to me.

Miranda wasn't very sympathetic. 'I should think you'd be thrilled to bits not to be friends with that boring old Lucy,' she said. 'You should see the way she looks at me now, like I'm some sleazy tart who's lured you away from the straight and narrow.'

'Well, you *have*,' I said.

We had a silly poking-finger fight. It started to get quite painful. Then Miranda coiled her little finger round mine.

'Hey hey! We're best friends now, remember?'

I thought Carl would be very pleased that Miranda was keen to go bowling, but he seemed totally taken aback when I told him.

'I was only *suggesting* it. I didn't mean it *definitely*,' he said. 'Maybe it's not such a good idea. I don't know how Miranda and Paul would get on. I think she's way too eccentric and gabby and flamboyant for him. He's basically quite a conventional guy.'

'So why do you like him so?' I said, puzzled.

'You don't like convention. And you certainly don't like football.'

'I don't like him "*so*",' Carl said crossly. 'He's just this guy in my class, that's all.'

'OK.'

'And I truly don't think it would work, the four of us. We're all too different. So put Miranda off, OK?'

But the next evening Carl came round to my house, still in his purple grammar uniform. He was usually pin-neat, but not today. His shirt was hanging out, his sweater sleeves rolled up, his regulation black school shoes badly scuffed and laced with bright-red cord. His cheeks were bright red too.

'Are we still on for Friday night?' he asked eagerly.

'You said you didn't think it was a good idea!'

'Yeah, well, I've changed my mind. I was having this chat with Paul and he was saying all over again that he'd like to go bowling. He said it would be fun to go bowling with a couple of girls and I said, "No problem, I'll fix it."'

'Well, make up your mind, Mr Fixit. Stop blowing hot and cold.'

I couldn't work it out. Carl seemed really keyed up about Friday night – and yet he hadn't seemed nervous about going to Miranda's party *last* Friday. He'd been totally cool about it. I'd been the one chopping and changing, not sure whether I wanted to go or not.

Miranda was the only one of us totally

committed to the bowling date. I couldn't help letting her think it had been *my* idea: I'd casually suggested including Football Paul just so she'd be particularly pleased with me. She *was* pleased too.

'Mind you, if he turns out to be cute but boring I'll swap you him for Carl,' she said mischievously.

I spent more than an hour getting ready after school on Friday, though I ended up wearing exactly the same outfit, my jeans and Mum's black sweater. It would be too hot again but it seemed more sophisticated than any of my T-shirts. It draped pleasingly over my chest too, making it look as if there were a proper pair of breasts underneath. I wondered if Mum might be planning to wear it for *her* date on Sunday. I hoped I wouldn't get it all sweaty under the arms.

I *felt* a little sweaty when I went to call for Carl. He seemed anxious too, fussing because Jules had thrown out some old army-style sweatshirt he wanted to wear. He was wearing his oldest jeans too, the pair that was torn at one knee and fraying at the ends.

'So what's this new look, Scruff Boy?' I said, ruffling his hair.

'Get off! I've been *trying* to gel it into place.'

'I don't like it gelled. It looks much better all shiny and floppy.'

'Yeah, well, maybe I'm sick of the little choir-boy look.' Carl raked his hair irritably. 'Right, shall we go? I've got heaps of cash by the way. Tonight's on me.'

'Thanks, Carl.'

Jules came to say goodbye. She gave both of us a happy hug. 'Have fun, darlings,' she said. 'Give us a ring if you're going to be really late.' She beamed at us both. 'Happy bowling!'

We set off a little self-consciously.

'I don't even know *how* to bowl,' I said.

'Simple. Roll the ball at the pins. That's basically it.'

'So why the big deal?'

'It's the, like, social occasion, innit?' said Carl, mock-Cockney. 'It's where you hang out with your mates and pull the birds, right?'

'Well, you're doing all right, definitely, seeing as you've got your mate all lined up and two birds.'

Carl grinned at me and checked his wrist-watch. 'We're meeting them outside at seven thirty? We're going to be ever so early. What do you want to do? We could always go and have a coffee or something.'

'Or a drink.'

'Or a meal.'

'Or go night-clubbing.'

'Or take the train to the coast.'

'No, take the plane to . . .'

'Paris?'

'No, Venice. We'll go to see the glass-blowers on Murano and buy the most beautiful chandelier.'

126

'We'll hang it in the palace and hold a grand ball and dance until the small hours.'

'And meanwhile Miranda and Paul will be down the bowling alley, rolling the balls at the pins.'

We laughed a little too uproariously. Then we were silent. We could see the alley at the end of the road, its blue and orange neon sign flashing hypnotically. We trudged towards it.

'We don't *have* to meet up with them tonight,' I said. 'We *could* just slope off and leave them to it. We don't have to go off to anywhere exotic. We could simply go home and hide out in the Glass Hut, just being *us.*'

'I know. Stop tempting me,' said Carl.

'You *don't* like bowling, do you?'

'No. I can't stand it.'

'So why did you start all this?'

Carl sighed. 'I suppose I wanted to impress Paul.'

I was baffled. I'd never known Carl try to impress anyone before. I imagined Paul in my mind, tall and athletic, in football strip, with one of those handsome, chiselled, square-jawed faces. I tried hard but I couldn't project any expression onto him. He lumbered stiffly through my thoughts like a soldier doll, tanned and plastic and ready for action.

'Hey, he's there already! He's even earlier than us!' said Carl, suddenly hurrying, almost running.

I squinted at all the guys hanging around

outside the bowling alley, lolling against the
wall, jumping up and down the steps, sitting on
the wall kicking their feet. None was a likely
candidate for Football Paul. Then a boy started
waving – and Carl waved back.

So this was Paul, this ordinary-looking boy in
a hoodie and faded jeans and scuffed trainers.
He was a little taller than Carl and a little
broader. He had darkish-blond hair, gelled and
spiky. He had a few freckles across his nose
and cheeks and a grin that showed a lot of his
teeth. I couldn't decide if he was good looking or
not. He didn't seem a *patch* on Carl.

They were messing around together, Carl and
Paul, doing a weird elaboration of a high-five
routine, and then playing some crazy kind of
kung fu, chopping thin air and making daft
sounds. I stared at them. I'd never seen Carl
acting the fool like this – he was normally way
too cool. He saw me staring.

'Hey, Paul, this is my friend Sylvie,' he said.

Why couldn't he say *girl*friend?

'Hello, Paul,' I said.

He held out his hand. I thought he was still
mucking around kung fu-ing so I kept my own
arm pinned to my side. He withdrew his arm,
looking disconcerted. He'd simply been trying to
shake my hand. I felt awful but it seemed
too late to start all over again. I nodded at him
instead, smiling manically to show I wanted to
be friends.

'Where's Miranda?' said Paul.

128

He was eyeing me up and down, obviously hoping Miranda would be more promising.

'She's meeting us here. We're still a bit early,' I said.

It was torture waiting for Miranda. Carl and Paul and I made stilted three-way conversation for a little while but this soon tailed away into awkward silence. So Carl asked Paul about some match he'd played that afternoon and they were off speaking boring football-lingo. I was surprised that Carl could talk it. He was a little too sycophantic, going on and on about Paul's astonishingly amazing brilliant performance, like he'd done complicated brain surgery while whistling the Hallelujah chorus. He'd just run around a field kicking a ball, for heaven's sake. Carl actually used the word 'awesome'.

I stared at him, wondering if he was actually sending Paul up. No, he seemed *serious*. I raised one eyebrow at him. He didn't raise one back. He edged away, practically turning his back on me, standing in a little huddle with Paul, cutting me out. He was treating me the way he treated *Lucy*. I was so hurt and cross I almost stomped off home by myself, but I felt I had to wait for Miranda.

We all waited and waited and waited.

'Is this Miranda actually going to turn up?' Paul said, turning to me.

'Yes, of course she is,' I said, though I was starting to wonder myself.

Miranda was ten minutes late.

I checked my mobile for messages. I sent Miranda a text, then another.

Fifteen minutes. *Twenty*.

I tried ringing her but she was engaged. Maybe she was sitting cosily at home, ringing Alice or Raj or Andy, having sensibly decided to give the bowling date a miss.

Twenty-five minutes.

'She's not coming,' said Paul, frowning. He obviously wasn't used to being stood up.

'Is she mucking us about?' Carl said crossly, glaring at me as if it was somehow *my* fault.

'How do *I* know?' I said.

I tried giving her one last ring on her mobile – and got through to her.

'Hi! Why are you phoning? I'm *here*,' said Miranda.

There she was, walking towards us, looking stunning in very tight jeans, a black satin shirt (mostly unbuttoned) and a crazy furry waist-coat. Her hair wafted past her shoulders in a mad cloud of curls. She took little swaying steps on account of the incredibly high heels of her killer boots.

Carl and Paul stared at her. Carl smiled. Paul shook his head, looking bemused. He gave a little whistle.

'*She*'s Miranda?' he said. 'Oh boy!'

Miranda came wiggling up to us, laughing and talking and hugging as if we were all her oldest friends, even Paul – *particularly* Paul. She didn't apologize for being so late; she didn't seem the slightest bit fussed about it. She let Carl pay for her to go into the bowling alley as if it was totally her due, not even bothering to thank him. She didn't take much notice of me either. She just nattered away to Paul and he nodded and smiled and preened in a totally sickening fashion.

'Happy now?' I said to Carl as we queued up.

'Sure,' he said, but he didn't actually seem sure at all.

I hated the noise and blare and stale chippy smell of the alley. I hated the game itself. I couldn't seem to get the knack at all. I tried to copy the others, bending down and then rolling the ball, but I was lousy at aiming – once my ball jiggled over into the neighbouring alley, causing four boys to start screaming abuse at me. I ignored them, though I knew my face was beetroot red. I stood with my hand on my hip, yawning every now and then, trying to pretend that the game bored me silly and I wasn't even going to try to play properly, but I didn't fool anyone.

It didn't help that the other three were so good at it. Paul was by far the best, aiming stylishly, effortlessly, his ordinary boy body suddenly taking on a Glass Boy grace. He spoiled it by punching the air and leaping about crazily each time he knocked ten pins down, which happened with monotonous regularity.

Carl did his best to copy his style, bending

exactly the same way, extending his head, flicking his wrist, like a Paul shadow. He could copy the technique but he didn't have Paul's natural ability. He looked good but he only ever demolished half his pins.

Miranda did things *her* way, of course. She could barely bend in her tight jeans and adopted an odd crouching position, her bum in the air, so that all the boys in the bowling alley started goggling at her. She was very aware of this and played up to her audience, tossing her hair and leaning further forward so that the remaining two buttons on her shirt strained and popped. Everyone expected her to bowl as badly as me, but somehow she had the knack. The ball left her hand, spurted up the alley and knocked the pins over with a satisfying thunk each time.

Miranda and Paul were level-pegging for a while, but then he started drawing ahead. Miranda laughed and clapped him, telling him he was absolutely fantastic in this silly breathy voice. I thought she'd been taken over by aliens, just like Carl, but when she looked at me she pulled a funny face, raising her eyebrows. She was obviously just playing a silly game with him, scoring her own jackpot.

The evening was starting to seem endless. It was all Paul's fault. He was making Carl and Miranda behave like cartoon morons. I hated the way he lorded it over Carl, jostling him, swearing, telling silly jokes. Carl tried hard to join in, though it was the sort of behaviour he'd always despised. I hated the way Paul looked at Miranda, as if she was a page-three pin-up. She played up to him, wiggling and giggling until I wanted to shake her.

I hated the way Paul treated *me*. He ignored me most of the time, as if I truly wasn't worthy of his attention, but when he felt it necessary he ordered me around like I was someone's little sister, only there under sufferance.

We went and had hot dogs and chips, and Paul squiggled red and yellow lines of ketchup and mustard up and down his dog and then started squiggling Carl's too. Carl just laughed, even when they were drenched. Then he grabbed the ketchup and started swamping Paul's meal in turn. I couldn't believe it.

Miranda sighed and started eating her chips delicately, one by one.

'Here, let's make them a bit tastier for you, Miranda,' Paul giggled, aiming the mustard at her plate.

'You squirt so much as a spoonful and I'll ram it down your throat and season your tonsils,' Miranda said calmly.

Paul blinked at her, taken aback. 'Hey, hey, lighten up, I'm only joking,' he said.

Carl was surreptitiously scraping the worst of the sauce off his food. I knew just how much he hated cheap ketchup and mustard.

'What about you, Sylvie?' said Paul, juggling the red and yellow bottles.

'No thanks. You're behaving like two-year-olds,' I said primly.

Paul pulled a face. 'Oooh, I consider myself severely chastised,' he said in a silly voice. 'That's rich, coming from the youngest of us.'

'I bet I'm *not* the youngest,' I said. 'How old are you? When's your birthday?'

It turned out I was the second oldest.

'So it's your birthday very soon, Carl,' said Miranda. 'What do you want? I know, some select and sparkling item of glasswear.'

I held my breath. If Miranda started talking about Glassworld then Carl would kill me. No, worse. He'd never play Glassworld with me again.

Paul laughed, thinking this was some kind of crazy joke. 'Glass?' he said. 'What are you on about? Why would he want glass?'

'Oh, our Carl's total Glass Boy, didn't you know?' said Miranda.

Carl's head jerked. Miranda saw it too.

'You love my stained-glass windows, don't you Carl?' she said smoothly. 'Didn't you say you had your own glass collection?'

'Sort of,' Carl mumbled.

'What, vases and stuff?' said Paul. 'Weird.'

'It's not weird at all. Carl's got an amazing collection,' I said. I thought of a way to impress him. 'Similar pieces go for hundreds on eBay and yet he bought them for a couple of pounds ages ago.'

'Really?' said Paul. 'I tried selling these little

134

pig money banks on eBay – someone said they were worth heaps, but the most someone offered me was five quid and it cost more than that to send the little beggars. I used to collect pigs when I was a little kid. Hey, Carl, I've got a glass pig. Would you like it? I'll give it to you for your birthday present.'

'Cool,' said Carl.

'That's a bit of a cheapskate birthday present,' said Miranda. 'Hey, I've thought of the most brilliant birthday treat for you!'

I didn't like the way she always tried to take things over.

'Will you have a party, Carl?' she asked.

'Probably not.'

'Yeah, you're not really a party guy, are you? So let's have an amazing birthday outing!'

'We've already got something planned, just Carl and me,' I said quickly.

Carl and I celebrated his birthday together, the two of us. There was usually a family meal but then Jules generally took us somewhere special. Last year we'd gone to the glass gallery in the V and A, magical rooms right at the very top of the museum with green glass steps and a glass balcony. Carl had performed a Fred Astaire-type tap dance all the way down the glass steps, ending with a high kick, a spin round, and then stretched his arms out in triumph while I clapped like crazy.

'What have you got planned?' said Miranda.

'Oh,' I said, stuck. I hadn't come up with a

new idea yet. 'Probably a museum. You'd be bored.'

'I probably would. No, I've got a *much* better idea than a stuffy museum. We'll go to Kew Gardens on one of their floodlight evenings.'

'Gardens?' said Carl. 'Thanks, Miranda, but I don't fancy that for my birthday.'

'You will. They've got a Chihuly exhibition there.'

'Oh wow!' said Carl.

'You what?' said Paul.

'Chihuly's this amazing American guy – he makes these extraordinary glass flowers,' said Miranda.

'There's this fantastic greeny-yellow gigantic whirly glass like thousands of snakes hanging in the entrance of the V and A. That's Chihuly,' said Carl.

'How did you know about him?' I asked Miranda.

She grinned. 'I asked my dad. He's a bit of a glass freak too. It's settled, right? We'll go on your birthday, next Friday night, yeah? You and me and Sylvie . . .'

Carl looked at Paul. 'Are you coming too?'

'Sure,' said Paul.

# 13

It looked as if Paul was now part of us, like it or not. When Carl and I were walking home together he turned to me and said, 'So, what do you think of Paul?'

I shrugged. 'He's OK.'

Carl looked crestfallen. 'Only *OK*?' he said. 'What's the matter? Why don't you like him?'

'I do like him. Sort of. It's just he's so . . .' I searched for the correct word. Dull? Ordinary? Boring? I settled for 'boyish'.

'Well. He's a boy. What else would he be?' said Carl.

'Yes, but he mucks around so. He's a bit manic, don't you think? What was all that hot-dog stuff about?'

'Oh, Sylvie, that's just his wacky sense of humour. He's always larking around. Even in mid-run on the football pitch he'll suddenly start capering about like a loony and Mr Grisby, the sports teacher, screams at him but then Paul whacks out a foot, kicks the ball and scores a goal.' Carl tried to demonstrate, looking ridiculous.

'You're not getting into football too, are you?' I said.

'No, of course not. I'm hopeless at it, you know I am. But it's good fun watching Paul. He's brilliant, he really is. The school want him to try out for the boys' team of one of the big football clubs. He's the best at football in our whole school and yet he's not a bit big-headed about it.'

'Fancy you being friends with a football jock,' I said.

'Well, why shouldn't we be friends?' said Carl. 'And he isn't a football jock. He's clever – he's in the top set in nearly all subjects. He reads a lot. He's into Fantasy. He's lent me a couple of his favourites. There's one that's a bit like Glassworld. I'll let you read it if you like.'

'I'd sooner make up *our* Glassworld.'

'Paul's quite good at writing too. He does this cartoon thing in the school magazine. We're thinking of doing a whole picture strip together.'

Carl went on burbling about Paul all the way home. It was almost as bad as having Paul physically with us. I wondered if he was taking Miranda all the way home or leaving her at the bus stop. I wondered what would happen when they said goodbye.

'Do you think they'll kiss?' I said.

Carl stopped. 'What?'

'Miranda and Paul.'

'No. Maybe. *I* don't know. Why, do you think he really liked her then? I thought she went totally over the top, all that waggling her bum about. I couldn't help feeling embarrassed for her – she's so *obvious*. She can be fun, I suppose, but I don't really know what you see in her, Sylvie.'

I was infuriated. Carl felt free to criticize my friends. He was rude about Miranda and totally cruel about poor Lucy, yet he didn't seem to like me being even mildly critical about Paul.

'Still, it's good we've got another girl. Threesomes can be a bit awkward,' said Carl. 'And it's a seriously cool idea going to see the Chihuly glass at Kew.'

'Can't we go on our own?' I asked.

'Well, it was Miranda's idea. And I've asked Paul now and he said he wanted to come.'

'What about me?' I said. 'You didn't ask me.'

'Oh, Syl, I didn't have to ask you. I knew you'd want to come,' said Carl, putting his arm round me. 'Come on, stop being Sulky Sylvie.'

He so rarely put his arm round me nowadays that I couldn't possibly stay stand-offish. I snuggled up as close as I could. He was wearing his denim jacket and the round metal buttons dug in painfully but I didn't care if they became permanently embedded in my flesh. We turned the corner into our street. I wished the road would stretch from here to China so we could carry on walking for ever, Carl's arm warm and protective round my shoulders.

When we got to our gates Carl stopped, looking me straight in the eyes, still holding me. I thought this was the moment at last. Our moment. Carl's lovely mouth puckered into a kissing shape. I started trembling. But then he just blew me a kiss, turning it into an affectionate joke.

'Night, Syl,' he said, and went indoors.

I went into my house, feeling so churned up. I wanted to go straight to my bedroom to brood in private but I bumped into Miss Miles shuffling in her slippers to *her* bed, cup of herbal tea in one hand, book in the other. She asked where I'd been, and when I said bowling she became surprisingly interested and said it was something she'd been considering taking up herself. This was such a totally bizarre idea I was struck dumb. It wasn't until she asked me if it was compulsory to wear all white that I realized she meant that bowling-green game for old codgers. I couldn't help snorting with laughter.

'Someone sounds happy,' Mum called from the living room. 'Come and have a chat, Sylvie. Did you have a good time, darling? Tell me all about it.'

Her computer was still on and it gave a little *ting* to show she had a message. Mum kept her eyes dutifully on me, not even glancing at it. I squinted at the screen suspiciously, hating the thought of some creepy guy sending lewd lovey-dovey messages to my mum.

'Hey, you're not meant to peer at my messages,' said Mum, pink and beaming. 'Gerry phoned me up tonight too. That was a huge relief, because I'd been a little bit bothered he'd have speech difficulties because of his stroke and I was scared I wouldn't be able to understand him. Thank goodness he speaks absolutely normally. He's got a lovely voice, actually, really warm and friendly. He's still very keen on us going swimming on Sunday.'

'Do you want to borrow my costume?'

'I'd never squeeze into it! No, I've treated myself to a new one.' Mum went and rifled in a plastic bag. 'Look, what do you think?'

It was scarlet with little white roses.

'It was so hard finding anything *decent*. I like the shape of this one but they only had it in red and it's ever so bright. Do you think it's *too* bright?'

I did my best to reassure her. Then she asked me all sorts of stuff about Carl and Miranda and Paul. She went on and on about Paul.

'What's he like? Is he good looking? What sort of clothes does he wear? Is he a *nice* boy? Did you have fun together?'

'We *weren't* together, Mum. It was him and Miranda, Carl and me,' I insisted.

'I know you're totally Carl's girl, darling, but maybe . . . maybe it would be good to start seeing other boys.'

'No thanks. I don't want to. Come on, Mum, you know I just want Carl.'

Mum sighed. 'Yes, I do know, but . . . Oh well. Whatever. I'm sure things will work out. I just want you to be happy, darling.'

When I got into my room at last my mobile rang. I hoped it would be Carl, but it was Miranda.

'Well, I think our little friend Paul belongs in an aquarium,' she said. 'Talk about an octopus! I let him have this little weeny snog when we were saying goodbye and it was suddenly hand up here, hand down there, hands all over the place. Is Carl like that, Sylvie?'

'Um. No. No, he's not a bit like that,' I said. 'So, do you like Paul, Miranda?'

'Mmm. Well. He's OK. Ish. I'd sooner have Carl though.'

'Well, he's taken,' I said.

'I know, I know.'

'Don't sound so disappointed! Miranda, this outing to Kew, do you think it's really going to work? I mean, maybe we could go bowling again? Or we could go for a pizza together? It's just that Kew's such a weird place for us, especially with Paul tagging along too.'

'Oh, Paul will like it all right. He'll be grabbing hold of me and whisking me behind the potted palms at every opportunity,' said Miranda, giggling. 'Oh well. It might be fun.'

It didn't look as if there was any way I could talk her out of it. Kew was *our* place, Carl and me. Jules had taken us there and we'd had a picnic under a willow tree and then we'd wandered in and out of the glasshouses. Carl and I climbed the rickety steps all the way up to the balcony under the roof. We peered down at all the palms while trapped birds flew in and out of the branches as if we were truly in the jungle. We'd introduced a glasshouse into Glassworld, a gigantic crystal palace where albatrosses soared overhead, casting shadows with their great white wings, and enormous red roses and white lilies and pink orchids bloomed in the artificial warmth while snowflakes patterned the outside of the glasshouse like lace.

Why hadn't *I* known about this special glass exhibition? Why did Miranda have to push in everywhere and take control? I wondered if I was sick of Miranda. But when she phoned on Saturday and asked if I wanted to come round I was pleased.

'Come right now! I'm soooo bored,' she said. 'Bring Carl too.'

'I can't. He's watching the Boy with the Golden Boots play flipping football,' I said.

Miranda chuckled. 'Just so long as *I* don't have to go and watch him. I find football the most tedious game on this planet. OK then, Sylvie, *you* come. Don't be long, will you?'

'OK, I'm coming now,' I said, though I wasn't sure how I was going to get there.

Mum was out, taking Miss Miles to visit her mother in some nursing home in Worthing. Miss

Miles seemed ancient enough to me. It seemed bizarre that there was an even older, wrinklier version propped up in a bathchair somewhere. I decided I was never ever going to get really old.

I wondered about nipping next door and asking Jules if she could possibly drive me to Miranda's. It seemed an awful cheek but she was almost like an aunty to me. I hurriedly changed into my best jeans and a T-shirt and an embroidered ethnic waistcoat thing that Mum used to wear way back before I was born. I hoped it might make me look vintage and funky. I suspected I just looked like I was dressing up in my mum's old clothes but I didn't have time to try out another look.

I grabbed my keys and ran next door. Jake answered, eventually, wearing a sweater over his pyjamas, his hair sticking straight up.

'Hi, Jake,' I said. 'I haven't got you *up*, have I? It's two o'clock!'

'Heavy night last night,' he said, scratching his head and yawning. 'We were rehearsing, working on my new number.'

Jake's part of this silly schoolboy band, playing the lead guitar. He talks like he's part of a mega-band playing to millions.

'Did it go well?' I said politely, as if I cared.

'Yeah, it did actually.' He paused, playing air-guitar. 'But we need to try it out on an audience. You should come, actually, Sylvie. Bring some friends.'

'Like . . . Miranda?' I said, guessing his game.

'Yeah, whoever,' he said.

'Well, maybe,' I said. 'Look, Jake, is your mum in?'

'Mum? No, I think she's gone up to town to see some art exhibition. Dad too. And Boy Wonder's watching football.'

'I know. Oh. I was rather hoping to beg a lift to Miranda's from your mum.'

'*I'd* give you a lift. If I could drive. You can hitch a lift on the handlebars of my bike if you like.'

'Oh, ha ha.'

'I'm serious. You're only a little titch.'

I winced at the nickname.

'I suppose I'll have to walk it,' I said, and waved goodbye.

It was a very *long* walk – all the way across town – to Miranda's house. I'd put on my boots with heels. I realized this was a serious mistake by the time I'd got to the end of the road but I didn't want to waste any more time going home and changing. I staggered on, and then ran for a bus. Big mistake. I'd come out without any money whatsoever so I had to get off again and carry on walking. I thought I'd take a short cut down the back streets but I got a bit lost. It was about half past three when I *eventually* rang the doorbell of the white house.

No one answered. I wondered if Miranda had gone off somewhere without me. I rang the bell again and again and then turned and started limping dejectedly back to the gate.

I heard the door open behind me.

'Dear God, you took your time,' said Miranda. She was wearing black but seemed oddly speckled with white.

'Fairy dust?' I said, touching it.

'Hey, you're making it worse,' said Miranda irritably, slapping my hand away. 'What took you so *long*?'

'I'm sorry. I got a bit lost. I hadn't realized it was so far,' I started, but she wasn't interested.

'Come *in*, then,' she said. 'We're in the kitchen. We're cooking. You have a lot of catching up to do.'

She'd called Alice when I'd failed to materialize within ten minutes. Miranda had made Alice a smoothie in her mum's special blender, and that had suddenly given them the idea of making cakes. They'd never made cakes before but that didn't deter them. They had flour and eggs and sugar and butter and jam spread all over the long kitchen table, with bowls and cups and spoons scattered all around.

Alice was listlessly beating a gloopy mixture in a bowl, her hair tied up in a topknot. Her face was as pale as the flour. She smiled at me wanly. It seemed obvious that she wished she had Miranda all to herself. They carried on making their cakes, chatting together, occasionally asking me to pass them more flour or milk as if I was their little scullery maid. I had half a mind to walk straight out, all the way home again.

Miranda flicked a little flour at me. 'Don't look sulky, Sylvie. I expect you've still got time to make a cake yourself if you get a mad move on. Although you seem in total *sloth* mode today.'

'I practically *ran* here, Miranda,' I said, flicking her back.

'Well, no one but a madman would *walk* all that way. Why didn't you get a lift?' said Miranda, flicking again.

'I tried, but my mum's out and so is Carl's. Look, *stop* it, I don't want to get covered in flour.'

'Why on earth didn't you get a cab?'

I very nearly grabbed the big bag of flour and tipped it right over her head. 'Because I don't have any money as I'm not a spoiled little rich girl like you!'

'Look, you two, don't get into a fight, for God's sake,' said Alice. 'And stop messing around with that flour. *I* need it. Look, my eggs have gone all funny. Do you think they've curdled?'

'They're coming out in sympathy with Sylvie,' said Miranda. She suddenly put her floury arms round me and gave me a big hug. 'Hey, sorry sorry sorry sorry! OK? Now, grab a bowl and get cracking, Sylvie. Do you know how to bake a cake?'

'Of course,' I said, though I'd only ever made little Barbie fairy cakes out of a packet mix. But Carl was a brilliant cook. He'd started off when we were seven with a Winnie-the-Pooh recipe book, making a really good quick-mix

147

birthday cake. Then he fell in love with Nigella and her chocolate cake, and then he got attached to Jane Asher and experimented with one of her cakes whenever any of us had a birthday. He wouldn't let me help, rapping my fingers with his wooden spoon, but I always licked out the bowl, and if I begged hard enough he let me play around with the icing bag when he was decorating.

I rolled up my sleeves and started measuring and mixing. By the time Miranda and Alice had finished faffing around with too many eggs and too much flour and way too much milk so you could drink their cake mix I'd caught them up. Miranda found three different cake tins. I bagged the best sponge tin quickly, badly wanting my cake to come out well.

'Does your mum make lots of cakes then?' I said, impressed with the assortment of tins.

'My *mum*?' said Miranda, flipping back her long hair, making a weird white streak at the front. 'You have to be joking. My ma's so afraid of putting on weight she rarely enters the kitchen. If she smelled our cooking cake fumes she'd need to scrub out her nostrils pronto.'

I thought Miranda was joking but when I went off in search of a loo I burst in on an extraordinary stick-thin woman tweezering her eyebrows in the Venetian glass mirror. She raised one of these beautifully arched eyebrows at me.

'Oh, I'm so sorry,' I stammered.

Her reflection smiled at me. 'It's OK, sweetheart. So who are you then?'

She was speaking slowly and kindly to me, like I was six.

'I'm Sylvie, Miranda's friend,' I said.

'Oh. Of course,' she said. Then she sniffed delicately. 'What's the smell, Sylvie?'

'We've been making cakes. I hope that's all right. We'll clear up all the mess,' I said anxiously.

'That's fine, darling. Making cakes! How *lovely*,' she said, as if it was anything but. She looked as if she lived on rocket leaves and Evian. She was beautiful in a weird otherworldly emaciated elfin way. She had Miranda's dark eyes and tilted nose and thick glossy hair but her face was all cheekbones and pointy chin. Her skimpy designer T-shirt and skinny jeans hung loosely on her.

I wondered what it would be like to have such a scarily glamorous mother. I thought fondly of my mum with her home-dyed hair and her round shiny face. She wasn't *fat*, but she had to yank hard at her Tesco jeans to get them to zip up over her tummy.

'I've just met your mum,' I said to Miranda when I got back to the kitchen.

Miranda paused, scraping the mixing bowl. 'Old Anorexic Annie?' she said.

'She is *ever* so thin. Is she, like, on a permanent diet?' I asked.

'Oh yeah. Plus the personal trainer at six in the morning, and colonic irrigation once a week.

149

She pays *money* to have some dimwit shove a hosepipe up her, imagine!'

We imagined it all too vividly and groaned and giggled.

'Still, she does look wonderful,' said Alice. 'I'd give anything to have a figure like hers.'

'*I* wouldn't,' said Miranda. 'I think she's off her head. It's not even like she's a model any more so she hasn't got her job as an excuse.'

'She was a real fashion model?' I asked.

'Yeah. From when she was fourteen. *Our* age. She's got huge glossy photos of herself all over her dressing room. How sad is that? I think she looks gross in the extreme.'

'Miranda!' said Alice.

'It's OK. She says *I* look gross. Do you know what she said to me the other day? I'd called out for a takeaway pizza after supper and she caught me stuffing my face. So she gives me this mournful lecture, right, and she finishes up, "You could be such a lovely-looking girl if you'd only watch what you eat, Miranda. If you'd only lose weight *you* could be a model!" Like I'd *want* to be a brainless clotheshorse!'

'What do you want to be, Miranda?' I asked, smearing my finger round and round my bowl.

'I rather fancy being a journalist,' said Miranda. 'I can write, I'm nosy, I'm pushy, I'm clever at getting people to do stuff. Yeah, I'll be a great journalist.'

'I'd much sooner be a model,' said Alice, striking a pose. 'Or an actress or maybe a singer.

Hey, Miranda, remember way back in the juniors when we sang that Cheeky Girls number and shocked all the teachers?'

'That's my speciality, shocking teachers,' said Miranda. 'I've been slacking recently at Milstead. OK, Sylvie, you can help me out. Shall *we* develop a Cheeky Girls routine?'

'You're too much of a Cheeky Girl already,' I said, putting down my bowl. 'Why do cakes taste better raw than cooked? I wish I'd left more in the bowl.'

'I think your cake is going to be the best,' said Miranda. 'You really know what you're doing, don't you? Hey, do you want to *be* a cook – like, celebrity chef, own your own restaurant?'

'No, I want to be a writer. With Carl,' I said.

'Oh yeah. You've written this famous book together,' said Miranda.

'Shut up,' I said. I didn't want her to talk about it in front of Alice.

'Don't tell *me* to shut up, Titchy-Witchy,' said Miranda, but she changed the subject. 'Come on, cakes, I'm *hungry*,' she said, tapping at the oven door. 'Shall I have a look to see if they're done?'

'No, they've only been in ten minutes tops. They won't rise if you let a draught in,' I said. 'We've got to sort out how we're going to decorate them.' I peered inside cupboards and drawers. 'Oh *great*, your mum's got an icing bag! So why has she got all this baking stuff if she doesn't like cookery herself?'

'She tries to get the au pairs to cook. And for

151

a year we actually had a proper cook-housekeeper. I think the cake stuff started then. She made all sorts – cheesecakes, banana bread, carrot cake, oh yummy yummy – but then Annie went on this mad macrobiotic diet and drove the cook daft with what she could and couldn't eat so she left and that was the end of my cake-fest.'

'You'll have to come round to our house. We've got this sweet Polish au pair now and she makes this fantastic apple-sauce cake – you'd love it,' said Alice.

It was so weird hearing them chatting away, like Victorian women comparing servants.

'Did you ever have au pairs, Sylvie?' Alice asked.

'Nope.'

'But your mum works, doesn't she? Who looked after you when you were little?'

'I went to a childminder and for a bit my mum was *like* a childminder – she looked after these twins, *and* she was their cleaning lady too.'

I wasn't being entirely truthful. Mum just scrubbed up after us if we made a mess with our dough and finger paints but I wanted to make a point.

Alice looked embarrassed, her pale face flushing, but Miranda burst out laughing.

'What's so funny?' I said furiously.

'*You* are, Sylvie, scoring points left, right and centre and putting us poor little rich girls in our places. OK, you win, you win. And you haven't even started on your great-great-granny in the matchstick factory getting phossy jaw and your great-great-granddad being shoved up chimneys when he was six months old—'

'Oh shut up,' I said, giving her a shove, but I burst out laughing too.

My cake was by *far* the best, pale gold and light and fluffy, risen to the top of the tin. Alice's was a pale soggy sad affair and Miranda's was squashed down at the very bottom of her tin.

'Someone's *sat* on it!' said Miranda. 'Oh, just look at yours, Sylvie! How come yours is so perfect? Ah, you're going to tell us your mum is a cook as well as a cleaning lady?'

'Of course,' I said, gently easing my perfect sponge onto a wire rack. 'No, actually, it's Carl. I've watched him cook.'

'You're *so* showing off today,' said Miranda. 'You and Carl! It's so unfair, it's *my* turn with him now. Can't we do a swapsie when we go to Kew? You have Paul the Ball. I'm tired of him trying to score goals with me.'

'No thanks. I don't really like him.' I paused. 'What do you think Carl sees in him? He's so . . . basic.'

Miranda and Alice exchanged quick glances.

'What?' I said.

'*All* boys are basic,' said Miranda quickly. She prodded her flat cake. 'Hey, I think I'm going to call this cake a biscuit, then it won't be so much of a failure. Shall I try to squeeze chocolaty bits into it so it can be a giant chocolate-chip cookie?'

'You could always ice it,' I said, finding a full packet of icing sugar in the cupboard. 'I'll make enough icing for all of us.'

'Cool,' said Alice. 'And have you got any decorations, Miranda, like those little silver balls?'

'Maybe. Let's have a peer,' said Miranda. 'We could use little sweets instead, couldn't we?'

Alice couldn't find silver balls, so she used little pink sugar flowers instead, stuck in a pattern around the edges of her white iced cake. Miranda's cake/biscuit was thickly iced and then piled high with Smarties, Liquorice Allsorts and Jelly Babies.

I decided to resist sweet decoration. I iced my sponge as smoothly as I could, put a drop of blue colouring in the remains of the icing, poured it into the icing bag and then piped *Happy Birthday Carl* as carefully as I could.

'Oh wow, why can't *I* do that?' said Miranda. 'Are you going to give it to him next Friday? Then we could maybe say it's from me too. It's all my ingredients, after all.'

'It might be stale by then,' I said quickly. 'No, I'll give it to him tomorrow.'

Mum was up terribly early on Sunday morning. She had a bath and washed her hair and then came and patted me awake.

'Help, Sylvie. My hair's sticking up all over. It won't go right. Please be an angel and wake up and style it for me.'

'Mum, you're going swimming. Your hair will get soaked in the baths. It won't matter what it looks like now,' I said, diving down under the covers.

'Gerry will see it *before* I go in the pool,' said Mum. 'Come on, Syl, *please* do it. And look, does this skirt look OK?' Mum tugged at the frills on her gypsy skirt anxiously. 'I don't look too girly, do I?'

'No, no, you look fine,' I said, sitting up. 'Well, maybe a bit dressed up to go swimming.'

'Dressed up, like way over the top?' said Mum. 'Oh God. Maybe I look like I'm about to . . . what do gypsies dance? The Fandango?' She raised her arms and stamped her foot and then groaned when she caught sight of herself in the big mirror. 'What should I wear then, Sylvie?'

'Casual clothes.'

'I haven't *got* any casual clothes. I've got fancy clothes and office clothes and very scruffy cleaning-the-house clothes. I *can't* wear them – Gerry will take one look and run a mile.'

'I didn't think he was up to running.'

'Stop that, Sylvie!'

'No. Sorry. I didn't mean . . . It's just so weird that you're, like, going on a date.'

'If it feels weird for you just think what it's like for *me*. It is mad, isn't it? Maybe I should phone him up and call the whole thing off.'

'No, no, you're going, Mum, and you'll have a lovely time and this Gerry will be lovely too and if you come here I'll make your hair look lovely as well. Which way do you want me to style it?' I said, kneeling up on my bed and tucking it behind her ears, trying it this way and that.

'*Any* way.' But then she saw me plaiting a lock and she twitched her head away. 'Any way except little plaits! I don't want to look like a middle-aged schoolgirl.'

'You're not middle-aged anything yet, Mum. You're *young*.'

'I've got middle-age spread already,' said Mum, patting her tummy ruefully.

156

I thought of Miranda's stick-thin mother. 'You're just right,' I said. 'You don't want to look *too* thin. Hey, Mum, why don't you wear your jeans and that black sweater?'

'It's kind of *our* black sweater now. And my jeans are all frayed at the bottoms.'

'That's a totally cool look.'

'Maybe on thirteen-year-olds. Don't forget we're maybe having lunch at the posh club.'

'OK, OK, stick with the gypsy skirt. Tell you what, get the tongs and I'll make your hair all wavy and then we'll stick a rose behind one ear!'

We didn't go as far as the rose but I did wave Mum's hair for her so that she could make a magnificent first impression – even if she doused the curls five minutes later.

She set off, smiling bravely, tossing her curls and swishing her skirt, but when she turned to wave at the gate she pulled a funny face of terror, like Munch's *Scream*.

'It's OK, Mum, you'll have a great time,' I said, giving her a thumbs-up sign.

I watched her head bobbing away above the hedge. I so hoped it would go well for her, though I wasn't at all sure about this Gerry.

I wondered what my father would think if he knew Mum was dating again.

I used to hope he'd come back – not as my *real* dad, who lied and cheated and couldn't be bothered with us half the time. I wanted him transformed into a new loving, caring dad who'd make a big fuss of Mum and come home on time and laugh and joke and take us out. I wanted a dad who'd treat me like I was really special. I'd heard Lucy's dad call her his Fairy Princess. He looked at lumpy old Lucy as if she really had golden locks and gauzy wings and a sparkly crown. I'd wanted to cry then, almost wishing I could trade places with Lucy.

I still felt guilty when I thought about her. No, I wasn't going to think about her today. I wasn't even going to think about Miranda. I wanted to concentrate on Carl.

I wondered if he'd be awake yet. I flopped back on my bed imagining Carl only two walls away lying in his own bed. When we were little we'd hang out of our windows as soon as we woke up and yell to each other. When we got older we'd keep tin cans by our beds and bash them in our own complicated code. We never said anything extraordinary – *Hi, are you awake? I had a funny dream. Have you done your homework yet? Yum, I think Mum's making pancakes* – but it felt great to be secretly communicating, even though we wore our arms out bashing those stupid tins.

We both had mobile phones now but we seemed to have got out of the habit of calling each other recently. I reached over the side of my bed for my phone in my school bag. I wondered about phoning Carl now, but if I woke him he might be grumpy. I wanted today to be perfect.

I tried sending him a tiny text: R U AWAKE? I waited, hanging onto the phone, willing it to *ching-ching* back at me. The phone stayed silent. I sighed and lay on my front. I tried to distract myself thinking up a new Glassworld Chronicle, but for once it was hard concentrating on King Carlo and Queen Sylviana. The idiotic Piper kept playing his shrill pipes wherever they went, even in their innermost private chambers, clowning like a jester and captivating the King. I banged my head on the pillow to try to rid myself of this irritating image. I didn't didn't didn't want to think about *him*.

Maybe Paul would sidle off with Miranda next Friday and Carl and I would look at the Chihuly glass together, just the two of us. I daydreamed about a new Ice Age in Glassworld, a winter so cruelly cold that everyone froze to death, iced into white statues – everyone but King Carlo and Queen Sylviana in their heavy sable robes. No, Princess Mirandarette escaped, skating across the iced-over sea to her own sunny land of Sangria, but Piper Paul blundered into a snow-drift and was never seen again, never never never.

I went to run a bath, hoping that Mum hadn't used up all the hot water. I looked down at my body and sighed. I still looked so *young*. Mum kept reassuring me, telling me I was simply a late developer. She told me I'd start getting a figure any minute now. Any hour, week, month, *year*? What if I *never* developed? What if I stayed stuck with the skinny body of a ten-year-old girl for ever? What kind of freak would I end up?

Imagine a fifty-year-old in kiddie clothes, travelling half price on the buses, turned away from cinemas and pubs. It was obvious why Carl couldn't take me seriously.

I peered down at my chest. '*Grow*, can't you!' I hissed, lathering myself with soap.

I shampooed my hair too and then experimented with the curling tongs, but they didn't work for me. I ended up with a head of crazy Tracy Beaker curls. I looked even *younger*. I washed my hair all over again and let it dry naturally into its usual limp long style, just past my shoulders. I wore my jeans and appropriated Mum's black sweater yet again, needing to look cool but not like I'd made any effort. I was simply going next door to see my oldest friend, for goodness' sake.

I wondered if Carl was awake yet. I checked my mobile. I tapped out: R U AWAKE NOW, SLEEPY-HEAD? I waited. Then the phone vibrated with a message, making me jump, even though I was holding it in my hand. The message read: EYES WIDE OPEN!

I jumped up and whirled round my bedroom, punching the air. I stuffed my school bag with pens and crayons and paper and then paused, looking at Carl's birthday present. I'd wrapped the champagne glass round and round in bubble wrap and then covered it with midnight-blue tissue paper patterned with silver stars. I'd bought a length of silver ribbon specially to tie round it. I didn't want to give Carl the glass with

Miranda and Paul watching and commenting. I decided to give it to him *now*. I wrapped my old fleece round the parcel as extra protection and then gently wedged it into my school bag.

Miss Miles was in the kitchen, munching her muesli and reading her book, a dog-eared paperback of *Great Expectations*. She was dotty about Dickens, reading him constantly. She was forever quoting him, though Mum and I generally didn't get this until she put her head on one side and said, 'As the great man says.'

'Hello, Sylvie. Mum's already off then?' she said.

'Bright and early,' I said.

'I hope she has a lovely time,' said Miss Miles. 'She deserves a bit of fun in her life.'

I smiled at her, wondering if she ever had a bit of fun in *her* life. 'Did you ever have a boyfriend, Miss Miles?' I asked.

She paused, stirring her lumpy breakfast. Her eyes looked misty behind the thick lenses of her glasses. I felt mean for asking her. Of course poor Miss Miles had never managed to have a man in her life.

But she surprised me. A little pink edged along her cheekbones.

'I've had my moments,' she said. 'There was one man in particular . . .' She sighed.

'It didn't work out?'

'Perhaps it was my fault,' she said. 'Maybe I should have been a bit bolder. Seize every opportunity, Sylvie, otherwise life rushes past before you've had a chance to live it properly.'

I nodded politely, eating cornflakes straight out of the packet. Then I had a quick peep inside the cake tin.

'Have you been baking?' said Miss Miles.

'At my friend Miranda's.'

'Can I have a peep?' She craned her neck upwards like a meerkat. 'Oh, I say! That's totally professional. Lucky Carl! Tell you what, if my old mum makes it to a hundred I'll get you to make a cake for her.'

'Do you think she will?'

Miss Miles shrugged. 'Probably. She's a determined old bat. I think she's decided to live for ever. Worst luck.'

I blinked. I'd assumed Miss Miles was devoted to her mother. 'Don't you like your mum?'

'Not much. And she doesn't like me, but I'm all she's got now to keep her in new nighties and talc and boxes of chocolates. Your mum's an angel to take me – it makes all the difference. It's so lovely that you and *your* mum are such good friends.'

I smiled and stuffed another handful of corn-flakes down my throat, feeling embarrassed.

'Why don't you pour yourself a proper bowlful, dear?' said Miss Miles.

'Well, I'm in a bit of a rush. I'm going next door,' I said. I felt a bit mean shooting off straight away and leaving Miss Miles on her own all day. 'Carl will be waiting for me,' I told her.

'What larks, Sylvie, old chap,' said Miss Miles. 'As the great man says.'

'Yeah. Mm. Whatever,' I said, grabbing my bag and the cake tin.

I didn't have a free hand to knock on Carl's door. I clattered the letter box with my elbow and almost immediately the door opened. Jake stood there, dressed in an old skimpy black T-shirt and black jeans. His brown hair was unaccountably black too. Even his hands were purply-black.

'Don't blink at me like that, Sylvie,' he said. 'I know, it looks a bit weird. I thought I'd dye my hair black to look kind of gothic for the band, but I didn't twig you need rubber gloves when you rub in the dye gunk.'

'Oh well, black hands are ultra-gothic. You should file your nails to a point and paint them black too,' I said, joking.

'Do you think that would look cool?' Jake said seriously.

I raised my eyebrows and edged round him. 'I hope Carl hasn't dyed *his* hair.'

'As if,' said Jake. 'He's still little Goldilocks. What's that you've got there – a cake? Let's see!'

'It's not for you,' I said, but he prised the lid off anyway.

'Oh yum! Did you make it yourself? Lucky Carl!'

'Carl makes better cakes than me.'

'He would,' said Jake. He reached out to break off a piece of icing with his black fingers.

'Don't!' I said, trying to hold the tin out of his reach.

'It's OK, only teasing. Will you make a cake for me when it's my birthday?'

'A black one, with black icing, and little black bats as decoration?'

'Cool!'

'Is Carl in his room or in the Glass Hut?'

'He's in the kitchen. Jules is making pancakes. Come on. There's heaps, so you can have some too.'

'I've already eaten,' I said, but when I breathed in the sweet eggy lemon buttery smell in the hot kitchen I decided to go for breakfast number two. Jules was standing at the Aga, her hair sticking up, wearing her purple painting smock, patched jeans and scarlet espadrilles. She blew me a kiss and poured more batter into her pan.

'Pancake, Sylvie?'

'Yes please!' I said, sliding onto the bench beside Carl.

He was wearing his jeans, a soft blue shirt with the sleeves rolled up, and an old bead necklace I made him years ago.

He grinned at me. 'See, I really am awake,' he said. 'What's all the stuff?'

'I made you something round at Miranda's. It's for your birthday.' I held out the tin to him.

'Shouldn't I wait?'

'No, it probably won't keep. Especially now Jake's had a peer. Go on, open it.'

He took the lid off the tin. 'Hey! It's beautiful.'

'Can I see?' said Jules, peering over from the pan. 'A birthday cake! Oh well done, Sylvie. I won't have to make him one now. Shall we have it for tea?' She tossed the pancake expertly.

'I could maybe try a weeny slice now,' said Carl.

'Pig! You've had two whacking great pancakes already,' said Jules.

'OK, make it three, and I'll save my cake,' said Carl.

'*I'm* having the pancake after Sylvie's,' said Jake. 'Know your place in the pecking order, squirt.'

'Pipe down, both of you,' called Mick from the living room. He was sprawling on the sofa with the *Observer* newspaper. 'You're both total squirts compared with me, the Alpha Male. It's *my* pancake next, isn't it, wife?'

Carl rolled his eyes at me. 'What's in the bag?' he said, gently patting it.

'Just stuff.'

'Stuff wrapped in special paper with a silver ribbon,' said Carl, investigating.

'Open it when it's just us,' I whispered.

Mick sometimes mocked Carl's glass obsession. He knew Carl always wanted money on his birthday to spend on his collection. He'd never give it to him. He'd spend a fortune on some gadget or sports equipment that Carl barely used.

Carl smiled. 'Dl-rows-salg,' he whispered.

It was our own old private word, Glassworld spelled backwards, meaning *fine, yes, OK, you bet*, whatever.

It was so wonderful that Carl was in such a good mood. We stayed eating pancakes, all of us laughing and chatting and bickering together. It was just the way it used to be. I was Carl's dearest friend and one of the family. I didn't even have to feel guilty about leaving Mum on her own because she was off having her own adventure.

After I'd eaten *two* pancakes and Carl one more we started to slope off to the Glass Hut, but Jake kept mucking about, going on and on about his boring band, wanting to play this new song he'd written. He sang it reasonably well – he's always had quite a good voice, though I think Carl's is better, so true and pure it makes me want to cry. Poor Jake made me want to *laugh*. He put on this ridiculous soulful expression, tossing his weird black tangled hair out of his eyes. He enunciated in an exaggerated way so we could appreciate every word of his lyrics, waggling his mouth around and showing a lot of his teeth. I had to bite the insides of my cheeks to stop myself laughing.

'What do you think, Sylvie?' Jake said when he'd finished at last.

'Yeah. It's great, Jake, truly,' I said, and then I rushed out of the room into the garden, spluttering.

'What a dork,' said Carl. 'He looks just like a

wild thing with all that mad matted hair and big rolling eyes and too many teeth.'

'Oh, Carl, *yes*, exactly, but you shouldn't be so *mean*.'

'Why not? He's always mean to me.'

'Yes, but Jake's so *sad*. He keeps showing off to me now, trying to make an impression, and he's so obviously wasting his time.'

'Is he?' said Carl.

'Well, of *course*. I can see he's dotty about Miranda, all the boys are, but *I* can't get him a date with her.'

'I think you're getting your wires crossed, Sylvie,' said Carl, opening the Glass Hut door.

I peered around, breathing in the lovely slightly earthy smell of the hut. There was something slightly strange. The glass collection wasn't arranged with pin-neat perfection. The Glass Boy was facing the wall, his back to us. The paperweights were clustered together, the vases were spread out unevenly and one of the tiny glass horses was hobbling along on three legs.

'Oh, Carl,' I said. 'The horse's leg's broken!'

'I know. Shame. Still, you know how fragile they are,' said Carl.

'But how did it happen? Who's been in here moving everything around?'

'Well . . .' Carl suddenly seized the feather duster in the corner of the hut. '*It was me, Miss Sylvie. I'm Plain Jane the Silly Servant Girl and I was a-doing of the dusting and I just flipped*

167

*the wee glass horsey with my feather duster and
down he toppled and broke his little fetlock—'*

'Shut up, Carl. It wasn't you. You're ever so
careful when you dust.'

'Yes, OK, well, whatever,' said Carl, tickling
my neck with the feather duster. 'Let me see my
birthday present then!'

'In a minute. Look, Carl, it's obvious someone's
been in here, moving stuff around. It wouldn't be
Jules, would it? Perhaps we'd better ask her,
because if she *hasn't* then I think someone's
broken in—'

'No one's broken in, silly. Paul was here,' said
Carl.

'Paul?' I blinked at him.

'Yes, he came round for a bit after his match
yesterday.'

'And you let him in the Glass Hut?'

'*Yes*. Don't act like it's such a big deal. It wasn't
*my* idea – he asked to see it, he was interested,'
said Carl, flinging himself on the sofa.

'So interested he mucked everything about
and snapped off the horse's leg?'

'He didn't do it deliberately. He can't help
being a bit clumsy. He was horrified. He says he's
going to get me another one.'

'Did you . . . ?' I swallowed. 'Did you show him
our Glassworld book?'

'No!' said Carl. 'No, of course not. It's ours.'

I breathed out.

'Besides, I didn't want him to think me
completely nuts,' said Carl.

I grabbed the cushion under his head and whacked him with it. He whacked me back and then we were messing around mock-fighting, somehow back to normal again. I still hated the thought that Paul had been bumbling around our private place, poking and prying, breaking things, but at least he hadn't stumbled through Glassworld, smashing everything.

'Can I have my present now, please?' said Carl.

I handed it over with a flourish. I didn't need to tell him to be careful. He delicately untied the ribbon, undid the wrapping paper, unwound the bubble wrap.

I waited, my heart beating fast. I knew Carl would be tactful and say he loved whatever I gave him, but I also knew him too well for him to be able to fool me. It was always risky buying him glass when I knew so little about it. *I* loved the champagne flute and I was pretty sure it was Victorian, but maybe it was just repro-duction, maybe it was just any old rubbish and Carl would secretly hate it.

'Oh!' he said when he saw it. 'Oh, Sylvie, it's lovely.'

'Really?'

'It's absolutely beautiful.' He ran his finger very gently along the vines curling round the stem. 'Where did you find it?'

'It was in the Cancer Research shop near my dentist's. I didn't have enough money on me but I went back.'

'How much did you pay?'

'You're not meant to ask that! Ten pounds. Was that too much?'

'Total wondrous bargain. Oh, Sylvie, you're the best friend in all the world.' He raised the glass to me and mimed drinking. He breathed in, as if savouring his sip of champagne, and then held the glass solemnly out to me.

I leaned over and sipped too. It was the way we used to play when we were little, melting ice lollies and pretending they were wine. It was so real I could almost sense the fizz of champagne under my nose, taste the delicate froth on my lips.

I looked at Carl. He looked at me. His face was soft and gentle, his eyes dreamy. He leaned forward a little. He had only to move a fraction more, angle his head sideways, and we would be kissing. I leaned forward too. Carl blinked and stood up suddenly.

'Let's play Glassworld,' he said quickly. 'OK, it's King Carlo's official birthday on Friday, but that's a bit of a public bore, all pomp and ceremony, so Queen Sylviana decides to give him a very special unofficial birthday celebration the Sunday before. Sunday is their only day off from royal duties, a day when they can leave off their glass crowns, kick off their glass boots, and indulge themselves. So they sleep late, and when King Carlo wakes, Queen Sylviana has her pet canary trill *Happy Birthday* to him. She brings him a special birthday breakfast prepared by herself, golden croissants in the shape of His Majesty's initial, and a bottle of the finest vintage champagne from the Glassworld cellars.

' "But you've forgotten the glasses, my dear Queen," says King Carlo.'

' "No, no," says Queen Sylviana, smiling, and she hands him a beautiful midnight-blue parcel tied with silver ribbon, and inside the parcel King Carlo finds the finest antique champagne flute blown when his great-great-great-grandfather was but a boy. It's the most beautiful birthday present from his dear Queen. It makes him very happy. He starts musing on all the past birthdays they've spent together, ever since they were first betrothed as small seven-year-olds. His first birthday present was . . . Come on, Sylvie, what was it?'

'I don't know,' I mumbled. He was indulging me, playing the game I loved most in the world, but it was all delicate diversionary tactics.

'Of *course* you know,' said Carl. 'Come on, start writing it. On King Carlo's seventh birthday his child bride Sylviana gave him—'

'She gave him a huge set of glass Lego bricks, hand-carved prisms with rainbow reflections, and he set to and made an amazing shiny glass palace. Then he fashioned two small figures out of modelling clay, one a boy, one a girl, and put them on two tiny thrones within the newly constructed glass palace, as representations of the infant newlyweds. He promised they would reign over Glassworld happily ever after.'

171

'And on his eighth birthday?'

We went through crystal bikes, alabaster snow-skis, a glass aviary filled with lovebirds, a tame snow leopard with a ruby-studded collar, a pair of polar bears with silver claws, a glass fountain with rainbow-hued water, an indoor garden of blue glass flowers, and finally the crystal champagne flute. It was part of an entire sparkling set of glass dishes and goblets. King Carlo and Queen Sylviana celebrated the royal birthday by drinking pink champagne out of the birthday flutes and eating strawberries and cream from glass dishes.

'Perfect,' said Carl. 'Maybe Mum can turn up trumps and give us real strawberries.'

'We've only just had pancakes. And we don't have the special glass dishes for the strawberries.'

'Oh fiddle-de-dee, Miss Fussy Knickers. We'll substitute china and *use our imagination*.'

Carl hurried off to find Jules.

I stayed in the Glass Hut, starting to write up the latest chronicle. I heard a little *ching-ching* on Carl's mobile. It had fallen out of his jeans pocket onto the floor while we were wrestling. I pressed the little button to see who was sending him a message. I wasn't really snooping. I did it almost without thinking.

WOT??? NEVER SENT U WAKE UP TEXT, U BERK. IVE BEEN IN SNOOZZZZZELAND ALL MORN. U DONE YR MATHS HOMEWORK? CAN I COPY? CHEERS. PAUL.

# 15

Mum didn't get home till late afternoon. She came to collect me at Carl's.

'Wow, look at you! Positively *glowing*,' said Jules. 'So what's he like, this Gerry?'

'Oh, he's very sweet,' said Mum, ducking her head coyly. Her cheeks were bright pink and she giggled.

'Look at you, blushing like a schoolgirl,' said Jules. 'So when are you seeing him again?'

'Well, next weekend, if it's OK with you?'

'Of *course*,' said Jules. 'Sylvie's part of the family, you know that.'

Mum looked at me. 'Is it OK with you too, Sylvie?' she asked.

'Mm. Yes. Whatever,' I said.

'We'll go home and talk about it,' said Mum, putting her arm round me.

'It's fine, Mum, truly,' I said, wanting to stay with the Johnsons, but Mum steered me firmly towards the door.

'Can't you stay for supper, both of you?' said Jules.

'Yeah, hang out, why don't you?' said Jake. 'Though watch out, Dad cooks supper.'

'I make a mean plate of butternut -squash risotto, even though I say it myself,' said Mick.

I was looking at Carl. He was carefully looking *past* me, as if observing something fascinating in thin air.

'Carl!' said Jules. 'I'm not sure the Johnson cellars can come up with champagne, but I'm sure we'll find a bottle of Cava lurking somewhere. Then you can sip from your lovely flute in style.'

'Mm. Great. Though actually, I might just dash over to Paul's for supper. He's having a maths crisis and I kind of promised to help him out,' said Carl.

'Do you really have to? Honestly!' said Jules, looking quickly at me.

I smiled as if I'd known all along and was perfectly happy about it. It wasn't really a big deal, was it? Carl had a perfect right to go round and see his friend. We'd spent nearly the whole day together and he'd been so sweet to me all that time. He'd obviously sneaked off at some point and texted Paul but that wasn't a crime. Miranda and I were always texting each other.

'It's fine,' I said. 'Thanks for having me, Jules,

it's been lovely. See you, everyone. Come on, Mum.'

Mum's arm was still round my shoulders. 'I can't come up with butternut- squash risotto but I'll do us a lovely plate of beans on toast,' she said.

It was our special comfort food. I hated it that Mum felt I needed comforting.

'I'm actually not really hungry. I'm still stuffed with lunch,' I said. 'Maybe I'll just go and get on with *my* maths homework,' I said as we went into our house.

It seemed so shabby and empty after a day at the Johnsons'. There were oblong patches on the walls where Dad's paintings and maps had hung, great gaps in the bookshelves, heavy indentations in the carpet where his desk once stood. Mum had bought a couple of paintings from the Hospice charity shop, Gwen John and Picasso reproductions, but they didn't quite fit the bare squares. The Gwen John woman looked hopelessly forlorn and the old Picasso lady had her head thrown back, her mouth wide open in agony. We were better off with bare walls.

We bought books from library sales but Mum's were mostly self-help paperbacks and diet books and mine were modern kids' books about broken families, so the bookcase had a sad air too. We didn't have enough spare cash for a proper new desk. We had a huge flatpack standing in the desk place, but we couldn't even work out how to get it out of its cardboard case, let alone erect it.

It was as if our lives had been put on hold since Dad cleared off. Mum kept insisting we were better off without him. She said she liked it much better with just the two of us. She said she didn't want to meet anyone else, ever.

But now she'd gone and got herself a *boyfriend*.

'He's not my boyfriend!' said Mum. 'He's my *friend*, that's all. For the moment, anyway.'

She brought a tray of baked beans on toast for two into my bedroom even though I said I didn't want it. The beans smelled so good I couldn't help eating them, giving up all pretence of working at my maths homework.

'So you like this Gerry, Mum?'

'Yes, ever so much. He's so *funny*,' said Mum. 'He just makes you feel comfortable straight away. I was a bit nervous about meeting him—'

'What?'

'OK, OK, I was totally terrified. I had to go and find the ladies twice on the journey I was so scared. I almost came straight back home. It wasn't just meeting Gerry. It sounds so terrible, but I didn't know quite how badly his stroke had affected him, and I was so worried I'd go to shake his hand and then find he couldn't use it, stuff like that. He'd told me he had a limp but I didn't know how bad it was. I wondered if he used a wheelchair and I tried to work out in my head if I should bend down to be at his eye-level when I said hello or whether that would look patronizing. But *anyway*, the moment we saw each other he gave me this lovely big smile and I smiled back and all my worries just seemed so stupid. It felt as if we already knew each other, as if we'd been friends for years. He doesn't have a wheelchair, he can manage with a walking stick. His limp's quite bad but it was good to walk slowly, especially as I was wearing my best shoes with high heels.'

'Is his face a bit wonky?' I asked. 'You know.' I pulled my own mouth down and to the side.

'Don't, Sylvie! Honestly! No, it's not a bit wonky, not that I'd really mind if it *was*. It's *him* that matters, not his looks, though actually I think he looks pretty special. He's eight years older than me and he's going a bit grey, but he works out a lot in the gym so he's got great arms and a really flat stomach. I *did* feel a bit shy then, coming out of the changing rooms and meeting up with him in the pool. I was so conscious of *my* stomach. I worried that I looked awful in that bright red costume. Still, once we were in the water I was fine. He's such a good swimmer, he can totally outpower me, flashing up to the end of the pool and back. You'd never think he had any kind of disability.'

Mum went on and on and on about Gerry while I speared baked beans moodily with my fork.

'Sylvie?' Mum said eventually. 'I thought you were cool with all this but now it looks like it's really bugging you.'

'No, I'm fine, I keep *saying*,' I snapped.

I *wanted* to feel fine. I wanted to reassure Mum and tell her I was happy for her. I *was* in lots of ways. It was just that I was jealous too. It felt so raw and painful and humiliating but that was the truth of it. I was jealous of my own mum because she'd gone out on a proper romantic date, just the two of them. I was still longing for Carl to ask me out on a date with him, just the two of us.

'Did he kiss you?' I asked suddenly.

Mum went bright red. 'No!' she said.

'Then why are you blushing?'

'Well, because I feel silly. OK, we *did* kiss, just when we said goodnight.'

'Did he kiss you first or did you kiss him first?' I asked.

'Look, I'm not spelling out all the details! And I don't honestly know. It just happened out of the blue. First we were saying goodbye, and then I think I leaned forward, maybe to kiss him on the cheek, but somehow we ended up *kissing* kissing.'

All right, I thought. That's the way to do it.

Jules drove us to Kew on Friday evening, Carl, Paul, Miranda and me. We stopped at Pizza Express on the way. I was so keyed up I could barely eat. I was sitting next to Carl but he was busy chatting to Paul about some stupid production of *A Midsummer Night's Dream* they were doing at their school. They started talking in cod Shakespeare.

'Oh, methinks 'tis a pizza! Marry, I love the dish.'

'Aye, my good fellow, let us nosh this excellent fare.'

They wouldn't stop, even when Jules begged them.

Miranda yawned. 'Canst ye not give it a *rest*, you guys?' she said, breaking off a piece of Carl's pizza, an extra cheesy bit.

'Get off! 'Tis *my* morsel!' said Carl. He prodded her gently with his fork.

'Thinkst thou I am frightened of thy weapon?' said Miranda.

Paul snorted with laughter and Carl joined in.

Miranda sighed heavily. 'Give us a break, guys, you're being so *boring*. Are you *in* this play?'

'We're rude yokels,' said Paul.

'That figures,' said Miranda. 'So which ones? Are you Bottom?'

'I'm Snout the Tinker, so I also play Pyramus's father. Carl's Flute, so he's got to play Thisbe, this bird that Pyramus is in love with, and he has to kiss her.'

'Shut up,' said Carl.

'Yeah, yeah, and it's Michael Farmer who plays Pyramus. Imagine snogging *him*! We're going to have to watch you, Carl, you might turn gay on us,' said Paul.

'Shut *up*,' said Carl.

'*Oooh*,' Paul said in a silly camp voice. '*My love! Thou art my love, I think. Kiss me, kiss me – oooh, Mikey, kissy kissy kissy.*'

Carl stabbed at Paul with his fork. Paul raised his own and they started up a silly fork fight.

'You boys and your forking fights,' said Miranda. 'Stop it!'

'Yes, stop. *Now*,' said Jules.

'I'll divert them,' said Miranda. She opened her big shoulder bag and brought out a small purple-velvet parcel. 'It's present time,' she said.

'Oh God, I forgot. I was going to give you that glass pig, wasn't I?' said Paul.

'It doesn't matter. I don't want presents,' Carl said quickly.

'I think you'll want mine!' said Miranda. 'Come on, open it up. *Carefully.*'

Carl cupped the purple present in his hands. It looked as if it might contain a piece of glass. My chest went tight. Carl opened the parcel slowly, stroking the velvet, then finding the black tissue paper inside. He slid a finger delicately under the sellotape, unwrapping until he held the present in his hand.

'Oh!' he said.

'Let's see. What is it?' said Paul. He peered. 'An old paperweight?' he said, sounding disappointed. 'That's a duff present.'

'No it's not!' said Miranda. 'Is it, Carl?'

He was too stunned to answer. The paperweight wasn't pretty with little glass rod patterns like a mosaic. It was plain and big and round, with *Remember Me* in white, and a laurel wreath and a tiny rose with green leaves. Carl was holding it as if real roses were flowering in his palms.

'It's a Millville paperweight,' he said hoarsely. 'American.'

'Yeah, the guy in the antique arcade said it was American,' said Miranda.

'Millville made Jersey Rose paperweights,' said Carl.

'Have you got some then?' Miranda asked.

'No, no. They're way too expensive,' said Carl.

'Oh, Miranda, it's incredibly kind of you, but I hope you haven't spent *too* much,' said Jules anxiously. 'There, Carl! Aren't you lucky? You've got your beautiful champagne flute from Sylvie and now your lovely paperweight from Miranda.'

'Mm,' said Carl, holding the paperweight up and examining it from all angles.

I knew Jules was trying to be tactful, mentioning my glass too. I'd tried so hard but Miranda had effortlessly trumped me.

'It's fine, Jules. I'm glad Carl likes it,' said Miranda. '*I* think it's a bit weird and clunky. OK, Birthday Boy, am I going to get a thank-you kiss, then?'

She leaned towards him, her mouth pursed. Carl didn't push her away. He didn't kiss her nose. He kissed her full on the lips right in front of me.

'Hey, stop snogging, she's *my* girl!' said Paul.

'I'm not anybody's girl, I'm my own woman,' said Miranda.

She was wearing dark lipstick. Some of it was smeared on Carl's lips, making him look astonishingly beautiful.

'*Oooh, Thisbe, thou art a luscious wanton-lipped wench,*' Paul scoffed.

Carl quickly wiped his mouth with the back of his hand. 'Thank you, Miranda,' he said.

'So will you?' she said.

'Will I what?'

'Remember me!'

'Yeah, yeah. How could I forget?' said Carl. He looked at her, then he looked at me, then he looked at Paul. 'I think this is definitely going to be a night to remember.'

Dear Jules paid for the pizzas and then dropped us off at the Victoria Gate of Kew Gardens. It was pitch dark in the street, but the paths in the gardens were lit by little lamps and the big glasshouses were ablaze. There were two amazing swirly glass towers at the entrance to the vast Palm House, one yellow, one orange, both extending great glass tentacles at every angle. Carl peered up at them, noting every bubble and twirl, his eyes following each extraordinary spiral.

'Boy transfixed,' said Miranda. 'So how does Chihuly do it, Carl? Why don't all the woggly feelers break off the pole?'

'He does them one at a time and then slots them in so they stay fixed for ever,' said Carl.

He went on explaining to her as they wandered round the Palm House pond, their heads close together, Miranda's hand tucked into his elbow, slotting in so it seemed fixed for ever too. Paul and I mooched after them, disgruntled.

'Do you like Chihuly's glass?' I asked desperately.

' 'S OK,' said Paul.

'I believe you saw Carl's collection in the Glass Hut,' I said.

'Yeah, yeah, it's kind of weird. I mean, like, obsessive.'

'Well, that's Carl. Totally weird,' I said. I meant it as a compliment but Paul frowned at me in the gloom.

'In what way?'

'In every way,' I said.

'You and Carl, you're, like, an item?' said Paul.

'Well . . . yes,' I said. 'We've known each other ever since we were tiny. We go w-a-y back, Carl and me.'

'So why is your mate Miranda making eyes at him and giving him flash presents?'

'That's just Miranda. She's so warm and generous. She's like that with everyone,' I said.

'I wish she'd warm up a bit with me,' Paul muttered. 'Has she said anything to you about me, Sylvia?'

'Sylvie. Well. She's said some stuff, you know, girl talk.'

'Do you think she reckons me then? More than Carl?'

'Definitely,' I lied.

'Well, tell you what, let's try separating them, because they're just going to rabbit on about *glass* all evening.' He took a deep breath. 'Hey, Miranda, wait for us!'

'Come over here. Come and look at the boat on the lake,' she shouted from the darkness.

'A boating lake – *great* idea!' said Paul, hurrying towards her.

I was left stumbling after them in the dark,

lonely and left out. Then Carl bobbed out of a bush and seized hold of me.

'Doesn't the glass in the boat look wonderful! And see all those round floating ornaments like giant glass figs? Chihuly calls them *walla wallas* – mad name, but don't you think they're brilliant!' Carl felt in the dark for my face, putting his lips to my ear. 'We'll float them up and down the rivers in Glassworld, thousands of them, then all the children can paddle their boats and collect them in a Glassworld walla-walla water race.'

'Carl? *There* you are!' Miranda said. 'Oh my, look at the lovebirds!'

'We can be lovebirds too,' said Paul. 'I wish there were more boats. I'm ace at rowing. Feel my pecs!' He raised his arms.

'You keep your pecs to yourself,' said Miranda. She consulted her map of the gardens. 'Let's go and find this sun piece that's meant to be even more fantastic.'

We walked along to the Princess of Wales Conservatory, jostling each other in the dark, darting forward and swapping places as if we were performing a complicated dance. We stood still when we glimpsed the enormous glass sun, the thousand yellow spirals shining. Carl clutched my hand in excitement, the way he used to when we were children.

'We'll have a huge party at the palace and the glass sun will shine over us,' I whispered.

He didn't say anything because Paul and

Miranda were pressed up close within earshot, but he squeezed my hand. We made our way all round the floodlit conservatory, spotting the tall glass reeds amongst the real cactuses, blue bird shapes stretching their necks out of the water, green glass grass everywhere. It wasn't just Carl who was enraptured. There were large crowds going *Oooh* and *Aaah*, and flashes from cameras.

'Let's go outside in the dark for a bit – this is doing my head in,' said Paul.

'Oh, for goodness' sake, Paul, can't you see how much this means to Carl?' I said.

'OK, OK, you stay with him. Miranda and I will go and get a breath of fresh air,' said Paul, grinning.

Carl turned away from the sun. 'OK, I'm ready, let's go.'

'No, we'll stay, Carl!' I said.

'No, it's fine, really. I've had a good look,' said Carl. 'Come on then, you guys.'

I could have shaken him. He followed Paul out of the conservatory with a craven look on his face. Paul turned momentarily and raised his eyebrows at me in exasperation. Miranda also looked irritated. She strode forward in her black buckled boots, Paul in pursuit, Carl keeping close and me stumbling after them as Sylvie-tag-along.

'Miranda? Wait! Look, let's explore a bit,' Paul said, taking hold of her arm and trying to steer her into the trees.

'No, it's *this* way,' said Miranda.

'But we've just *seen* the whirly things and the boat,' said Paul.

'Past them. We've got to see the Temperate House. Come on, the gates close in an hour.'

'Oh, flipping heck,' said Paul – or words to that effect.

'Hey, mate, we can go off exploring if you like,' said Carl. 'Maybe we've seen enough glass.'

I stared at him. He never used the word *mate* and mocked anyone who did. And I knew he was desperate to see and marvel at each Chihuly piece.

'No we haven't!' said Miranda, seizing him by the arm. 'For God's sake, you moron, it's the best bit! They've got the Cherry Walk all lit up!'

It was like walking into a carnival dreamworld. The trees were lit with coloured lamps so they glowed royal blue and emerald green. There were strings of fairy lights and fire-eaters swallowing flame and men on stilts striding ten foot tall through the undergrowth. It was so strange and magical that Paul stopped moaning and Miranda stopped being bossy. We walked together, all four of us, in the midst of the crowd drifting down towards the Temperate House.

We stepped inside and gasped. Gigantic glass flowers bloomed everywhere amongst the real plants and trees. A great green chandelier hung from the ceiling like a gigantic bunch of grapes. A tangle of gilded glass balloons spiralled almost down to the ground. Strange glass vegetation drifted in the little stream.

187

'Look at the floats,' Carl whispered, bending down and staring at the huge blue spheres, like the biggest glass bubbles in the world. 'How can he make them this big?'

'I like the ones like real flowers, the pink one and the turquoise one. Let *us* have flowers like this,' I said.

I meant in Glassworld, but Miranda took me literally.

'They'd be way way too expensive, silly. Even the simplest Chihuly piece costs thousands.'

'Especially the *Macchia* flowers,' said Carl. 'They've got contrasting colours on the outside and the inside. I think they use opaque glass in between, but I can't quite work out *how*.'

'It doesn't matter *how*. Let's just enjoy them,' said Miranda. 'They're so beautiful! Even you have to admit they're beautiful, Paul.'

'*You're* beautiful, Miranda,' said Paul, batting his eyelashes in a ridiculous fashion.

'You are such an idiot,' said Miranda, but she blew him a kiss all the same.

Then she blew one to Carl and he blew one back to her and then blew one to me until there was a flurry of kisses flying through the air and we were all mouthing madly, people staring at us.

'Let's get out of here before they cart us away,' said Paul. 'Where's the way out?'

'Here's the way *up*,' said Carl, and he started climbing the little white spiralling stairs all the way up to the balcony right at the top of the Temperate House.

We followed, me next, then Miranda, then Paul, climbing until we were right up high in the glasshouse, a few trapped sparrows circling our heads, and below us a dazzle of bright glass amongst the intense green of the spotlit foliage. We stood peering down from our balcony like royalty. I felt for Carl's hand.

'I feel as if we're really in Glassworld,' I whispered.

Miranda took *my* hand. Paul already held hers. We stood still, all of us linked, no one speaking.

*I'll remember this moment for ever*, I thought. *I am holding Carl's hand and I am happy happy happy.*

It felt so magical. Anything seemed possible. We could all four step straight off the balcony and fly like birds, our hands still linked.

*When we are outside in the dark I will keep holding Carl's hand. We will walk into the trees and I will kiss him*, I vowed to myself.

We walked all the way round the balcony, and then down the winding stairs and out underneath the glass spirals and bubbles and chandeliers, through the door into the darkness.

The Cherry Walk was crowded with people trying to see everything before the gates closed.

'Let's go down this path, where it's quieter,' said Paul

'You're going the wrong way. You'll end up lost in the Woodland Glade,' said Miranda.

'Let's all get lost, just for a little while,' said Carl.

'Yes, yes, let's!' I said.

'We'll play Hide and Seek – Sylvie and Carl, Miranda and me,' said Paul.

'No, no, that's for chickens, hiding in pairs. We'll *all* split up,' said Miranda, eyes glittering in the moonlight. 'We'll all run off in different directions and the birthday boy has to count to a hundred, eyes closed, and then catch each of us.'

'No, that's just a baby game,' said Paul.

'Oh, go on. Humour her. So what do I get if I catch everyone, Miranda?' said Carl. His eyes looked oddly bright too. Maybe it was just the eerie light.

'You get whatever your heart desires, of course,' said Miranda, smiling. 'Right, I'm off.'

She suddenly started running, surprisingly quick in her boots, dodging round the corner of the Temperate House and out of sight before we could stop her.

'Go on, you two,' said Carl. 'I'll start counting. One, two, three . . .'

Paul sighed but started running, rounding the Temperate House too.

'Carl,' I whispered, my mouth dry.

'Four, five, six – go on, Sylvie.'

'Look, we could *both* run off, they're not to know,' I said. 'Come on!'

'That's cheating,' said Carl. 'We've got to play now. It's OK. If I haven't found you in ten minutes come back to the Temperate House, right? Don't look like that. You're not scared, are you?'

'No!' I said, and ran off the other way, down the whole length of the glasshouse, turning the corner up Holly Walk. I slowed down, counting in my head too. I stood still when I got to a hundred, standing behind a small tree, pretending to hide.

I waited for Carl to come and find me. I waited and waited and waited. He must have gone the other way, Miranda's way. He'd have caught her soon enough, and Paul too. So why weren't they all coming to seek me out?

I wished I had my mobile with me. I listened hard to see if I could hear them calling me. I couldn't. I couldn't hear anyone now. I wasn't wearing a watch so I wasn't sure what the time was, but I knew the gates would be closing soon. What if I got locked in? What if I had to spend all night circling the glasshouses in the dark, fumbling through the plants, stumbling in the silent groves until dawn.

I called out, 'Carl! Carl! Carl!' My voice was high-pitched and panicky. I sounded like a bird calling in alarm. *'Carl!'*

I was sure I'd been hiding at least ten minutes. I ran towards the Temperate House. It was still lit up, and I could see people inside. I stood there, taking deep breaths, trying to calm down. I was getting into a ridiculous state over nothing. Why did I have to be such a *baby*? If the others could see me now, how they would laugh at me.

There was no one waiting at the entrance. I stood there, dodging out of the way whenever anyone needed to come out. People were looking at their watches and sighing. Where were the others? They couldn't all be lost. They wouldn't be so mean as to play a trick on me, would they? Why on earth had we all agreed to play such a silly game?

I suddenly realized this mightn't be the only entrance to such a large glasshouse.

'Excuse me, is this the *main* entrance?' I asked desperately, seizing hold of a couple.

'I think there's one on the other side too.'

'Oh no!' I thanked them and then started running all the way round the great glasshouse. More people were pouring out. There was someone using a loud-hailer, telling people that the Temperate House was about to close.

'You're going the wrong way, girlie, the gate's down there.'

'Yes, yes, but I'm meeting someone,' I gasped, but I'd circled the whole glasshouse and there wasn't a sign of Carl or Miranda or Paul.

I didn't know what to do. Jules was picking us up from the Victoria Gate. Should I make my way there by myself? But Carl had told me to meet up with him here.

I stood still, my face screwed up, unable to decide. I felt tears welling and swallowed hard, scared I was going to start howling.

'Are you all right, dear?' a woman asked. She had fluffy hair and flowery trousers like Jules. I hung onto her for help.

'I've lost my friends,' I blurted out.

'Oh well, I'm sure you'll find them soon. Where were you supposed to meet them?'

'Here! I *think* so, anyway. But they've been gone ages.'

'Have you got a mobile phone?'

'Yes, but I didn't bring it with me.'

'What about your friends, do they have mobiles?'

'Carl does!'

'Well, Harry, lend us your mobile a sec.' She turned to her husband. 'Come on, dear, your mobile.'

He didn't look too happy about handing it over to me. I dialled Carl's number. I knew it by heart but I had to try it twice because my fingers were trembling so.

His mobile was switched off.

'Oh no, I can't get through to him!' The tears were starting to trickle down my cheeks.

'What about the other friends?'

'I could try Miranda. But I'm not sure I can remember her number.'

I tried once but a total stranger answered.

'Oh dear, maybe I've got the twos and threes muddled up.'

I tried a different combination.

'For goodness' sake, how many friends are you going to try?' Harry said impatiently.

'I'm sorry, I'm sorry, it's just I'm not sure of the number,' I sniffed.

'Stop bullying the poor little mite, Harry!

Try again, dear. Take your time.'

I tried once more. After three rings Miranda
answered.

'Yep?'

'Oh, Miranda! Thank goodness! Where *are*
you?'

'Hey, hey, what's up? Are you crying? What's
happened? First Paul goes all weird, then you.
Where's Carl?'

'I don't know! I've been looking and looking,
going round and round the Temperate House
but I couldn't find *any* of you. Where are you
now?'

'We're outside, Paul and me. We thought we'd
push off by ourselves. Paul said it was cool with
you. It *is* OK, isn't it?'

'But . . .'

'We won't go back with Carl's mum, we'll get
the train, OK?'

'But where *is* Carl? He said he'd come back for
me but he isn't *anywhere*. Oh, Miranda, don't
go!'

'But we're nearly at the station now. Paul, you
pig, you said Sylvie *wanted* us to clear off. Paul?
Stop it! Do you mind?' Miranda giggled. 'Hang
on while I prise him off me.'

'Does he know where Carl is?'

'I don't know and I don't care,' I heard Paul
say.

'What was that? Why's he being like that?'

'I think they've had some sort of fight,' said
Miranda.

194

'What about?'

'I don't know. He won't say. *Us*, maybe?' said Miranda. 'Anyway, I'm tired and my boots are rubbing and I got bored of stomping round the gardens—'

'Look, you'll really have to ring off now, this is costing us a fortune. Quarrel with your friends on your *own* phone,' said Harry.

Miranda giggled. 'Who's that? He sounds a royal pain. Anyway, I've got to go, Sylvie.'

'But what will I *do*? Something might have happened to Carl.'

'Don't be daft. He'll be by the gate, waiting. You go there too. Find his mum and go home together like good little kiddywinks. Bye!'

The phone went dead. I didn't dare try re-dialling on Harry's phone. I gave it back, thanking his kind wife, and then I started running all the way back up Cherry Walk towards Victoria Gate. I peered around desperately as I went, calling for Carl whenever I could draw breath. There was still no sign of him.

There was a little crowd of people near the gate, all saying their goodbyes. I dodged in and out of them, looking and looking, but still couldn't see Carl.

'Sylvie? Sylvie!' There was Jules standing on the other side of the gate, looking anxious, her hair wilder than ever. 'Oh, Sylvie, come on! Find the others and let's go. I couldn't find anywhere to park so I've left the car just up that street

195

blocking someone's drive. I'll *have* to move it in a minute.'

'But I can't come! I'm not with the others. We all got lost. Miranda and Paul are OK, they've gone off to get the train, but I can't find Carl *anywhere*. Oh, Jules, what are we going to do? I just know something terrible has happened to him.'

'Don't be silly, Sylvie,' Jules said briskly. 'There he is, behind you!'

I turned. There was Carl. I went limp with relief – until I saw his face. His eyes were red, his eyelashes spiky, his cheeks flushed. It was obvious he'd been crying.

I knew there was no point asking Carl what was wrong. He sat in the back of the car, fists clenched, lips tightly pressed, frowning hard with the effort of keeping it all in. Jules tried to make cheery general conversation, peering at Carl in her rear-view mirror. He stared resolutely out of the window into the darkness outside.

I tried reaching out to him, resting my hand on the seat between us. He didn't respond. I tried nudging a little nearer but he tensed up even tighter. I sat staring at him miserably, trying to work out what had happened. He had been so happy and carefree wandering around all the glasshouses.

I thought back to that moment only an hour ago when the four of us had held hands at the

197

top of the Temperate House. Why had we all agreed to play that stupid game of Hide and Seek? It was all Paul's idea, just so he could get Miranda on her own. Had Carl and Paul had some kind of argument over Miranda? But Carl didn't really care about Miranda, even though she wanted him. Still, she seemed happy enough to clear off with Paul now. Why couldn't Carl be happy with me?

The moment Jules drove up outside our houses Carl leaped out of the car and ran up the path, his key in his hand. He didn't say goodbye to me. He didn't even turn round.

'Oh dear,' said Jules, sighing. 'Do you have any idea what's happened, Sylvie?'

'No,' I said.

Jules put her hand on my shoulder. 'Sylvie, do you think . . . ?'

'What?'

I heard her swallowing. I didn't want her to say any more. I knew what she was going to suggest.

'Don't let's talk about him. He'd so hate it,' I said.

'Yes, you're right,' said Jules.

I mumbled a thank-you to her and went into my own house. I didn't want to talk to my own mum either. She was on the computer, probably emailing Gerry. I shut myself in my room. I lay on my bed, staring up at the ceiling. I thought of Paul and Miranda together. I thought of Carl alone in his bedroom, only a couple of metres away from me, yet he felt far away, in a different country altogether.

I didn't realize I was crying until the tears started trickling sideways down my cheeks.

Very early on Saturday morning I tried texting Carl.

R U AWAKE?

I tried every half-hour. I thought he *was* awake. I was sure I heard him opening his window. I tried opening mine, peering out. I couldn't see Carl but I thought I heard the *click-click* of his computer. I tried calling softly but he didn't reply.

I went downstairs to the living room and typed on our computer:

What happened, Carl? Have you and Paul had a fight? I don't care, whatever it is, I swear I don't, I just want to help. I can't stand it when you're unhappy. Please please please talk to me or write to me or text me.

He emailed back five bleak little words:

Please just leave me alone.

I tried to do just that. I kept to myself. I went back to bed and didn't get up till the afternoon. Miranda kept ringing but I didn't want to talk to her. I switched my mobile off.

'Are you having a mope, love?' said Mum,

coming into my room with a cup of coffee.

'I'm just *tired*, Mum,' I mumbled.

I let my coffee go cold and put my head under my pillow, trying hard to tunnel my way back to sleep. I kept having weird half-waking dreams about Carl and Miranda and Paul, until I started banging my head, trying to dislodge them from my brain. I had a headache from crying and sleeping so long, and when I got up at last I found I had two huge new spots on my nose. It was the final indignity. I felt so tragic and I just looked comically ugly. I tried squeezing the spots and made them worse. I smothered them with thick foundation and turned into a clown – with spots.

'Miranda's on the phone again,' Mum called.

'Tell her I've gone out,' I hissed.

'*You* tell her,' said Mum.

'Oh for heaven's sake, how can I if I'm pretending I'm not here!' I shouted down.

I knew Miranda might hear my voice in the background. I decided it was just too bad. I heard Mum mumbling some excuse on the phone. Then she came trekking up to my bedroom again.

'Why don't you want to talk to Miranda all of a sudden? I thought you two were such total bosom buddies?'

'Mum! I can't stick that expression. And as a matter of fact, I can't stick Miranda right this minute,' I said.

'OK, OK. And you've obviously fallen out with Carl too. I was talking to Jules this morning and *he*'s just flopping around in *his* room, not wanting to talk to anyone either. Honestly, you kids!'

Mum sighed, but she didn't look sad. Her eyes were shining and she had a silly smile, as if someone was telling her a private joke. It was as if she had her own private hotline in her head to this wretched Gerry.

I needed to get away from her. I didn't want to go next door. I didn't want to go over to Miranda's.

I decided I'd go and see Lucy. She was very lukewarm when I phoned. I couldn't blame her. I'd been practically ignoring her recently.

'Can I come round this afternoon, Lucy?' I asked.

'Why?'

'Well, because – because we're friends. Friends hang out together, don't they?'

'I suppose Miranda's busy,' she snapped.

I thought she might put the phone down on me but then she weakened.

'OK. Come round if you really must.'

I didn't really want to go at all. I felt I'd been mad to think of it, but I couldn't back out now. I went over to Lucy's, and when she opened the door I made an effort to put on a big smile and be sweet to her. It wasn't easy. She was still acting very off-hand and talked to me in monosyllables, sitting primly on the end of her bed, picking at the stitching on her gingham patchwork quilt.

I found it harder and harder to make bright friendly conversation. I wandered restlessly around the room while Lucy played her favourite new album, nodding her head and snapping her fingers and tapping her feet. She was never quite on the beat, which made it even more maddening. I turned my back on her to stop having to watch this twitchy performance and started rearranging her three bears on the windowsill, making them cosy up together.

'Hello, Bobby, hello, Billy, hello, Bernie,' I said. I made them each wave a furry paw. *'Hello, Sylvie,'* I said in a big booming bear voice. *'Hello, Sylvie,'* I said in a soft middling bear voice. *'Hello, Sylvie,'* I said in a teeny-tiny squeaky bear voice.

'I suppose you think you're funny,' said Lucy. 'They're all the same size so they all have the same sort of voice. And what are you doing *now*? They don't *kiss.'*

'Yes they do,' I said, making them cosy up together and rub snouts.

'You're *so* weird,' said Lucy, bouncing up off her bed and snatching her bears from me.

'OK, I'm sorry. Let's *do* something, Lucy. Shall we go shopping?'

'I've already *been* shopping this morning, with my mum.'

'Well, how about we look at some magazines then? We could cut stuff out and start up a scrapbook each. You could do one on all your favourite pop stars.'

Lucy perked up a little. 'I've got scissors and Pritt. I've got one proper scrapbook. I bought it to stick Christmas cards in but I never got round to it. But what can you use?'

She searched through all her stationery and eventually found me a big drawing pad from years ago, though she'd used up nearly all the pages. Little-girl Lucy had drawn endless pictures of a red house with frilly curtains at each square window, a line of blue sky at the top and a line of green grass at the bottom, with red and yellow flowers in regimental formation. Each picture was practically identical.

Lucy and I divided a huge pile of magazines between us. She commandeered all the teenage ones devoted to pop stars. I flicked through her mum's cast-off *Hello!* and *Heat* and her dad's car magazines. I decided to use all Lucy's bland little-girl houses, though I customized each one as I went. I cut out the Osbourne family and gave their house fancy extensions, with a gothic bat-decorated music studio for Ozzy. I gave them a car each and added lots of dogs cut from an old Ladybird book of dogs.

'You shouldn't cut up *books*,' said Lucy, snipping carefully round a heart-shaped photo of a blond boy band. Her lips opened and shut in time to the snip of her scissors.

'You can't tell me you still read it, Lucy,' I said. 'Do you have any crayons?'

I scribbled a little brown swirly pile beside each dog.

'Don't! That's disgusting!' said Lucy, but she couldn't help laughing.

I turned the page and cut out Elton and David for the next house. I extended it in every direction, making it as plush and palatial as I could. I found an old *Gardening Monthly* and filled their house with as many flowers as I could pick out from the shiny pages.

I started on the Beckhams next, giving them thrones in the garden, two huge golden chairs and three little ones for the children. I drew Victoria her own walk-in wardrobe and snipped out some dinky designer outfits for her. I stuck a lot of green at the back of the house so that David had his very own pitch for playing footie with his sons.

'Honestly, Sylvie!' Lucy kept exclaiming. She kept giggling too. 'You are so so so *weird*.'

When I was with Miranda I was the little titch meek mousy friend. When I was with Lucy I was the weird outrageous girl. I liked the way it made me feel.

Then Lucy's mum came in with a tray of Ribena and chocolate finger biscuits, as if we were still both six years old.

'Whatever are you up to, girls?' she said, frowning at the snippets of paper.

'We're making scrapbooks,' said Lucy. 'Oh, Mum, you should see what Sylvie's done, it's such a scream.'

Lucy's mum looked as if *she* might start screaming.

'Oh no!' she said. 'You've stuck all these silly pictures in Lucy's drawing book! Oh dear, why couldn't you have used the empty pages at the back? Why did you spoil all Lucy's drawings, Sylvia?'

'It's Sylvie, actually. I'm sorry. I didn't mean to spoil them. I was just turning them into collages,' I said.

'Don't fuss, Mummy. I don't mind,' said Lucy, embarrassed. 'It's only a dumb old book I did in Year Two.'

'I want to keep all your drawings and stories, Lucy; they're very precious to me.' Lucy's mum put the tray down on the dressing table so crossly that the purple Ribena splashed over the rim of each glass, and then stomped out of the room.

There was an awkward silence. Lucy and I looked at each other and then looked away.

'I'm sorry,' I said again.

I picked up the drawing book to see if I could peel off the pictures but they were stuck fast. They didn't seem so witty and inventive now.

'Don't worry, Sylvie, you know what mums are like,' said Lucy.

I was so glad I had my mum, not Lucy's.

# 18

I started planning Saturday evening on my way home from Lucy's. Mum and I could have a girly night in together. We could watch some silly romantic film, eat chocolates, try out new hairstyles on each other.

Mum had other plans.

'I'm supposed to be seeing Gerry, Sylvie.'

'I thought that was tomorrow. Aren't you going swimming again with him?'

'Yes. But he's suggested we go out tonight too. I told him the other day I like Abba and he's managed to get tickets for *Mamma Mia!*. But I don't have to go. I can easily ring him up and cancel.'

'Don't be daft, Mum. Of course you can't cancel! You go and enjoy yourself. You'll love it,' I said.

'I feel so guilty going out and leaving you. Still, I know you'll be fine next door. Though I'm not sure Carl will be there. Jules said he was out somewhere.'

'Oh. Well. I don't have to go round there. I'll stay home.'

'I can't leave you all by yourself. Do you maybe want to have someone over for a sleepover? Miranda keeps phoning. I'm sure she'd like to.'

'You would so live to regret Miranda on a sleepover. She'd bring a bottle of vodka and half a dozen boys,' I said.

'I hope you're joking,' said Mum. 'All right, what about Lucy?'

I thought about having Lucy to stay, doubtless with Billy and Bobby and Bernie Bear.

'I'll be fine by myself,' I said.

'Well, I know you're a sensible girl, and responsible enough to be left. It isn't as if you'll be *alone* in the house. Miss Miles will be in her room.' Mum paused. 'If you felt it was cosier I could always ask Miss Miles to fix a bit of supper for both of you and then you could watch television together.'

'Mum, no offence to poor Miss Miles, but I'd sooner cut my throat than sit eating one of her omelettes and watching her old *Midsomer Murders* videos. I keep telling you and telling you, I'll be *fine*. Go, Mum, go!'

So she went. I managed to stay all smiley until the front door closed, and then I lay on the sofa and cried. I felt so lonely and left out. I wondered if Carl was still out. Had he made it up with Paul? I kept thinking about them.

Miss Miles put her head round the living-room door. 'Are you all right, Sylvie? Not too lonely now that Mum's out? You can come and sit with me if you'd like?'

'No thanks,' I said.

Miss Miles sighed. 'Not that I'm exactly exciting company for you,' she muttered.

Then I felt really mean. 'It's not that at all. I'm just really tired – in fact I'm going to bed now,' I said.

I did go to bed early. I didn't get to sleep. I was still awake when Mum got in, way after midnight. I didn't call out to her. She came creeping into my room and hovered above me. I kept very still, my eyes shut.

'Are you asleep, Sylvie?' she whispered.

I stayed motionless, breathing very deeply.

'Night-night darling,' Mum whispered, and crept out again.

I heard her spinning round and round on the landing, whisper-singing *Dancing Queen*. I stuck my fingers in my ears. I didn't want to hear any Abba songs, especially not that one.

Mum woke me up early the next morning. She had her hair tied up with a ribbon and wore a T-shirt and skinny jeans. She looked like my big sister, not my mum.

'Hi, sweetie,' she said, sitting cross-legged on my bed. 'Were you OK last night? I looked in

on you when I got in but you seemed sound
asleep. I had just the most fantastic time. I
loved *Mamma Mia!*. I'll have to save up and take
you some time – it's such fun. I just know you'd
love it too – *and* Carl. Maybe I can try to take
you for your birthday treat. Though I expect it's
really pricey. Gerry wouldn't let me have the
tickets to see how much they were. He wouldn't
let me pay anything towards the evening, not
even our drinks.'

'Oh, what a perfect gent,' I said. It sounded
sourer than I meant it to.

Mum paused. 'Well, I think he *is* the perfect
gent,' she said. 'I can't quite believe this is
happening to me. It's mad, I know you'll think
me totally crazy. I hardly know him, but I
think I'm falling in love with him, Sylvie.
I know all sorts of things could go wrong, and it
probably won't last, but I don't care. I've never
felt this way, not even when I first met your dad.
You've no idea what it's like. I just look at him
and I absolutely melt. Don't laugh at me,
please!'

I didn't feel like laughing. I felt like crying. I
knew exactly what it felt like.

I burrowed down in bed so Mum couldn't see
my face. She misunderstood.

'Sorry, sorry, sorry! Oh, God, I know nothing's
more disgusting and pathetic than your own
mother rambling on about *true lurve*.' She said
it the silly way, sending herself up, trying to
ease the situation.

'I'm very happy for you, Mum,' I mumbled underneath the covers. 'I just wish you wouldn't go *on* about it.'

'Yes, I know. I'll shut up, I promise. But I can't *wait* till you meet him, Sylvie, just so you can tell me if I'm making a total fool of myself. In fact . . . we were thinking, Gerry and me, would you come and join us today?'

'No! Don't be silly. You don't want me.'

'We do! Gerry's dying to meet you. I've told him so much about you. You could come swimming with us. You love swimming, and it's such a fantastic pool. Then we could all have Sunday lunch together. Yes, it'll be great! Hang on just one tick and I'll phone Gerry—'

So it wasn't properly arranged. Maybe they hadn't even discussed it. I could just imagine Mum's furtive whispering on the phone: *'Yes, I know, I'm sorry, darling, I wanted it to be just us too, but I feel so bad about leaving Sylvie again. It's so sad, she just keeps moping after her childhood sweetheart when anyone can see that isn't going to get her anywhere.'*

'No, Mum!' I said angrily, as if she'd actually said it.

'Why not?' Mum said. 'You'll like him, I know you will. And you'll have to meet him *some* day, won't you?'

'Well. I will. If it lasts,' I said.

Mum had expressed exactly the same doubts but it was mean of me to say it back to her. She didn't get cross with me or tell me I was acting like a horrible jealous baby. She kept smiling at me bravely, and patted my shoulder.

'OK then, pet. Well, I'll let you get back to sleep. I'll come and say goodbye when I'm off, right?'

She walked slowly out of my bedroom, waiting for me to snap out of it and say something sweet. I kept quiet. She trailed down the landing to the bathroom – but after five minutes I heard her singing *Knowing Me, Knowing You*, in her bath, even doing a funny voice for the *Ah-ha!* part.

I put my head under my pillow and tried to blot her out, to blot out Carl and Paul and Miranda, to blot myself out entirely until I was the blackness and the blackness was me.

Mum lifted the pillow an hour later. 'Anyone hiding in the burrow?' she whispered, breathing fresh smells of coffee and perfume and toothpaste into my black lair. 'I'm off, sweetie. I feel terrible leaving you, but I'm still going to do it! I've just had a chat with Jules—'

'No!'

'She says lunch is around half one, but come round any time.'

'*No!*'

'Oh, for God's sake, stop being so difficult,' Mum said. 'Now, I have to go, I'm late already. Give me a kiss goodbye, eh?'

I sucked in my lips until they disappeared.

Mum burst out laughing. 'You used to do that when you were cross with me when you were *two*!' she said. 'OK then, don't kiss me. Love you, babe.' She patted the duvet above my bottom and then walked to the door.

'Kiss kiss,' I mumbled under my pillow.

Then I went back to sleep, down down down, though there was a ringing and a banging, and then a knock-knock-knocking.

'Sylvie, dear, are you awake?' Miss Miles was at my door.

'I'm having a bit of a lie-in,' I said.

'Your friend's downstairs, dear,' she said.

I jumped right out of bed, tugged on jeans and a T-shirt, and ran barefoot out of my room, past Miss Miles, down the stairs – but it wasn't Carl.

Miranda was sprawling on our living-room sofa, her boots propped up on the arm.

'What are you doing here? And get your boots off that sofa, you're making all dirty marks,' I said.

'*You* certainly got out of bed the wrong side this morning,' said Miranda, raising her eyebrows. 'Dear, dear. Shall I make you a cup of coffee? You look as if you need one.'

She swung her legs off the sofa and waltzed off to the kitchen as if it was *her* house.

'Would you like a cup of coffee too?' she asked Miss Miles, who was hovering in the hall.

'Thank you, dear, but I'll leave you two girls to have a nice chat together,' she said, starting back up the stairs to her own room.

I went up the stairs, too. 'I wish you hadn't let her in,' I whispered.

'Well, I didn't exactly. She was knocking very hard at the front door so I had to open it. Then she immediately barged straight past me, demanding to talk to you. I just about managed to make her wait in the living room. I had to use my fiercest teacher's voice too. She's one formidable young lady. I'm sorry if I've made things awkward for you, Sylvie.'

I softened towards her. 'I'm sorry I moaned, Miss Miles.'

'Not to worry,' she said brightly. 'It's good to have friends, you know, even very pushy ones.'

I took her point. Miss Miles didn't seem to have many friends at all.

I went to the loo and washed my face and cleaned my teeth and brushed my hair, so that I looked marginally better when I went downstairs again.

Miranda had a mug of coffee waiting for me on the kitchen table.

'Has your granny gone upstairs?' she asked.

'Who? She's not my grandma, she's our lodger.'

'Oh, yes, the *lodger*!' said Miranda, as if it was the most eccentric thing to have, like a pet llama in the living room.

'What do you want?' I said coldly.

'Well, let's hope the granny-lodger stays upstairs, because I've got an eye-bulging tale to tell.'

'You and your stories,' I said. 'Maybe I've heard enough of them.'

'Why are you being so *mean* to me?' said Miranda. She put down her own cup of coffee and threw her arms round my neck. 'You're meant to be *nice* to me. You're my best friend!'

'Yes, I thought we *were* best friends, but then you cleared off when we were all playing that stupid game of Hide and Seek and left me all alone in Kew Gardens!'

'Oh, Sylvie, you poor little diddums, did you get fwightened?'

'Yes, I was frightened!' I said, shaking her off. 'It was horrible and I couldn't find any of you and the gates were about to close. How could you just walk out on me and leave me there?'

'I thought that was what you *wanted* so that you and Carl could cosy up together. I thought you'd fixed it all up with Paul. That's what *he* said, I swear. You mean that was all a dirty great lie?'

'Well. Not exactly. He *did* talk about us pairing up. *You* were the one who insisted we all hide separately.'

'Yeah, yeah, well, that's me, baby. I like to fly solo,' said Miranda, striking a pose and tossing her hair, sending herself up. 'Not that it really worked out that way. I did hope I might just catch your Carl and indulge in a teeny bit of hanky-panky in the shrubbery, but no such luck. I couldn't find him. I hung around for *ages*. You weren't the only one, chum. Then Paul found me and he was in a really weird state, all fired up and telling me how much he fancied me. He actually said he *loved* me, truly. No one's ever said the l-word to me before so I thought, OK, we'll go with the flow on this one. I thought you must have caught up with Carl by this stage so I was happy to head off with Paul. And wait till you hear what happened!'

'You said you thought they had a fight?' I said quickly.

'What? Oh, Paul and Carl. Well, something happened, but Paul just clammed up and wouldn't say. What did Carl say then?'

'He wouldn't say anything either.'

'Boys! They can be so *moody* at times, especially your Carl, if you don't mind me saying so. *Anyway*, Paul was absolutely all over me, saying such sweet stuff. He can be really romantic when he puts his mind to it. Yes, I know, it doesn't seem likely but I swear it's true. He offered to walk me all the way home from the station, and I said I had taxi money, but he wouldn't hear of me going in a taxi on my own. So he came home too. Mum and Dad were out at some boring dinner party, and Minna, our au pair, was holed up in her bedroom, crying on the phone to her boyfriend back home, so I asked Paul down into the den and ... well, we did it!'

'Oh yeah, like I believe you.'

'We *did*.'

'I'm not Patty and Alison and all that gang. I know you like to kid people you do all sorts of stuff.'

'I don't kid you, Sylvie. I swear to you, we did it. Well. Sort of.'

'Aha.'

'We *tried* to do it. We lay on the sofa and snogged for a while. It's all a bit hazy because we had quite a lot to drink, and for the first time ever it all started to *mean* something. I wanted him to do it and he kept mumbling that he'd be careful—'

'I can't *believe* this!'

'Yes, all right, I know, I've had all the safe-sex lectures too, but somehow in the heat of the moment I didn't really care. But then the moment got *too* heated, if you see what I mean.'

I looked at her blankly.

Miranda sighed impatiently. 'It was all over before he could quite get started. I didn't realize at first. I wondered why he didn't get *on* with it. It was all a bit embarrassing, actually. I didn't mind too much – in fact I kind of sobered up and decided it was maybe just as well. I was a bit scared it might hurt, and I decided I could *sort* of count it anyway. But Paul got angry, punching the arm of the sofa and swearing.'

'Angry with *you*?'

'Angry at himself, I think. Though he didn't seem to want much to do with me, I must admit. So much for all the sweet-talk! He cleared off. Goodness knows how he got home. I did wonder about phoning him but I didn't want him to think I was chasing him. Maybe you could get Carl to phone him?'

216

'No.'

'Oh, go on. Look, let's pop next door and see Carl.'

'Absolutely not,' I said.

'Go on, go on, go on,' said Miranda. 'I'm dying to see his Glass Hut.'

'He certainly won't take you there,' I said.

'How do you know?' said Miranda.

'I know Carl,' I said. 'And he wants to be on his own right now.'

'Why?'

'He's upset.'

'Then he'll want to see us because we're his friends,' said Miranda. 'Come on.'

'You can't just barge in on him.'

'Why not? He can always tell us to get lost. You're hopeless, Sylvie, you always make things so complicated. You think things over and over in your head and dither about and end up not doing *anything*. Why won't you just go for it?'

'All right,' I said. 'Come on then. We'll go next door.'

# 19

If I'd been by myself I might have gone the back garden way to see if Carl was in the Glass Hut, but I wasn't going to do that with Miranda.

I took her out of our house and round to the Johnsons' front door. I rang the bell. I heard Jules shouting from the back of the house. Nothing happened. Miranda rang the bell again, insistently.

'Miranda!' I hissed, grabbing her hand.

Jules opened the door awkwardly, her hands white with dough, as if she was wearing pastry gloves.

'I'm busy making a pie, and will any of my idle men folk stir themselves to answer the door? No!' She smiled at us both. 'Hello, Miranda. I didn't know you were coming to lunch too.'

'Neither did I, but thank you very much

for asking me,' she said, marching in.

'Well, it's very kind of you to ask us both, Jules, but really we just popped round for five minutes to see Carl.'

'Ah. Well. I'm not sure he's in the mood for visitors,' said Jules. 'He's a bit down at the moment.'

'Then we'll cheer him up,' said Miranda. 'Is he upstairs?'

'Yes, but—'

She was already bouncing up the stairs, short black net skirt swaying, her fishnet calves taut above her killer boots.

'Well, maybe she'll divert him,' Jules muttered, raising her eyebrows.

'I'm so sorry,' I said, and ran after Miranda.

She went flying off in the wrong direction, briefly knocking at the first door she came to and then bursting in without waiting for any response. Jake was stretched out beside his bed wearing his boxer shorts, doing press-ups. He stared boggle-eyed at Miranda, lost all concentration, and crashed onto his chin.

'Whoops! Wrong guy!' Miranda giggled.

'No, no, feel free! Invade my bedroom any time,' said Jake, rearing his head up like a seal and rubbing his chin. 'Hi, Miranda. Hi, Sylvie. Give me one second to find my jeans and I'll be able to stop blushing.'

'It's actually Carl we're chasing,' said Miranda. 'But thanks for the open invitation.' She marched out again.

219

'How about you staying, Sylvie?' said Jake. 'I'll serenade you with my guitar.'

'Er, maybe not,' I said, and rushed after Miranda.

Carl must have heard us rattling along the corridor. I heard the quick click of his door key. Miranda tried to barge into his room but she couldn't get the door open.

'Hey! Carl! It's Miranda. Miranda and Sylvie. Come on, let us in,' she said, rattling the door handle impatiently.

Carl said nothing. I wondered if he was standing right the other side of the door. Miranda had the same thought. She went down on her knees and tried to peer through the keyhole, but the key on the other side was blocking her view.

'Carl, come on. We know you're in there. Please!' Miranda started knocking hard on the door. She tapped with both hands, making an insistent drumming beat.

'Don't make so much noise!' I said.

'That's the point. He'll open that door in a minute just to shut me up,' said Miranda, banging harder.

She underestimated Carl. He stayed silent behind his battered door. Miranda had to give up eventually. She stood there, breathing heavily, shaking her hands in the air.

'All right, *don't* come out,' she said. 'See if we care. We'll go round to Paul's instead.'

I thought I heard Carl's intake of breath, but he still said nothing. Miranda sighed heavily, rolling her eyes. She stamped down the corridor, motioning me to do the same. She stopped at the top of the stairs, her finger on her lips, waiting.

'What?' I mouthed at her.

'I bet he'll look out in a minute, just to check we're gone,' she whispered, as if *she* was the one who'd known Carl ever since he was a small boy.

Jake came out of his room, now dressed in his jeans and baseball boots and his coolest biker T-shirt, obviously intent on impressing Miranda. He took hold of both her hands. Their palms were still red.

'Great drumming,' he said. 'You can play in my band if you want.'

'Ssh!'

'Look, if you girls are hoping for a glimpse of the rare Greater Spotted Carl Tit you'll be here all day.'

'He's right, Miranda,' I said.

'He'll have to come out to have a pee sometime,' said Miranda.

I blushed, hating the way we were talking about Carl, worrying that he could hear us.

'He's got a sink in his bedroom,' said Jake.

'Oh yuck, that's revolting,' said Miranda, laughing, forgetting all about being quiet.

'Let's go downstairs,' I said. I raised my voice. 'Let's all give Carl some peace.'

So we went downstairs, out into the garden, where Mick was sitting in a deckchair marking essays. His eyes slid past Jake and me. He stared at Miranda.

'This is Sylvie's friend Miranda,' said Jake.

'I'm Carl's friend too,' she said.

Mick raised his eyebrows. 'Are you and Sylvie in the same year at school?' he asked, as if this was astonishing.

'Yep. I'm the new girl,' said Miranda. She sat down beside him, picking up his essays and peering at them.

'Hey, don't get them out of order,' he said crossly, but she just laughed.

'God, these look boring,' she said.

'They are,' said Mick, yawning. 'And I've got twenty more to go.'

'Are you a school teacher then?' said Miranda. She was sitting in a consciously kittenish way, hands round her plump knees, boots neatly pointed, head tilted up at him.

'I teach at the university.'

'Ah, a lecturer. Cool,' said Miranda. She was practically batting her eyelashes, chatting him up.

'In Politics,' said Jake. *'Boring!'*

Mick glared at him. 'What does your father do, Miranda?'

'Oh. Telly stuff.'

'He's an actor?'

'No, no, he makes documentaries. My mum's an actress – well, sort of. It depends what mood she's in, who she wants to impress. She used to be a model but she's too old now. She'll say she's an actress or a jewellery designer or an artist, but she hasn't been any of them *properly*, she just plays at it.'

222

'No harm in that,' said Mick. 'My wife Jules is an artist and you would probably say she plays at it because she's not recognized or hung in galleries and she doesn't make any money selling her paintings but she doesn't think that matters. She teaches art to kids as a day job and then paints for the sheer joy of it.'

I loved it that Mick spoke about Jules so proudly.

'I paint too,' said Jake, desperate to impress. He'd always done big sploshy work with paint dribbles and smudges all over. He used to paint dogs and rabbits and horses and big coiled snakes, his fantasy pets, but now he painted great pink women with breasts like watermelons, his fantasy girls.

His painting style couldn't have been more different to Carl's careful illustrations in coloured ink, as exquisite as illuminated manuscripts.

'I hear Carl paints too,' said Miranda. I sometimes felt she could read my mind. 'Where does he keep his paintings? In this special Glass Hut? Let's go and look.'

'No!' I said. 'No, you can't, Miranda. They're private.'

'OK, OK,' said Miranda, standing up and showing a great deal of her legs in the process. Mick averted his eyes, sighing. Jake stared.

'I won't look at a single painting then – but I simply *have* to see the famous glass collection.'

'No, that's private too,' I said.

'Don't be silly, Sylvie, it's just *glass*. And I've contributed to his collection, haven't I? I want to see where he's put my paperweight.'

'But it's Carl's private place. He doesn't want anyone to go there, especially without him,' I said.

'*You* go there. And he's taken *Paul* there too. So why can't *I* go? I won't touch anything, I just want to look. Where is it?' She squinted down the bottom of the garden to the yew hedge. 'Behind the hedge!' she said. She marched off, bottom waggling beneath her short net skirt.

'Come back here, Miranda,' said Mick. He said it quietly, but there was a steely tone to his voice.

She took a few more steps forward defiantly, but then stopped. She turned her head, flipping back her hair, her cheeks flushed. 'Mm?' she said, as if she hadn't quite heard.

'The Glass Hut is Carl's. It's private, as Sylvie says. No one goes there unless Carl expressly invites them. I think you'll have to wait for your invitation, Miranda.'

Miranda raised her eyebrows but didn't argue. She nibbled her lip, suddenly looking childish. Then she walked back to Jake and tucked her hand into the crook of his elbow.

'It looks like I'm settling for a tour of your paintings as I'm denied a glimpse of the famous glass collection,' she said.

'Sure,' said Jake.

She started tugging him towards the house. It didn't look as if I was included in this invitation. Then Jake turned, nearly at the house.

'Aren't you coming too, Sylvie?'

'In a minute,' I mumbled.

I waited until they'd both gone in the back door. Then I looked at Mick. He was gathering his essays, tapping them on his lap, getting them neatly squared up. He caught my eye and went 'Phew!' cartoon style, blowing up into his own nostrils.

'Your friend Miranda makes quite an impact, Sylvie,' he said.

'I know,' I said. 'I'm sorry I didn't ask you and Jules about her coming to lunch. She just kind of asked herself.'

'I can well believe that. She's a bit full-on, isn't she? I'm not sure our Jake can handle her — although I gather it's Carl she's really interested in.'

I shrugged.

'Well, she's wasting her time,' said Mick, and he reached out and gave my shoulder a little pat. Then he paused, his hand resting lightly on my arm. 'Sylvie, I don't know what's going on with Carl. Is he just being a bit of a drama queen, shutting himself away like this, barely talking to anyone? Or is he really unhappy about something serious?'

'I don't know,' I said miserably. 'He doesn't seem to want to tell me stuff any more.'

Miranda and I stayed to lunch. Carl didn't join us. Jules put his meal on a tray.

'I'll take it up to him if you like,' said Miranda.

'Thank you, dear, but I think Sylvie had better do it,' said Jules.

I jumped up quickly and took the tray upstairs. I put it down outside Carl's door. I didn't knock. I simply put my mouth to the door and said, 'Here's your lunch, Carl. I've left it just outside. I'm so sorry that we came and banged on your door. I promise we'll leave you alone now.'

I wanted to add, *I love you*. I mouthed the words, but didn't dare say them out loud.

Miranda left shortly after lunch. She didn't like Mick and Jules being firm with her and she got bored of flirting with Jake. I left too. We went back to my house but Miranda was still fidgety and restless.

'Maybe I'll phone Paul.'

'I thought he was going to phone you.'

'Yes, but you know what boys are like. They *say* they'll phone but they never do.'

'Do you want to go out with Paul again?'

'Yes. Well. Not really, but he'll do until someone more exciting comes along.'

'I don't like him one bit,' I said. I paused, rehearsing the next words in my head, needing them to come out as casually as possible. 'Why do you think Carl likes Paul?'

'Because he's . . .' Miranda waved her hands around for inspiration. 'He's a *lad*. He's good looking and he's sporty and he likes a laugh.

He's just got this cheeky fun thing about him. I know you don't like him, Sylvie, but don't *you* think he's pretty fit looking?'

'He's nowhere near as good looking as Carl.'

'Mm. Yes. But Carl's more your blond choirboy good looking. I think Paul's more sexy.'

'Even though he couldn't do it properly?'

'Well, most boys are hopeless at it at first.'

'In your wide experience,' I said.

'It's a whole lot wider than *yours*,' said Miranda.

She tried dialling Paul. He didn't answer, so she left a message.

'Hey, you, it's Miranda, and it's three o'clock and I'm bored bored bored. Do you want to get together somewhere? Call me then, asap.'

'You're bored bored bored?' I said.

'I was just *saying* that as an excuse to ring him, silly,' she said. 'Still, I'd better go home, in case he comes round calling for me. Plus the parents might actually be a bit twitchy seeing as I promised to be back by lunch time.'

I felt relieved when she went. I was starting to wish we hadn't made friends. I didn't want to be friends with Lucy either. I just wanted Carl for my best friend.

I lay down on my bed. Albert Bear was on my pillow but I flicked him overboard. I reached out for my old teddies on my windowsill and remembered the games Carl and I had first played together when we were little. We were jungle explorers and these tattered nursery-world creatures, pink teddy, baby blue ted, a Scottie dog with a tartan ribbon and a floppy sheep that looked as if it had been run over – they were our wild animals.

The softest and littlest, baby blue ted, was the most lethal. One bite from him had a devastating effect. We took it in turns to froth at the mouth and fit while the other performed complex medical procedures with a spoon and a pair of plastic scissors and a skipping-rope stethoscope.

My soft animal collection sometimes morphed into our children, Alice Pink, Benjamin Blue, Charlie Scottie, who threw terrible barking tantrums, and Michael Sheep, who was very very stupid but sweet-natured. We must have had our four children out of wedlock because we sometimes played Weddings. I made Alice a bridesmaid's dress out of a pink silk scarf. Benjamin, Charlie and Michael were pageboys until we got to church, and then Benjamin became a very short vicar, wearing a black glove over a white tissue so that he had a proper clerical collar.

Carl did Benjamin's voice and asked if I wanted to marry Carl Anthony Johnson. I stood there in my white nightie with a bouquet of dandelions and said, *I do, I do, I do*, promising to love and obey him until death did us part.

I wondered if Carl was still lying on his bed on the other side of the wall. Maybe he was even remembering the same games, thinking the same thoughts.

My mobile went *ching-ching*. I jumped and pressed the message key, heart leaping, but it was only Mum asking if I was OK and had I had a good lunch at Jules's. She promised she'd definitely be back by tea time and how did I feel about her bringing Gerry back to meet me?

Oh God. I texted back: PERHAPS NOT. LOVE S.

I lay back on my pillow and felt so lonely I started to cry a little, tears seeping slowly sideways. Then I fell asleep and dreamed about Carl. We were in Kew Gardens. I was lost again and I was running, running, running, trampling my way through jungle plants, Chihuly glass smashing all around me, and there, just ahead of me, I saw Carl. He was running too, away from me. I couldn't catch up with him, try as I might. He dodged up the spiral staircase in the glasshouse and I pounded after him, hauling myself up two steps at a time. Then I was at the very top, running along the narrow balcony, gaining on him now. He looked over his shoulder, slipped, lurched backwards, up and over the low rail. I watched, screaming, as he spiralled down and down and down through the great green leaves.

*Ching-ching.*

I woke with a start, my throat aching as if I'd really been screaming. I grabbed my mobile, but it was Miranda sending me a text to say she was sending me *Paul*'s text. For the next fifteen minutes I was forced to read their silly texting banter. I wanted to switch off my phone, but I still hoped Carl *might* text me . . .

*Ching-Ching.*

Not *another* stupid Miranda-and-Paul message! I touched the display button, all set to erase it.

SORRY SORRY SORRY, S. C U IN G H ? C X

*Yes!*

I rubbed at my face, ran down the stairs and through the kitchen, giving Miss Miles a quick nod as she made herself a cup of tea. Then I was out the back door, down our garden, through the gap in the fence, until I stood breathless outside the Glass Hut. The light wasn't on inside. Perhaps I'd got there before Carl? I tapped timidly on the door.

'Come in,' Carl whispered from inside. 'You are on your own, aren't you?'

'Of course I am,' I said, slipping inside.

It was so dark I couldn't see a thing. I felt for the light switch.

'Don't,' said Carl. 'Let's stay in the dark.' He reached out and found my hand. 'Come and sit with me.'

I sat on the sofa, close beside him.

'Oh, Sylvie,' he said, sounding hoarse. 'I'm sorry.'

'*I'm* sorry,' I said. 'I was mad to bring Miranda with me. I couldn't stop her banging and banging like that. It was so awful.'

'It was awful *my* side of the door,' said Carl. 'I

thought she'd start hacking her way through with an axe any minute. I know it was silly and childish hiding away from everyone but I couldn't face her. Did she tell you what happened at Kew?'

'No. Well, just that she went off with Paul.'

'So maybe he didn't tell her.'

I swallowed. 'Tell her what?'

I heard Carl swallow too. We sat hand in hand in the dark for several long seconds.

'I've been such an idiot,' he said. It sounded as if he might be crying.

'Oh, Carl, it's OK. Please don't,' I said. I wanted to put my arms round him but he was clutching my hand as if he could never let it go.

'It's not OK. I've ruined everything. He hates me now. And I love him.'

I felt the blood beating in my head. He'd said it out loud. We couldn't pretend any more. This was it. The end of all my dreams.

'I know you love him,' I said, trying to keep my voice steady.

'You're shocked, aren't you?'

'No, no, don't be silly,' I mumbled.

'*I* was shocked. I mean, I kind of knew I liked boys, not girls – apart from you, I mean – but I didn't *want* to be different. But I couldn't help it. I just saw him that first day and it was like he was the only boy in the whole school. I couldn't stop watching him. It was OK because *everyone* watched him. He was the big-time football hero and everyone was desperate to be

231

in his little gang. It was fine then, when we never even spoke to each other. But then we were paired up by this teacher in drama. I couldn't believe it. I was thrilled and yet so scared too. I was sure I'd make a complete berk of myself. Well, I did, I didn't have a clue what to say—'

'Oh, Carl, stop it, you're the most articulate person I've ever met.'

'I can say all sorts of stuff to *you*, Sylvie, but at first with Paul I could hardly say two words. Then we had to do this daft trust exercise when you take turns falling and the other guy has to catch you. You've no idea what it felt like, holding him in my arms. I can't explain, just touching him, it was electric. You wait till you feel that way about someone, then you'll understand.'

I was glad it was dark.

'Sylvie?' He didn't understand. 'You *are* shocked, aren't you?'

'No, no, it's just . . . a bit of a surprise.'

'It's a surprise for me too,' said Carl. 'I never ever thought I'd feel like this. I thought I'd just coast along somehow. I've always been careful not to act too girly or whatever. I hate being teased. I felt so safe, you and me and our own private world. I didn't have a clue what it's like to fall in love. It's frightening because it's so intense, it kind of takes you over. It's just like every stupid cliché, every silly song. You can't eat, you can't concentrate, you can't sleep. You just think about the other person all the time, even though you know it's crazy. You just can't help it. It's especially crazy to fall for Paul because he's the straightest boy ever. He's one of the worst for making stupid jokes. I knew I didn't stand a chance of him ever feeling the same way about me, and yet I still sort of hoped that somehow it would happen. How mad is that?'

'It's mad,' I said.

'So I thought I'd just carry on, us being friends, Paul and me. I thought I could make it work. But it was so *difficult* never being able to say what I really felt. It made me feel so hopeless sometimes. I mean, even if Paul were gay too you could never ever come out at our school. You can call any of the guys any four-letter word you choose and they don't blink, but call one of them gay and he'll punch your head in, even if he *is*. I used to get called gay a lot because I'm arty and swotty and not too good at football, but they didn't really *mean* it. *Paul* called me hopelessly gay whenever I muffed a football move, but it was OK if I just laughed and clowned around with limp wrists, going *whoopsie* all the time to try to be part of the joke.'

'Carl, how can you love someone who treats you like that?'

'But I keep telling you, he didn't *mean* it. He didn't dream I was really gay. He always went on and on about girls and what he'd like to do to them so I did too.'

'About me?'

'No!' he said. 'I'd never talk about you like that, Sylvie, you know I wouldn't.' He said it fiercely, to be reassuring.

'So who did you talk about?'

'Oh. Just anyone. It was all so stupid and tacky. Whoever came into my head.'

'Miranda.'

'Well, she was an obvious candidate.'

'Did you tell Paul about kissing her at the party?'

'Yes, I did vaguely mention it.'

'So what did you tell him it was like?'

'Oh, Sylvie, I can't remember. It didn't mean anything to me. It felt a bit weird and threatening, if you really want to know. She opened her mouth so wide I thought she was going to swallow me whole. Plus she was wearing all this slippery lipstick. I was scared she was going to get it all over me. It tasted disgusting.'

I felt a pang for Miranda, but I couldn't help being pleased.

'So you tried to set Paul up with her instead?'

'I know it was mad and stupid but I hoped that the four of us could be friends and all go round together. It seemed a great idea at the time. I mean, I love Paul, I love you, you like Miranda, she likes *any* boy who pays her attention. I thought it might work.'

The Glass Hut whirled round me as I replayed what he'd said inside my head.

'You love me?' I whispered.

'Yes! Of *course* I love you, Sylvie. You know how much you mean to me. You're the one and only girl for me, ever. You know that.'

'But you're not *in* love with me?'

'Not the way I'm in love with Paul.'

'Still?'

'Yes. And you don't even know how he acted. You see, I tried to kiss him and—'

'You did *what*?'

'I know, I know. It was totally crazy. I didn't mean to. It was just a spur-of-the-moment thing. It was so lovely in Kew Gardens in the moonlight. I felt as if we'd stepped into another world and anything could happen.'

'I felt that too.'

'It was like our own Midsummer Night's Dream. Then Miranda suggested playing Hide and Seek, and we all scattered and I didn't plan anything, I just set off and I spotted Paul almost straight away. It was as if he was waiting there in the bushes for me. He laughed when I walked up, and pulled me in to the bushes with him so we were all squashed up, hiding together. My head was right next to his and we were still laughing and fooling about, and without even thinking I kissed him. I couldn't believe it was happening. It felt so incredible – but then he pushed me away. He punched me. Then he said all these awful things.'

'Oh, poor poor Carl,' I said, but I couldn't help adding, 'Still, what did you *expect*?'

'I know, I know. I was just totally mad. I kept

telling him I was sorry and I'd never do it again but he kept on saying stuff, acting like I was this weird sick pervert.'

'You're not, you know you're not.'

'But *he* thinks I am. He acted like it's some contagious disease and I was trying to infect him too. He was so *angry* with me. I fell over and he actually started *kicking* me, even though we'd been best mates just two minutes ago. Then he stormed off, saying he never ever wanted to see me again.'

'Well, that's a bit silly, seeing as you're in the same form at school.'

'That's what I'm so worried about. It's not just the awfulness of making Paul hate me—'

'That's mad. I think you should hate him for being so horrible to you,' I interrupted.

'No, listen, what if he tells everyone at school that I kissed him?'

'He won't,' I said firmly. 'Look, I know he didn't tell Miranda. He just said you'd had a fight. She thought it was over her.'

'That's so typical of Miranda. I don't know what you *see* in her, Sylvie.'

'Well. I don't get what you see in Paul. Especially now,' I said. 'You *still* want to be friends with him, don't you?'

'Yes, but he won't want anything to do with me. Yet the weirdest thing of all . . . for a second he kissed me back like he really cared about me too.'

# 20

I didn't want to talk about Carl to Miranda. Luckily she was too caught up with her own affairs. She was still texting Paul all the time. He kept asking her to send a photo to his mobile.

'What *kind* of photo?'

'Oh, he's just trying it on. He wants a quick flash of my chest.'

'*What?*'

'Don't look so shocked. It's a boy thing. That's what they all want.'

'Yes, so they can show it round to all their dirty mates.'

'Do you think he'll show Carl if I oblige?'

'No! Miranda, you're not *serious* about this?'

'It's no big deal. It's just a bit of fun. It's like a mobile status symbol. You get the right handset, the right ring-tone, the right photo of your girl—'

'Yeah, if that's how you want to be thought of – the right topless girl – then you're crazy.'

'I'm not saying I'll go *topless*. I could just undo a few buttons, show off a bit of cleavage ... Don't look like that! You're just jealous because you haven't *got* any cleavage – and even if you *had*, Carl doesn't seem very interested.'

'Why do you say that?' I said, my heart thumping.

'Well, I know you two have been lovebirds since the cradle, but you just don't *act* very lovey-dovey when you're together. I haven't even seen the two of you so much as holding hands.'

'You have no idea what we do when we're alone together,' I said hotly.

'Well, what *do* you do? How far have you gone with him? Why won't you ever *tell* me?'

'It's private. I'm not a kiss-and-tell girl like you.'

'You don't kiss so you haven't got anything to tell,' said Miranda snippily.

I worried about people kissing and telling all day. When I got home from school I didn't even wait to text Carl. I went round to the Johnsons' house straight away. Jake answered the door. He actually smiled at me.

'Ah! Hi, Sylvie!'

'Don't look so excited, Jake. Miranda's not with me,' I said, pushing past him.

I called for Carl.

'He's upstairs, Sylvie,' Jules said. She looked worried. 'He came home from school early. Said he was sick. I hope he hasn't got anything catching. Here, take him some fizzy water, sweetie.' She poured a glass and then gave me a second look. 'You don't look very well either. Do you feel sick too?'

'A bit,' I said truthfully.

'Oh dear. You drink some water too. I hope you're not both going down with something. Still, at least you could keep each other company. Do you remember the time you both had chickenpox when you were little? We popped you one in each end of Carl's bed and you played together, all over pink spots,' Jules sighed. 'I wish you were still little kids. Well, you're still OK, Sylvie, you're lovely, but both my boys have changed so. Jake's this great noisy untidy bear stomping round the place, playing his awful music. Carl's gone to the other extreme, hiding in his lair, barely saying two words to anyone, looking so white and anguished all the time, like some boy martyr with a wolf gnawing away at his chest. If I try to ask him what the matter is he just rolls his eyes at me and won't *say*.'

She put the two glasses on a tray with a plate of water biscuits and black grapes. 'There! A small snack for the two invalids. Try very hard to have girls when you get married, Sylvie. I'm sure it's a lot easier.'

239

'I don't think I'm going to get married now,' I said. I tried to say it lightly but my voice wobbled. I felt dangerously near tears. We both looked at my little-girl wall painting of my wedding in the corner of the kitchen.

'You'll be a beautiful bride one day,' said Jules softly.

I smiled at her wanly and carried the tray upstairs.

'Here, let me,' said Jake, bounding out of nowhere and hoisting the tray high, like a waiter. The two glasses clinked together, water spilling.

'Stop messing about, Jake. Give it back,' I said.

'I'm only trying to help.' He clicked his heels together and bowed low, spilling more.

'For heaven's sake, do you have to mess about all the time?' I snapped.

He straightened up, looking surprisingly hurt. I thought he was being deliberately annoying, peeved because Miranda wasn't there.

'Sorry,' he mumbled, and sloped off.

I sighed and went on up the stairs and along the landing.

'Carl?' I said quietly, outside his door. 'It's Sylvie. I've got a tray for you.'

I wasn't sure he'd let me in, but the key clicked and the door opened a few centimetres. I slipped inside. Carl was still wearing his school uniform – the white shirt, badly cut grey trousers and purple tie that took away all his style and individuality. His hair was standing up at odd angles, as if he'd been running his hands through it. He sat down on the edge of his bed, arms folded, knees together, and stared into space.

I put the tray on the floor and sat down beside him. I reached out for his hand and held onto it. He didn't squeeze my hand in return. He just sat there, rigid.

'Was it awful?' I whispered.

He nodded.

'You told Jules you were sick.'

'I was. I threw up all over the floor of the boys' bogs.'

'So you're really ill?'

'Paul thinks I am. Sick. A perve. A poof.'

'Stop it!'

'He said much worse things. He's still so angry with me. He thinks I set out to befriend him and turn him gay too.'

'That's ridiculous.'

'He really hates me, Sylvie, it's so awful.'

'Well, you've got to start hating him back.'

'How can I do that?' Carl said helplessly.

'Easy!' I said, wanting to shake him. 'He's horrible, Carl, crude and stupid and hopelessly prejudiced. He's not even that bright or witty or interesting. He's just a boring, cruel idiot. He's the easiest person in the world to hate.'

'Look, you're so sweet, you're trying to be kind, but truly, you haven't got a clue. You can't just stop loving someone and start hating them instead. I hate *me* more than I hate Paul, for being such a fool and putting him in this situation when he just wanted us to be good mates. He's scared that everyone will start talking about us, calling us both queer. He said he's not going to say another word to me ever. He said if I ever tried to so much as touch him he'd ram my head down the toilet. He said I disgust him. That was when I threw up. So of course I disgust him even more now,' said Carl. 'Imagine, throwing up right in front of him. I think some of it splashed on his shoes.'

'Good. Serve him right. Aim at his head next time. Look, even if he was gay he *so* wouldn't be the right boy for you, Carl. He's nowhere near good enough. You're acting like you're under some stupid spell or something.'

'That's what it *feels* like,' said Carl, smacking the heel of his hand against his forehead. 'I don't want to feel like this. If you only knew what it was *like*, Sylvie.'

'What makes you think I don't?' I said.

I'd meant to say it in my head, not out loud. Carl focused on me, frowning. We looked at each other. His eyes widened. Then we both looked away, ducking our heads, both of us blushing. He cleared his throat, ready to say something.

'Here, have a glass of water,' I said hastily.

I drank myself, so quickly that I gave myself hiccups. 'Oh God, not again,' I said.

I made much of the hiccups, holding my

breath, gulping from the wrong side of the glass, all the party tricks, to divert us both from the painful embarrassment of the situation. Carl saw that I didn't want to discuss it and acted as if he hadn't understood. But when I stood up to go he whispered, 'I'm so sorry, Sylvie. If only—'

There was no point in him even finishing the sentence.

I went home and made desultory small talk with Miss Miles in the kitchen. When Mum came home she was in the mood for *big* talk. She was obviously feeling guilty for going out with Gerry at the weekend, so she was now determined to spend quality time with me to compensate. She started all sorts of Sylvie-centred topics, asking about Carl and Miranda and Lucy, about school, about my reading, even about my Glassworld writing.

I didn't want to talk about anything at all and became increasingly monosyllabic. Mum misinterpreted my attitude, thinking that I was in a sad little sulk because she'd been neglecting me.

'Oh, Sylvie, darling, you do know you'll always always come first with me, no matter what,' she said, trying to hug me.

'Don't be daft, Mum,' I said, wriggling free.

'But it's true,' she said. 'Gerry or no Gerry.'

'So I take it he's now a close second?'

'Well. Yes. He is so special, Sylvie. *Please* will you meet him next week? You could come out with us or he'll come over here, whichever you'd prefer. I just know you'll get on with him. He's so funny and yet so gentle. He's *so* different from your dad. *He* was always so bossy and belligerent, and he'd never listen to me properly. Oh, I'm sorry, I shouldn't say that. He's your father and no matter what's happened between the two of us you're still his daughter and he loves you very much.'

'Mum. Stop it. I'm not a little kid any more. You don't have to say all this stuff. Dad doesn't give a toss about me. He hasn't even *seen* me for years. He'd probably walk straight past if he saw me in the street. Ditto me him. I don't *care*.'

'OK, OK,' Mum said gently, as if she was soothing a silly toddler.

'I don't need my dad any more. I don't need a *new* dad either. I don't need anyone. I'm perfectly happy as I am,' I shouted.

Then I burst into tears. I wouldn't let Mum comfort me. I stamped upstairs, aware that I was behaving ridiculously but unable to stop. I kept hearing *If only if only if only*. I kept seeing the pity in Carl's eyes. It made me want to curl up and die.

I cried until I gave myself a headache. I ached all over, my chest, my stomach, my back. I wondered if I was really ill. Heart-sick. It had a melodramatic, glamorous ring. I peered at myself in the mirror. I *looked* ill, very pale, with dark circles under my eyes. I hoped they made me look a little older.

My tummy was really sore now. I wondered if

I was going to be sick like Carl. I went to the bathroom and found that I'd started my period. I stared at the stains on my underwear. I'd waited for this moment for so long. I was the last girl in our whole class to start. I'd begun to think I was going to be a freaky new phenomenon, stuck in little-girlhood for ever. Here at least was real proof that I was turning into a woman. I touched my sore chest, wondering if that was suddenly metamorphosing too, but sadly it felt as flat as ever.

I washed myself and then took Mum's box of tampons and puzzled for ten minutes over the instructions. I put my leg up on the side of the bath. I seized the tampon, trembling, as if I was holding a hand grenade. I tried to insert it but couldn't work out exactly how to do it. I didn't want to push too hard in case it was the wrong bit of me. I couldn't see what I was doing – and didn't really want to anyway. Maybe I wasn't formed properly. Maybe I really *was* a freak, a girl doll minus the proper working pieces.

I gave up and used the horrible pad thing from the packet that Mum had put on the top shelf of my wardrobe. They'd been waiting there untouched for a good two years. I felt as if I was wearing a nappy. We had PE tomorrow. How on earth was I going to manage?

I wished I wasn't a girl. If I was a boy I wouldn't have to cope with such a sore and messy and embarrassing problem once a month.

245

If I was a boy Carl might love me back the way I loved him.

I tried hard to imagine what I'd be like as a boy. It would be even worse being so small and skinny. I wondered what my hair would look like chopped short. I'd look like some weird little pixie person. I wouldn't be able to hide my sticking-out ears. I'd never be good looking like Carl. I wasn't bright or talented or witty. The other boys would hate me. Carl might hate me too. No, worse, he'd feel sorry for me and hang out with me sometimes, just to be kind.

I would be no use as a gay boy. No one would ever fancy me. I would have even less success with girls. Someone like Miranda would make mincemeat of me. I saw her squashing me into a mincing machine and turning the handle, squeezing me out at the other end as a string of limp little sausages. She'd despise me as a boy. Thank goodness she liked me as a girl, so long as I played along with her.

I liked her too. I thought about the possibility of loving her. I thought she was beautiful in her own dark dramatic way. I loved the glossiness of her red hair, her even white teeth, her wicked dimples. I loved her clothes, especially her exotic underwear and her bold buckled boots. I tried to imagine taking her in my arms and kissing her. I wasn't sure it would work. Her lips would feel too full, her body too soft, her hair too long. I longed to look like Miranda, even to be Miranda, but I didn't want to love her.

It was so silly. You couldn't help the way you felt.

I loved Carl. Carl loved Paul. Paul maybe loved Miranda. I wasn't sure Miranda loved any of us. She just wanted us all to love her.

I fell asleep long before Mum came upstairs. I woke up when she crept into my room, but I kept my eyes closed. I could sense her standing there, looking at me. She sighed softly, then bent over and kissed my hair. I wanted to reach round and cling to her neck and have a good cry, the way I'd done when I was little. But in those days Mum could always make it all better for me. There was nothing she could do to change Carl. I didn't even want to tell her I'd started my period because she might gush in an embarrassing way.

She found out anyway.

'So you've started your period, Sylvie!' she said in the kitchen at breakfast.

She didn't lower her voice at all. Miss Miles could easily have heard upstairs in her room.

'There no need to blush, darling. There's nothing to be ashamed about. We should be celebrating your becoming a woman.'

I squirmed. 'I don't want to be a woman,' I said. 'Shut up about it, Mum. How do you know, anyway?'

'The toilet was blocked up with bits of sanitary towel. I knew it wasn't me and dear Miss Miles is way past that stage in her life.'

'I wish I was too,' I said.

I was tired of being a teenager. It was too sad, too complicated, too worrying. I wanted to fast-forward fifty years and be really really old. Then it wouldn't matter if I was small and scraggy. It would be a positive advantage if I still looked young for my age. It wouldn't matter if I didn't have a boyfriend. I could just shake my head enigmatically when anyone asked about my past love life and say 'I had my moments' just like Miss Miles. I wouldn't have to make friends to prove I was popular. I wouldn't have to fit in at school. I wouldn't even be at work any more. I could simply please myself and do what I wanted. I could read for hours. I could write and draw and paint. I could live all day in Glassworld. I could stay eternally young as Queen Sylviana, and King Carlo would love me, only me, and we would live happily ever after.

I went to school with a couple of horrible pad things in a plastic bag. The outline of the one that I was wearing showed horribly through my knickers. I wondered about asking Lucy how she coped. We rarely talked about intimate things but I knew she'd started her period last year. She called it 'her visitor'.

I leaned over as far as I could during double maths to ask for advice.

'Hey, Sylvie, are you copying from me?' she said, shielding her answers.

I was hurt that she should think this, or indeed would mind sharing her solutions with me. I was also irritated. I am bad enough at maths, but Lucy is worse. Only a total fool would choose to copy down her answers.

'I just want to ask you something, Lucy,' I hissed. 'Look, what do you do when we have PE if you've started?'

'Started what?' said Lucy.

I sighed. '*You* know.' It was no use. I had to use her twee little phrase. 'When you've got "your visitor".'

'Oh!' Lucy went a little pink. 'Well, I always wear two pairs of knickers.'

'Ah.' I thought about it. It was a reasonably sensible solution, though it sounded hot and uncomfortable. I only had the knickers I was wearing. I couldn't really ask to borrow an extra pair from Lucy.

'It stops the pad thing showing?' I whispered, pink myself.

'More or less. And it helps if you start flooding.'

'Oh God.' So far the blood had been a small trickle. Was it about to start gushing everywhere like a scarlet Niagara? 'Do *you* flood, Lucy?'

'Oh yes, it's terrible. Mum had to take me to the doctor's. It kept going all over my *bed.*'

I started to feel ill. The classroom spun round. Maybe I was going to faint. Then at least I'd have a reasonable excuse for getting out of PE.

I went flying to the girls' toilets at break time, not waiting for Lucy or Miranda or anyone. I was starting to imagine great gushing and clutched my plastic bag desperately.

249

'Sylvie? Sylvie! Hey, hey, slow down!'

It was *Jake*.

'I've got to dash, Jake,' I said, trying to dodge past.

'But I've got to tell you something,' said Jake.

I did stop then, wondering if he had a message from Carl. Maybe he'd decided to stay away from school, pretending he was still sick. If so, perhaps I could risk playing truant again. I had to be with him. He needed me. I was the only one he could talk to.

'What is it?' I asked.

'Wegotagig!' Jake said.

'What?' The words didn't make sense. It sounded like gobbledegook.

'We've got a *gig*,' Jake said, grinning proudly. 'They rang up yesterday evening, after you'd gone. They want me and the boys to play at this birthday party and they're *paying* – fifty quid, how cool is that!'

'*Your* band?' I said. 'Oh. Well. Good for you.' I tried to edge round him.

'Will you come, Sylvie?' said Jake.

'Come where?' said Miranda, materializing behind me.

'This party. My band's playing,' said Jake proudly. 'You can come too.'

'I don't think I can make it, Jake,' I said, rushing past. There! He could get Miranda to go – that was surely what he wanted.

'But you don't know when it *is*!' Jake called after me.

I pretended not to hear him. He couldn't very well follow me right into the girls' toilets. I charged into the cubicle and faced the worst. It wasn't as bad as I'd feared, but I still had PE to contend with.

'Sylvie?' Miranda called, outside my cubicle. 'Why don't you want to go to Jake's party?'

'It's a *birthday* party. It'll probably be some little kid wanting to do a bit of head-banging with all his mates. No one sane would employ Jake for a real party. His band is unbelievably awful.'

'OK, point taken. I expect I'll be on some heavy date with Paul anyway,' said Miranda.

I muttered a very rude sentence.

'What? Hey, that's my boyfriend you're describing so graphically,' said Miranda. She didn't sound too perturbed. 'What's he done to upset you?'

'He hasn't done anything to *me*.'

'To Carl? Hey, have you found out about this fight?'

'No,' I said quickly.

'Are you *sure* you don't know something?' said Miranda. 'Hey, Sylvie, what are you *doing* in there? Have you got galloping diarrhoea or something?'

'Shut up! I've got my *period*,' I hissed.

'Oh. Right. Have you got a tampon then?'

'No.'

''S OK, I've got one in my school bag. Half a tick.' She passed one under the door.

'I can't use them,' I whispered.

'What? I can't hear you.'

'Miranda! Look, I don't want to announce this to the whole *world*. I don't use tampons, I can't get them to work, OK? They're too big or I'm too little, whatever. Shall I broadcast it on the Tannoy system?'

'Yes please,' said Miranda, giggling. 'Try my tampon. Go on, it's a special little one.'

She gave me full instructions on how to use them. I prayed no one else was in the toilets. But eventually I triumphed.

'Yay! I've managed it. Oh God, what a palaver!' I said, coming out of the cubicle and washing my hands.

'You're acting like you've never had a period before, Little Titch,' Miranda teased.

'Well. It is my first time if you must know.'

'*Really!* I started when I was ten.'

'Typical. Precocious brat.'

'That's me, babe. You come to your Aunty Miranda whenever you need practical advice. What lesson have I got next? I can never remember at this stupid school.'

'I've got PE,' I said grimly.

'Poor you. I hate prancing around in those awful baggy school knickers. God, they're such depressing garments.'

'Lucy wears two pairs of knickers when she's got her period,' I said.

'Oh, Lucy would. She'll wear two pairs of knickers the first time she goes out with a boy,' said Miranda.

252

We giggled unkindly. I knew I was being mean but it made me feel so much better.

I was still desperately worried about Carl, but I told myself he'd manage somehow. Boys had fights all the time. No one would know *why*.

I went round to see Carl as soon as I got back from school but he wasn't there.

'Isn't it his drama night?' said Jules. 'Do you know when *A Midsummer Night's Dream* is going to be performed?'

'Oh God, an all-boy *Midsummer Night's Dream*?' said Jake. 'What's Carl playing? Please tell me it's not Titania.' He started running about the kitchen, flicking back imaginary long hair and flouncing non-existent skirts, proclaiming, '*Begone, proud Oberon. Where are my fairies?*'

'Do you really think you're *funny*, Jake?' I said, and slammed out of their kitchen.

I went and made myself a sandwich at home and sent Carl a text.

R U OK? HOW IS PAUL SITUATION? C U L8R. LOVE S

He didn't reply. I got a text from Miranda instead.

RAJ JUST TEXTED ME THIS!!!

SOME YR 9 BOY IS SENDING ROUND IMAGES OF YOU TOPLESS TO ALL HIS GRUBBY LITTLE MATES — WITH COMMENTS. SHALL I SUMMON FORTH HIT SQUAD AND EXTERMINATE HIM? LOVE R. P.S. HE'S ALSO STARTING GAY-BASHING YR NICE PAL CARL.

I rang Miranda immediately.

'Oh God, Miranda, what's he *saying*?'

'I don't know exactly, something about me and my figure and what he'd like to do. In his dreams, matie! As if I'd let him near me now. Still, it's kind of *weird* being a telephone pin-up.'

'No, no—'

'I *know* you told me not to, but that was kind of like a dare. It was just a bit of fun—'

'Never mind about you and your silly photo! What's he saying about *Carl*?'

'It's not silly. It's rather a good photo, actually. I'm not *totally* topless. I've got this silky little jacket and my boobs just peep out. I tell you, the *Sun* would pay a fortune for it. Maybe this is the start of a whole new career—'

'Miranda. Please. Tell me about Carl.'

'Well, there's nothing to tell. Raj says they're just all picking on him, saying he's gay. I must admit, I have wondered myself, but you've always gone on and on about him being your boyfriend, you funny girl.'

'You wanted him as *your* boyfriend!'

255

'Of course, because he's gorgeous and funny and imaginative – which, come to think of it, *definitely* makes him gay. Still, it's every girl's fantasy, isn't it? You're the one girl in the world who can make him change his mind. *So*, is he utterly gay, Sylvie, or simply undecided? And why do you think Paul has suddenly grown three heads and is acting so grossly? I mean, I understand if he wants to send a photo of my tits to all his pervy little pals because they *are* pretty spectacular, but I never thought he'd be a creepy fascist fag-hater. They were best friends, for God's sake.' Miranda paused. I could *hear* her mind going tick-tick-tick.

'Oh!' she said. 'Did he try it on with Paul?'

I said nothing. I didn't need to.

'So that's why they had the fight! Oh God, Paul's *pathetic*! Well, I think we'll cross him off my list. To be honest, he always came a very poor second to Carl.'

'How was Carl taking it? Did Raj say he seemed very upset? What *exactly* were they saying?'

'I don't know. You know how stupid boys can be. Oh dear, everything's adding up now. Poor Carl. Shall I come round?'

'No, no! He isn't at home anyway, he's out at his drama club.'

'Paul's in that too, isn't he? Oh dear, they'll be acting out their own little drama. You go round later though, and give Carl a big kiss and hug from me and tell him Paul's a little shit and

256

I'm not having any more to do with him, OK?'

I tried sending another text to Carl the moment Miranda got off the phone but he still didn't reply. I tried phoning him in case he was on his way home but the phone switched straight to his message service. I didn't know what to say. I didn't want to tell him that all these people were talking about him, he'd hate it so. In the end I just said, 'Hi, Carl, it's me. I'm thinking of you. Phone me as soon as you can. Lots of love.'

Mum was late getting home from the building society. I nibbled at another sandwich. I wondered if I should start getting anything ready for supper. There didn't seem to be anything promising in the fridge. I found some old cheese, hard as a brick. I rifled through the cupboard to see if we had any macaroni but I couldn't find any.

I heard Mum's key in the door. She started talking to someone in the hall. Miss Miles was up in her room with 'Richard and Judy' – I could hear the faint buzz of her television.

'Is that you, Carl?' I shouted, wondering if he'd come straight round to talk to me.

It wasn't Carl. It was a total stranger, a tall dark man limping towards me. Oh God oh God oh God.

'This is Gerry, Sylvie,' Mum said brightly.

I glared at her but reluctantly held out my hand. Gerry shook it enthusiastically, smiling at me. His hand was damp, as if he was nervous.

'Why didn't you tell me Gerry was coming round, Mum?' I said.

'I didn't know! He came to pick me up from work as a surprise,' said Mum quietly. 'I thought it would be nice if we all had supper together.'

'We haven't got much in,' I said. 'I hope you like bread and cheese, Gerry.'

'No, no, we stopped off at Marks,' said Mum, lugging carrier bags into the kitchen. 'Take a look at this!'

Gerry obviously had a large wallet. There was smoked salmon, chicken, salads, rolls, peaches, cherries, white chocolate, fruit juice and wine.

'Feast time!' said Mum, happily unpacking.

'It looks fantastic,' I said. 'I hope you both have a lovely supper.'

'It's for you too, silly,' said Mum.

Gerry was giving her a hand, unwrapping all the food carefully to show he was a well-trained new man.

'No, I've said I'm eating next door,' I said.

'Sylvie,' said Mum. She took a deep breath. 'Eat with us. You've eaten round at Jules's enough recently. Come on, help lay the table.'

'Well, I'll just nip next door to explain—'

'For heaven's sake!' said Mum. She rubbed her forehead for a moment. 'Lay the table, please.'

'I can lay—' Gerry started.

'No, Sylvie can do it. She knows where the plates and knives and forks and everything are kept,' said Mum.

'OK. I'll lay the table. In a minute. I *have* to see if Carl's back.'

'When will you learn to stop running after Carl?' said Mum. 'Where does it *get* you? Honestly! Stop behaving like a five-year-old, please.'

I laid the table, slamming the plates down and rattling the forks and knives. It was so unfair. She didn't understand – though there was enough truth in what she'd said to make my eyes sting. It *didn't* get me anywhere. But I was still Carl's friend, no matter what. It sounded as if he'd had a terrible day. He *needed* me.

But Mum wasn't going to let me go. She made me sit down with her and Gerry and we ate the salmon and the chicken and the salads and the rolls and the fruit and the chocolate. Well, Mum and Gerry ate. I just picked at the food, a forkful of chicken, a tiny tomato, a bite of roll. Mum kept looking at me reproachfully, her eyes bright as if she was near tears. I wasn't picking *deliberately*. I was just so het up and anxious that I could barely swallow.

'Eat some cherries, Sylvie,' said Mum, pushing the plate towards me.

'No thanks.'

'Well, what about a peach?'

'No, really.'

Mum looked as if she'd like to ram the pound of cherries and all four peaches down my throat. Gerry tried to make polite conversation, asking me questions about school and favourite subjects and friends and hobbies. My answers were monosyllabic. He changed gear and chatted about his job and shopping and swimming while I shifted around in my chair, barely nodding. He eventually ground to a halt, exhausted.

There was a long silence. I wondered if I dared ask if I could go next door again.

'Would you like a cup of coffee, Gerry?' said Mum.

'I'll make it,' I said. 'You two go and sit in the living room. I'll bring it in.'

Mum hesitated. It was the first move I'd made towards being a good daughter.

'All right,' she said.

They took their glasses and what was left of the wine into the living room. I heard Mum murmuring and Gerry saying, 'No, no, she's lovely. I expect she's just shy, that's all.'

I didn't want him to defend me in that patronizing way! Why did Mum feel she had to parade me for his approval? He was nothing at all to do with me. I didn't mind Mum having a boyfriend. She could keep company with an entire football team if she was so inclined. It was fine with me, just so long as I didn't have to meet any of them.

I got the coffee percolator out and started shoving coffee grounds in. I knew Mum would fuss if I made His Lordship a quick mug of Nescaff. I piled the dishes in the sink, leaving the water running. Then I cautiously turned the key in the back door and inched it open. I couldn't risk going out of the front door. Mum would be bound to hear me, no matter how engrossed she was with Gerry, but hopefully she'd not know I was sneaking out the back with all the kitchen noises going on.

I crept furtively down the dark garden, dodging round the old apple tree, stumbling over a little pile of flowerpots, till I got to the hole in the fence. I edged through it into the Johnsons' garden, jagged wood catching at my school cardigan.

I looked up at Carl's bedroom. There was no light on, but that didn't necessarily signify anything. He could well be lying there in the dark.

Then I saw a dim light in the Glass Hut window. I ran across the grass and tapped our Morse code password on the door. I waited.

'Carl?' I whispered. 'Carl, can I come in?'

He didn't answer me. I stood listening, waiting for a rustle, a sigh, a sob. I could hear a distant dog barking and the faraway strum and wail of Jake playing his guitar in his bedroom.

'Carl, I'm going to come in,' I said, and I turned the hut handle.

I opened the door and stepped into the hut. Something crackled under my feet. I stared around, blinking in the light, catching my breath. The five shelves were heaped with shards and fragments, a grotesque kaleidoscope of colour. The little glass animals were all mutilated. The elephant was minus his trunk, the giraffe's head missing, the pelican beakless, the rabbit lop-eared, the crocodile without its tail.

The drinking glasses were keeling over drunkenly, the stems snapped off. Two vases rolled on the floor in a jumble of red and blue glass. The ashtrays were chipped, a paperweight smashed, millefiori flowers scattered like confetti. And the Glass Boy, oh the Glass Boy, Carl's special irreplaceable Glass Boy was smashed into splinters, his beautiful glass face gone, his arms shattered, his legs stumps, one bare glass foot still fixed on his glass plinth, uselessly poised on tiptoe.

I reached towards him with one trembling finger. I touched a jagged edge. I didn't know I'd cut myself until the red blood started pooling on the pad of my finger. The pain made me see it was real, not a terrible nightmare. Someone had smashed Carl's glass, the beautiful special pieces he'd collected for years, the glass he dusted so carefully. He knew each swirl and bubble, every mark. He'd held each piece to the light and marvelled at it. He'd searched endlessly in charity shops and jumble sales. He'd spent every penny of his birthday and Christmas money on his collection. It meant the whole world to him. Someone had smashed it all.

Who could have done such a terrible thing?

Who could possibly hate Carl so much?

I was sure I knew.

I started running up the garden, screaming.

Mick came rushing out of the back door.

'What in God's name . . . ? Sylvie? What's happened?'

He tried to catch hold of me but I pulled away from him. I ran through the door and there was Jules in the kitchen and Jake leaning against the fridge, drinking from a carton of milk. He stopped in mid swig and stared at me.

'Sylvie!' said Jules, seeing the blood on my cut hand. 'Come here, over to the sink.'

'Who hurt you, Sylvie? Tell me!' Jake said urgently.

'No one. It's not me. It's the glass. It's so awful. It's smashed, all Carl's collection – *all* of it – even the Glass Boy.'

'Oh my God,' said Jules. 'What about Carl? Where is he?'

'I don't know, I don't know!' I sobbed.

She had hold of me, keeping my hand under the cold tap, doing all the careful motherly things – but she started shaking too.

'Jake, you take care of Sylvie. Oh God, what can have happened to Carl? Mick?' She went to the back door. 'Shall I call the police?'

Mick came back in from the garden. 'Yes, right now. Sylvie's right. Everything's smashed. I can't understand it. How did anyone know the glass was in there? It just looks like a garden shed from the outside. *We* know about Carl's glass, Sylvie does – but no one else.'

Jules was looking at me. 'Who else knows, Sylvie?'

'Paul,' I whispered.

'Carl's friend.'

'Not any more. He hates Carl now. He's saying all sorts of hateful stuff about him at school. He's been so horrible. But I never ever thought he'd do *this*.'

'There now, Sylvie,' said Jake, patting me.

'You think he crept into the garden and smashed everything?' said Mick. 'For God's sake, is this boy some kind of psychopath? How did he get *into* our garden?' He peered out into the dark and then suddenly lunged forward. 'Bloody hell, he's still there! Look, over by the bushes!'

Mick started running. Jake followed him. They pounced on the figure hiding in the bushes, dragging him out.

'Oh God,' Jules whispered.

It wasn't Paul. It was Carl. He was muddy and dishevelled, stumbling and shaking his head. His sleeves were covered in something dark. Mick and Jake tried to help him up the garden. He was crying, his nose running, and he was holding out his arms oddly. The dark stuff was blood.

He struggled to get away when he saw us staring at him. He ducked his head desperately.

'Carl! Let me see your arms,' Jules said. She took one look at his blood-soaked sleeves. 'Right. The hospital. I'll drive us there – it'll be quicker than an ambulance.'

'I'm not going to any hospital!' Carl shouted

264

hysterically. 'I'm OK. I'm just cut a bit, that's all. Look, I'll wash it off, right?' He ran the tap hard on his arms, splashing water everywhere.

'Carl, love, you're going to have to go, you're going to need stitches,' said Jules. 'Your fingers are a mess – and look at your wrist!' She tried to hold him but he was flailing wildly.

'Did he cut him? I'll punch his head in,' said Jake, nearly in tears himself.

'I'm going to call an ambulance if you won't let me take you by car,' said Jules.

'We'll call the police too,' said Mick, getting his mobile out of his jeans pocket.

'Why in God's name phone the *police*? Are you going to have me arrested?' Carl shouted.

'We have to report what's happened. Sylvie thinks your friend Paul smashed everything,' said Mick.

Carl looked astonished. 'You idiot,' he said to me. He stood up straight, wiping his eyes and nose, blood dripping from his arms. 'Isn't it obvious? *I* did it.'

We all stared at him.

'Don't be ridiculous, Carl,' said Mick. 'What are you trying to do, protect this so-called friend?'

'You wouldn't smash your own collection, Carl,' said Jake. 'It would be like me smashing my guitar.'

'Oh, Carl,' said Jules. 'Whatever made you do it?'

There was a sudden loud knocking on the door.

'You didn't call the police already, did you?' said Carl.

'No, no. Jake, go and see who it is,' said Mick.

We heard my mum's voice, very cross.

'Oh no,' I said.

'Let's call in all the neighbours. Let's get the whole street to come and gawp at me,' said Carl.

Mum came storming through to the kitchen. 'Sylvie, how *dare* you disappear like that—' she started. Then she stopped, seeing Carl and the state he was in. 'Dear God, what's happened?'

'We're not quite sure,' said Jules. 'Some of Carl's glass collection got smashed and he's hurt himself picking up the pieces. Sylvie's got a little cut too, but I think she's fine. Still, maybe she'd better come with us to the hospital just to make sure she doesn't need a tetanus jab or whatever.'

'I'll take her. Oh God, no, I've had too much wine. Perhaps Gerry can drive us. I don't think he's had as much as me.'

I went to Mum and put my arms round her. 'Mum. You stay here with Gerry. I need to go with Carl. *Please.*'

Mum started arguing but Jules was surprisingly firm.

'There's no point all of us sitting in A and E for hours. I'll take them.'

She put a hand on Carl's shoulder, a hand on mine, and steered us out of the house. Carl tried to pull away when we were at the gate but she hung onto him.

'You're coming to that hospital, Carl. You're badly cut. It looks like you've got splinters of glass in your fingers. For God's sake, you're my artist son, you need to get your hands fixed properly. You could have severed a tendon. Now get in the car, both of you.'

She drove us to the hospital while we sat shivering in the back of the car. Carl was still sobbing, though he was trying hard to stop. I got the car rug and wrapped it round him.

'There now,' said Jules when we pulled into the hospital car park. 'Let's get you sorted out, sweetie.' She put her arm round Carl, tucking the rug tighter round him. 'Come on, Sylvie.'

We had to give our details to a woman at reception. Then we sat in a crowded waiting room with babies crying, drunks swearing, mad people muttering. Carl hunched up inside his rug. Jules sat between us, her arms stretched out round both of us. We still didn't talk. We were too dazed by the whole situation. Carl shut his eyes as if he was trying to blot it all out. Jules kept looking at him anxiously, her teeth nibbling at a piece of loose skin on her bottom lip. He was still shivering violently.

'There now,' she whispered. 'There now.'

Then we were led into a small cubicle and a woman in a white coat gently peeled back Carl's bloody sleeves and looked at his arms and hands.

'Ooh dear, you've gone to town here, matie,' she said. 'What have you done to yourself, eh?'

'He tripped and knocked over a glass collection,' said Jules. 'That's why he's in a state of shock.'

'I should think you are too!' she said. 'Well, we'll get you thoroughly examined and stitched up and you'll eventually be as good as new. I wish we could do the same for your mum's glasses! And now what about you, young lady? Oh, this is just a little nick. Still, we might give you a tiny stitch, just so you can keep your brother company.'

'He's not my brother,' I mumbled.

'Uh-oh! Boyfriend, then?' she said.

I took a deep breath. 'No. Best friend,' I said.

Carl opened his eyes and gave me a wry little smile.

'I'm afraid you'll have to wait a little while until there's a doctor free to stitch you up. I'm not sure if the cafeteria is still open, but you can get a tea or coffee from the machine down the corridor. That's it, try to cheer up. It's not the end of the world.'

'She's right,' said Jules when she'd gone. 'Now, I think we could all do with a cup of tea, don't you? I'll go and see what I can rustle up. You two look after each other. If either of you start violently spurting blood holler for a doctor, OK?'

She went off, and Carl and I were left together.

'I'm sorry I called you an idiot,' Carl

whispered. 'You're not the idiot, Sylvie. *I* am. I've just been so stupid. I feel so ridiculous. It's so awful. I'm not used to being like this, feeling so much, making such a fool of myself. I just couldn't bear it though. He's told everyone.'

'But *why* did he?'

'I don't think he intended to. He kept quiet and ignored me in class. Then he told the drama teacher he didn't want to be in *A Midsummer Night's Dream* any more. He said it interfered with his football practice, but then one of the Neanderthals in the team said to him, "What, don't you want to be in your fairy play any more, you little poof?" He didn't *mean* it, he was just mucking around, but Paul took him seriously and practically punched him. Then some of the others started joining in. They were just *teasing* – they all think he's fantastic, and they *know* he's straight – he's been showing stupid Miranda's tits to everyone, for God's sake. All he had to do was laugh, but he got more and more wound up. I was watching him and he saw me and he blushed. Someone said, "Why have you gone all red?" and someone else said, still teasing, "Ooh, it's the sight of his fairy playmate," meaning me. You could tell they weren't serious, they weren't putting two and two together, but he was scared and he just started yelling stuff.'

Carl stopped and took a deep shuddery breath.

'Stuff about you?'

'Yes. That I was gay and I'd tried to snog him and it made him sick. Then they all got started on me. Only this time they weren't teasing. This time it was for real. And Paul joined in. He said the worst things. And he told them stuff about me, told them about my glass collection. They started calling me Glass Boy. Then one wag said, "No, no, *Ass* Boy," and that's caught on in a big way.'

'Oh, Carl. What did you do? Did you get angry? Did you cry?'

'I just stood there like a dummy, trying to ignore them. I tried to make out that it was no big deal. I didn't really care so much about all the others. It was Paul saying it. I held it all in. I went to drama and all the boys there knew and they couldn't say too much in front of the teacher but there was a lot of whispering and no one would come near me. Then on the way home on the bus some of them were saying stuff and cracking jokes, really stupid crude jokes—'

'How can they all be so *horrible*?'

'It's just the way things are. But I still didn't react. I sneaked in at home while everyone was in the living room watching something daft on the television. I couldn't face them. I grabbed a bottle from the kitchen cupboard – cooking sherry, for God's sake – and I went out to the Glass Hut and I started drinking.'

'Why didn't you *phone* me?'

'I wanted to hide away by myself. I tried to get drunk but the sherry tasted disgusting, so sweet and syrupy, it was hard to get it down. I wanted to blot out all their voices, all the stupid crude things, all the ugliness. I kept seeing Paul and the dirty things he was shouting, and there was the Glass Boy right in front of me. It's so like Paul – I don't know whether you've ever noticed. I couldn't bear it. I didn't really know what I was doing, I just flung the sherry bottle, and it smashed him. It was so awful, I couldn't bear it, and yet I couldn't *stop* smashing, and then I cut myself and—'

Carl stopped. Jules was standing there, trying to balance three polystyrene cups of tea.

'You cut yourself, Carl?' she said. The cups wobbled, spilling tea onto the floor.

I took them from her. She sat down beside Carl.

'Tell me. I won't tell anyone else. Not even Dad. But did you cut yourself on purpose?'

'What? You mean, was I trying to slit my wrists? Well, I made a bit of a botch of it, didn't I?' said Carl, waggling his congealed fingers. 'No, Mum, I wasn't trying to kill myself. I didn't really care that I was getting cut to ribbons, but I wasn't doing it deliberately.'

'Thank God,' said Jules. She put her arm round Carl and rested her head against his. 'I know you haven't been very happy recently. I've been very worried about you. Obviously something horrible's happened to get you in this state. You don't have to tell me about it if you don't want to. Just so long as you realize you've

271

got everything to live for. You're a fantastic, bright, gifted boy, you've got a family who love you to bits, and Sylvie's your best friend in all the world.'

'Yes, Mum. I know. It's just—' Carl struggled, shivering still.

Jules gave him his tea. 'Here, drink.'

She gave me my tea too. 'Do you know what's wrong, Sylvie?'

'Well. I do now. Sort of.'

Carl took a few sips of tea. 'The thing is, Mum – oh God, I don't know how to say it. It all sounds so corny. You see, I fell in love with someone.'

'Ah. And . . . they don't love you back?'

'They hate me,' said Carl. He took another sip. '*He* hates me,' he whispered.

'Ah,' said Jules again. She took a big gulp of her own tea. 'Well, it's awful that it hasn't worked out for you this time, but I promise you you'll fall in love again – and again and again and again. It might not be quite so intense, quite so painful, but it will be *better*, just you wait and see.'

I stared at Jules. Carl stared at her too.

'Mum? I've just told you I'm gay and you're being so *matter of fact* about it.'

'Well, it *is* a matter of fact. I've thought you might be.'

'Oh God, you haven't been discussing me with Dad, have you?'

'No. Well, not your love life.'

'And you don't mind?'

'Of *course* not. You're my Carl and I love you just the way you are. I mind a little bit for Sylvie.' She reached out and held my hand. 'It's maybe a bonus for me. Gay sons are always lovely to their mums.'

'What about Dad? Do you think he'll mind?'

'Mm. Maybe a bit. He prides himself on being totally PC and non-judgemental but it might take him a while to get his head round it. He'll probably want you to keep quiet about it while you're still at school.'

'Chance would be a fine thing,' said Carl. 'They all know. Paul told them. And now they're all saying stuff.'

'Awful things,' I said.

'I never wanted you to go to the wretched school,' said Jules. 'I wish you'd stayed at Milstead with Sylvie.'

'I wish I had too,' said Carl. 'I wish we were back in the infants, doing our finger painting and pouring water out of teapots, playing house together.'

'You always bagged the best Barbie doll even then,' I said.

It wasn't a funny joke but we all laughed a lot because it was easier than crying.

Mum was waiting up when I got home at last. I'd phoned her from the hospital and told her truthfully that I only needed a single stitch, though poor Carl lost count of the number of stitches he had to endure. He was so brave too, barely flinching.

'Let me see your hand, Sylvie,' said Mum, fussing.

'It's *fine*, see.' I waved it at her. I looked around the room. There was no sign of Gerry, but I'd seen his car outside. 'Gerry's still here?'

'Yes, he's staying the night,' Mum said, going pink. 'He's gone up to bed.'

*Her* bed.

'I thought I could maybe sleep on the sofa down here,' she said.

'Oh, Mum. Don't be silly. I'm not a little kid.'

'Well, it's a bit embarrassing. Gerry didn't plan to stay, but I was in a bit of a state and he wouldn't leave me. But contrary to what you're thinking, we haven't – we're not—'

'Mum!' I put my hands over my ears. 'Don't talk about it!'

'I know. Look, it's very embarrassing for all of us. And it's obvious it is a big deal for you Sylvie. You were so *hostile* at supper.'

'No I wasn't.'

'Come *on*! We could barely get a word out of you.'

'I had other things on my mind. I'm sorry. I didn't mean to be rude,' I said.

'So you don't absolutely hate Gerry?'

'He's OK. He seems quite nice.'

'That's a bit lukewarm. He thinks you're lovely.'

'Then he's either lying or mad, because I admit I wasn't *acting* lovely. But it was truly because I was so worried about Carl.'

'Right. Carl. Are you going to tell me what's going on?'

'It's private, Mum.'

'Does Jules know?'

'She does now.'

'That's good, because she's been so worried about him. How badly has he hurt his hands? It looked like a lot of blood.'

'He's cut all his fingers. They had to tweezer some splinters out. He was so brave. I'd have cried my eyes out.'

'But he was crying earlier.'

'You've no idea what he's had to put up with, Mum. I wish I could tell you. I feel so sorry for him.'

She tucked me up into bed, giving me lots of little kisses the way she'd done when I was little. It was very late and I was exhausted, but I still couldn't get to sleep. My finger throbbed and I tucked it into my armpit for comfort. If *my* hand was hurting then Carl must be in agony.

I thought of all those boys shouting stupid insults at him. I hated Paul. I hoped Carl would start to hate him too. At least he'd be able to stay away from school for the next week or so, while his hands were healing.

I got up very early even though I was still exhausted. I wanted to be in and out of the bath-room without any embarrassing encounters with Gerry. I made myself a quick breakfast, hoping to rush off before seeing anyone, but Miss Miles came in to make her early-morning cup of tea. She usually had a few Kirby grips skewering her thin grey hair into place and wore an old fleece over her limp nightie, but today she'd fluffed out her meagre curls and was wearing a silky kimono dressing gown.

I raised my eyebrows.

'Yes, I'm in my best bib and tucker in case I frighten our special guest,' she whispered. 'I met him last night when I went to make my Horlicks. He's *very* nice, isn't he?'

'Mm,' I said, shrugging.

'Now, now, Sylvie, don't play the surly teenager. He seems like a lovely man, and very fond of your mother.'

'They've only just met each other. It's not like they're getting *married*,' I said.

'Well . . . in the fullness of time . . .' said Miss Miles.

'Oh, please!' I hadn't quite got that far. It was one thing Mum having a boyfriend, but I wasn't ready for her to get *serious*. 'I'd hate that,' I said.

'Well, if I'm being totally selfish, I wouldn't be keen either, because I'd have to find a new home and I like it so much more here! It's been lovely, almost as if I'm part of the family.' She smiled at me sweetly.

I wondered if I should say she was just like an aunty to me but I couldn't quite get the words out.

'Did you ever have your own place, Miss Miles?'

'My salary wouldn't stretch to it, dear. I always thought I'd inherit the family house, but that had to be sold for Mother's nursing care. Ah well.' She sighed. 'Something will turn up, as dear Mr Micawber always says.'

Miss Miles treated Charles Dickens characters as if they were part of her family too. Still, I lived with King Carlo and Queen Sylviana . . .

I tried to conjure them up. I could see them but they stood as still and silent as waxworks. I simply couldn't will them to life. I couldn't bear it if they were all over too.

'I'm going to see how Carl is before I go to school,' I said. 'Can you say goodbye to Mum for me?'

I was astonished to find Carl up already and dressed in his purple school uniform. His bandaged hands looked like comical white gloves.

'You're not going to *school*, are you?' I said. 'Are you crazy?'

'That's exactly what I said,' said Jules. 'Oh, Carl, do see sense. There's no *point* in your going to school – you can't even write your name.'

'Yes I can, with a bit of effort,' said Carl. He flexed his bandaged fingers. 'See. They still work.'

'Don't give me that. You were ages in the bathroom. You can barely brush your own teeth. Mick, tell him he can't go.'

'I think Carl's the one who's got to decide for himself – and it looks as if he has,' said Mick.

He put his arm round Carl's shoulders and looked him straight in the face. 'You've got guts, Carl. I'm proud of you,' he said, and then he hurried out of the door.

'Oh God, spare me that macho nonsense,' said Jules. 'You're *not* going into school today, Carl, not in that state. They'll make mincemeat of you.'

'Shut up, Mum,' said Carl as Jake ambled into

278

the room, his shirt flapping, tie hanging off, shoelaces trailing.

'Now what?' said Jake. 'Hi, Sylvie.'

'We're both telling Carl he can't go to school with his hands so bad,' said Jules, shoving cornflakes and milk in front of Jake.

'Yeah, you're mad, Carl,' said Jake. He paused. 'But if you *are* going, do you want me to come with you? In case these guys are waiting in the playground or whatever? I'd love an excuse to duff up a few of those snotty grammar-school twats.'

Carl blinked. 'Thanks, Jake. But no thanks,' he said. He poured his own cornflakes and milk. His bandaged hand slipped and the jug tipped.

'There!' said Jules, dabbing with a J-cloth. 'You're proving my point, Carl. Look, let me do it for you, love.'

'For heaven's sake, Mum, I just spilled a drop of milk. It's no big deal. I've only got cut hands. You're acting like they've both been amputated. Stop flapping so,' said Carl. 'Look, I'm not hungry. I'm going now. See you tonight. And don't *worry.*'

He stood up and gave Jules a quick kiss on the cheek. She patted him helplessly. He went to the kitchen door. I got up too.

'Bye, Sylvie,' said Jake. 'Bye, Carl. Hey. Keep cool, little guy.'

'Cheers, Jake,' said Carl.

I walked with him to the gate. 'Can *I* come with you, Carl?'

'What? Are *you* offering to duff them all up, Sylvie?' said Carl. 'Hey, do you think Jake knows *why* the boys at school are picking on me? Do you think Mum told him? Or did he hear us?'

'Whatever. I expect he just put two and two together. He's not *that* dim.'

'He seems to be acting OK about it.'

'What, did you think *he*'d start beating you up?'

'Oh, he's done *that* all my life. What about Dad? He seems to know too. Oh God, I feel like all the neighbours are suddenly going to pop out of their front doors and start waving rainbow flags at me.'

'I'm waving mine,' I said.

'Sylvie – I'm sorry.'

'Don't start,' I said, patting his bandages very lightly.

'I'm not sure how much I smashed. Was it absolutely everything?'

'Pretty nearly.'

'I'm such an idiot.'

'You're being an idiot now, going to school.'

'I'm scared stiff, Sylvie. But if I don't go now they'll all *know* I'm too scared to face them.'

'You don't have to go at all. I'm sure Jules wants you to come back to Milstead. Oh, Carl, please, that would be so wonderful. And no one would make a big deal of stuff there. They all know you and think you're really special.'

'Look, I'd give anything to be back at

Milstead. I've hated it at the grammar. It's just such a weird atmosphere, all boys together. You *breathe* the testosterone, along with that awful smell of stale beds and smelly feet. The conversation's equally murky. Everyone wants to score off everyone else and there's all the joking and the shoving and the crazy rushing around. You can't get any peace anywhere, and you can't say stuff you really feel because they say it's so *gay* to talk about your feelings.'

'So what on earth's stopping you coming back to Milstead? You know they'd have you back like a shot.'

'I don't want them to think I'm scared of them at Kingsmere.'

'That's crazy! You're just letting your stupid pride stand in your way. Oh, Carl, why do you have to be so stubborn?'

'Oh well. Maybe they'll start throwing junk at me and shoving my head down the bog and it'll be so awful I'll be out of there like a shot.'

'Do you think they really might do that?' I asked.

'No, I was just joking. Sort of. They can't do too much in lessons, can they? I'll charge out as soon as school finishes, don't worry.'

'What about lunch times?'

'Well. That won't be so great. Maybe I'll try eating my lunch very very slowly, chewing each mouthful a hundred times, so I get to spend the whole hour in the canteen.'

'I know! Come and meet me at McDonald's.

We can both get there and back at lunch time. Go on, Carl, please. Then I won't worry so.'

'OK. I'll see, anyway.'

'No, *promise*. See you there – one o'clock?'

'All right, one o'clock. Happy now?'

He blew me a kiss and then started running down the road. I waited until he turned the corner. He didn't glance back, but he waved his bandaged hand at me, knowing I'd be watching.

I wished he could wear his magic Glassworld boots so that he could outrun everyone. I wondered if we'd ever be able to play Glassworld again. I tried to invent a new chronicle in my head but I couldn't come up with any idea at all. I tried re-running old adventures but the King and Queen stared at me blankly and wouldn't speak.

I wondered if the book itself was all right. What if Carl had ripped the pages, intent on destroying everything? I wondered about creeping back indoors and going through the hole in the fence in our garden to see for myself. No, I couldn't face all that shattered glass just yet.

I trudged off to school instead. Miranda was waiting for me, surprisingly early.

'Hey, why wouldn't you answer your mobile?'

She'd texted again and again while I was waiting in the hospital with Carl, but I didn't know how to reduce the horror of what had happened into several lines of text-talk.

'I'm sorry, Miranda. I couldn't. I was at the hospital.'

'What? Did you hurt yourself? What happened?'

'It was Carl,' I said. 'He was hurt.'

Lucy was standing nearby, moodily flipping through a gossip magazine with Jenny Rawlings, a sad spotty girl who didn't have any other friends. Lucy looked up at the sound of Carl's name.

'Carl's hurt?' she said.

'What? No. No, he's fine,' I said quickly.

'Come over *here*,' said Miranda, tugging at me.

'Some people think they're it, bossing everyone around,' said Lucy. 'Yet she's just a silly *slag*. Imagine, Jenny, showing your boobs off on a mobile phone!'

'Why shouldn't I? They're lovely boobs,' said Miranda, sticking her tongue out at them both.

But when she'd dragged me to a private corner over by the canteen she took a deep breath. 'I think this photo might have been a bit of a mistake. I meant it as a laugh just to tease Paul. I didn't *really* think he'd show everyone. I wouldn't have minded just one or two of his mates – Carl, for instance – but I don't want to have them *all* ogling. Sylvie, do *you* think I'm a slag?'

'No, of course not.'

She squeezed my hand gratefully. It was the sore hand with the stitched finger. She saw me wince. 'Sorry! Hey, you *are* hurt!'

'Only a little bit. Carl's the one who's really

hurt. His fingers were cut to ribbons with all the glass.'

'Not *his* glass? His collection?'

'Don't tell anyone else ever, Miranda, swear? Paul was so hateful, him and all the others in their form, calling Carl all sorts of names – you know what they're like – and Carl got a bit drunk and then he smashed up all his glass—'

'*All?* My *Remember Me* paperweight? Bloody hell, it cost a fortune!'

'I don't know if it got broken or not. I just saw glass everywhere. All the little animals were smashed, and the Glass Boy's broken.'

'So is Carl in hospital then?'

'No, they've stitched him up. He's got these big bandages on his hands and yet he's gone to *school*.'

'He's brave. Crazy, but brave. Oh God, I love him more than ever now, don't you?'

'You don't *love* him, Miranda!' I was suddenly furious with her. 'He's *my* boyfriend.'

'No, he's not. Don't get ratty. We can both love him, can't we? I wish I could have seen him all worked up like that. He's always seemed so in control.'

'That's what's so awful. Paul's taken everything away from him. I hate him.'

'I hate him too. You'll let me hate him, right, even if I can't love Carl?' Miranda said, giving me a little shove. 'He is just so uncool, turning on Carl like that. You'd think he'd be flattered. He must be terribly insecure about his own sexuality, making such a fuss. Maybe he didn't fancy me at all? Maybe he was just trying to prove to himself he wasn't gay? Well, Carl's well rid of him. I am too. Poor, poor Carl, it'll be horrible at school for him.'

'I'm going to meet him at McDonald's at lunch time.'

'Good plan. Yeah, we could maybe go somewhere great for the afternoon, the three of us.'

'I think Carl just wants *me* to meet him. He doesn't want anyone to know.'

'I'm not *anyone*. You're my best friends,' said Miranda. 'I'm coming.'

I couldn't stop her. I half wanted her to come anyway because I was scared about bunking off school on my own. Miranda walked boldly out of the school at lunch time, as if on some official errand. I dithered along beside her, anxiously peering over my shoulder. She paid our fare on the bus and then bought us both French fries and Coke in McDonald's. Carl wasn't there yet. There weren't any grammar school boys in their purple uniform today.

'He said he would come?' said Miranda.

'He promised.'

'Text him.'

'I *have*. He's not answering.'

'What do you think they'll be *doing* to him? They can be so horrible at their school – it's like it's still in the Dark Ages. Raj said there was even one little gang that kept calling him Paki, and making out he was some kind of terrorist. I don't think they *really* thought that, but every time he put his hands in his pockets or opened up his school bag they'd shout *"Duck"* and drop to the floor, like he was going to throw a bomb at them.'

'What did he do?'

'Oh, he was so brilliant! He bought this pretend hand grenade from some tacky joke shop and pulled the pin out and hurled it at them. It made this wonderful screeching noise. They nearly wet themselves. Raj is so funny.'

'Why can't you have *him* for your boyfriend?'

'Oh, I did go out with him for a bit, but his mum and dad started fussing. They thought I was a bit wild for their precious boy.'

'Well, you are!'

Miranda smiled, taking it as a compliment. She took a mouthful of French fries and then choked. 'There's Carl!'

I turned. He was walking towards us, his bandaged hands poking awkwardly out of the sleeves of his blazer. When he saw us looking he waved his hands in the air like a minstrel, clowning.

'Wow! Impressive bandages!' said Miranda, running up to him. She gave him a big hug, kissing his cheeks, pressing her face close to his, all the things I never dared do spontaneously. Carl played up to her, making a fuss of her too. I had to stand there, waiting my turn. Carl smiled wanly, not so good at pretending with me.

'How did the morning go?' I asked.

'Fine fine fine,' said Carl, sitting down. 'Hey,

feed me a few chips, will you? Can't get my bandages all greasy.'

'*Really* fine?'

'Of course not really fine. The bastards will be making his life hell,' said Miranda.

'Well, they *did* stuff my head down the loo, but hey, my hair needed washing anyway. No, only joking. They did all scream, "*Backs to the wall, boys*", when I walked down the corridor but it was obvious they all wanted to face front to admire me. And there was mass hysteria in the changing rooms for football, with Paul locking himself in the bog to change into his football strip. Perhaps he had a violent stomach upset and needed his privacy.' Carl said it all lightly, on one note, like a camp comedian.

'Oh, Carl,' I said.

'Is Paul being a total pig?' said Miranda.

'He hasn't really got any alternative. If he's nice to me, or just mildly friendly, then all the others will call him gay too. So he's got to be the guy who starts all the rubbish behaviour and says the worst things,' said Carl.

'Stop being so insufferably understanding,' said Miranda. 'He's behaving like a little shit and we both know it. We hate him, Carl.'

'I'm the only sane one. I've always hated him,' I said.

'Oh well. Simple. I'll hate him too then,' said Carl. He couldn't keep his voice totally expressionless. I prayed he wouldn't start crying in front of us, in the middle of McDonald's.

'That's right. Hey, hey. I'll make it easy for you,' said Miranda, holding a chip in front of his face. 'Look at the chip, Carl. Follow it with your eyes.' She wafted it slowly from left to right and back again. 'See the chip. There now. You're falling into a trance. A soft and starchy potato sleep.'

'Do McDonald's fries *contain* potato?'

'Shut up and concentrate! Follow the French fry with your eyes. Follow, follow, follow, follow, follow the yellow French fry. Now you're in a trance and you will believe everything I say, even when you wake up. You hate Paul, OK? You love *Miranda*,' said Miranda.

'No, you love *me*,' I said.

'OK, you love Miranda *and* Sylvie – but she's your old old old girlfriend, I'm your exciting new girlfriend, all set to entice and beguile you.'

'You're both lovely,' said Carl. 'But—'

'No buts!' said Miranda. 'Look, you can't be rock-solid decided yet that you're totally one hundred per cent gay.'

'I know.' Carl looked at me. 'Mum says I might just be going through a phase.'

'And might you?' said Miranda, eating her hypnotic chip.

Carl shrugged. 'How should I know? I just know what I feel now. What I think. What I want.'

'You want to shag Paul?' said Miranda.

Carl blushed painfully, going as red as if she'd slapped him.

'Shut *up*, Miranda,' I said, giving her a shove.

'Maybe,' Carl mumbled. 'No, actually, I just want to kiss him.'

'Well, his loss,' said Miranda. 'You're a great kisser.'

I felt as if she'd stabbed me in the stomach. I hated the way she always had to be the leading part, centre stage. I stuffed cold French fries in my mouth even though I wasn't hungry.

'Have you had any proper lunch, Carl?' I asked.

'Here, get him a burger,' said Miranda, giving me money.

'*You* go and get it for him!'

'I don't want it. Can I have a sip of your drink though?' said Carl.

He put his big bandaged hands on either side of the paper cup and raised it carefully. He drank it down steadily. 'I wish it was beer,' he said.

'We could get some,' said Miranda. 'Yeah, let's go and buy some. We'll go to the park this afternoon. I've got heaps of money. We could buy some vodka too, get really really wasted.'

'Not a good idea,' said Carl. 'No, I'm going back to school.'

'We don't have to do the drinking bit,' I said. 'Let's go to the park, though. Go on, Carl.'

'No. Thanks for the offer though, girls. See you, Miranda.' Then he looked at me. 'See you tonight, Sylvie.'

He walked off, his cheeks sucked in, his chin up.

'He looks like a cowboy going to a shoot-out,' said Miranda. 'Oh, wouldn't he look great in a cowboy hat and denim and boots. He's going to be *such* a hit at the Alhambra.' She looked at me pityingly. 'It's this pub in town where all the gay guys go.'

'I know,' I said, though I'd never heard of it.

'It's such a cool place. You can dance there too, and they have drag acts. It's great.'

'Have you been there?' I asked.

'Yes,' said Miranda. 'Well, I haven't actually been *inside*, but I've seen it. I wanted Raj and Andy to go there with me for a laugh, but they wouldn't. Maybe we could go with Carl, Sylvie?'

'Oh yeah, like I'd be allowed in a gay pub – in *any* pub,' I said.

'I don't know. I think you're starting to look a *little* bit older,' said Miranda, tucking my hair behind my ears and staring at my face.

I started to believe her, thinking that all my misery over Carl had given me a new knowing expression, but when I went to the ladies' toilets in McDonald's I looked as baby-faced as ever. I stuck my tongue out at myself unhappily. Miranda came out of her cubicle and laughed at me. She stuck her own tongue out. I crossed my eyes and made my tongue touch my nose. She screwed her face sideways and stuck her tongue out of the corner of her mouth, drooling.

'The great kisser?' I said.

Miranda waggled her tongue around lasciviously, looking revolting.

'Stop it!' I shrieked.

A woman came into the toilets with her little girl and frowned at us. We giggled weakly and escaped.

'Are we going back to school?' I asked.

'Are we hell! No, I've just had a brilliant idea for later. But first let's have that picnic in the park.'

'With vodka?' I asked anxiously.

'Of course.'

'I don't like it.'

'Don't be silly, it doesn't have any taste. You can't *not* like it.'

Miranda marched us off to Oddbins. She whipped off her school tie, rolled up her sleeves, undid the top button of her blouse and tucked her skirt up at the waistband so it was even shorter. Then she looked me up and down. 'You stay outside,' she said.

I watched her saunter inside, strolling around, peering at bottles of white and red wine, tossing a packet of peanuts from one hand to the other. Then she picked up a half bottle of vodka and took it to the counter.

I watched the bored guy behind the counter say something to her. She laughed at him, tossing her hair, sticking out her chest. He said something else. Miranda flushed and banged the vodka down hard on the counter. She flounced out of the store, marching straight past me in her buckled boots. I had to run after her.

'*Creep*,' Miranda muttered.

'What?'

'Not you. Him. What a jerk. He called me a little kid, can you believe it!'

'So, no vodka?' I said, very relieved.

'Don't worry. We'll go to Waitrose.'

Miranda got a wire basket in the supermarket and threw some chocolate and crisps in too, plus a couple of magazines. Then she walked over to the wine section, while I hung back. It wasn't any use. As soon as she put her hand on a bottle a middle-aged woman came over and told her she wasn't old enough to purchase alcohol.

'But I'm eighteen,' said Miranda.

'Yes, and I'm Queen of the May,' said the woman. 'Go back to school, you silly little girl.'

'You can't tell me what to do, you sad old woman,' said Miranda, but she had to put the bottle back on the shelf.

She abandoned the wire basket in the middle of the aisle and walked out. She had her head held high, tossing her hair. I shuffled along after her, worried that everyone was looking at us. Miranda swore under her breath as she stomped out of the exit. First all the four-letter words she could think of. Then she embellished them with adjectives. Then she made up new swear words of her own, inventive and disgusting. Then she tailed off into childish invective.

'Old snot-nose suck-a-toe sniff-a-bum,' she said.

I burst out laughing and she did too.

'Oh well. Third time lucky,' said Miranda.

I rolled my eyes. 'Miranda. It's not going to happen. They won't let you buy any.'

'I'm not going to buy it. We'll go home and *take* it. It's a bit of a bore trailing all the way back, but it can't be helped.'

'Won't your parents mind?'

Now she rolled her eyes at me. 'They won't notice. No one will be there. Dad's at work. Anorexic Annie will be at her yoga class. The cleaning lady will be done by now and Minna's got the day off. So come on. We haven't got all day. We've got to be back in town by three thirty.'

'Why?'

'You'll see,' said Miranda.

'Tell me.'

'I said, you'll *see*,' she said.

We caught the bus to her end of town. The posh end. I walked along Lark Drive, wondering what it would be like to live there.

'You're so lucky living here,' I said.

'*What?* It's so *boring*. I'm leaving home as soon as possible. I want to live in London in one of those great warehouse apartments with high ceilings and shiny new furniture and views right over the rooftops. It will be so cool. I can't wait to get my own *space*.'

Miranda seemed to have a great deal of space already. I thought about my own tiny box room at home. I could touch both side walls when I was lying in bed. I thought of Mum squashed into the small bedroom so she could charge Miss Miles that bit extra for her big room. We could all do with high ceilings and shiny new furniture and any kind of view, not just the similar shabby semis opposite.

'What sort of a bedroom have you got, Miranda?'

'Oh, that's so boring too. It's all deep purple and bead curtains and velvet cushions and fancy glass mirrors,' said Miranda, shuddering. 'I thought it divinely decadent when I was, like, *eleven*. I keep nagging to get it all redecorated.'

I thought it sounded divine, full stop. 'Can I see it?' I asked as we got to her front door.

'Sure,' she said, twisting the key. 'Funny. It's not double-locked.'

She stepped inside, into the beautiful cream hall, the stained glass in the door panels casting lozenges of red and blue and green on the pale carpet.

'Come on, then,' she said, starting up the stairs.

Then she stopped, so abruptly that I bumped into her.

'What?'

'Ssh! Listen,' she said.

We stood still. There was a sound upstairs, a little gasp, two voices whispering.

'Is it burglars?' I mouthed. 'Oh God, should we dial nine-nine-nine?'

'No, we don't want the real police. We want

the *moral* police to come and give my mother a good bashing with their truncheons,' said Miranda, not bothering to keep her voice down. 'Yoga class! Well, she's up there in her bedroom with someone. I'm sure they're simply trying out the lotus position together – *not.*'

'You mean—'

'Yes. Honestly! I wonder who it is *this* time,' said Miranda.

'Miranda? Is that you, darling? I'll be down in a minute, sweetheart.'

'Darling! Sweetheart!' Miranda muttered. She marched back down the hall. 'I'm not going to wait to find out.'

She darted into the living room, grabbed a bottle of vodka from the drinks tray and then went to the front door.

'Aren't you going to say anything?' I asked.

'Absolutely not,' said Miranda, slamming the door hard behind us.

'Will you tell your dad?' I asked.

'I might,' said Miranda. 'But then again, he has girlfriends, I know he does.'

'So did my dad,' I said.

'But your mother left him,' said Miranda, taking a swig out of the vodka bottle straight away.

'Actually, he left her.'

'So, that's men for you. I bet *your* mum doesn't have boyfriends. I bet she does real mumsie things like cooking and cleaning and fusses around you and kisses you goodnight.'

'She does. But she *has* got a boyfriend, actually.'

'She has?' Miranda looked surprised. 'You've never mentioned him.'

'I've only just met him.'

'What's he like?'

I shrugged. 'OK, I suppose. You know. A bit dull and boring. My mum keeps on about how funny he is but I can't see it myself.'

'I bet your mum doesn't sleep with him though.'

'Well. He spent the night at our place.'

'And you don't mind?'

'I didn't really think about it. I was at the hospital with Carl. I was too busy worrying about him.'

'Don't worry. We'll fix things for Carl,' said Miranda.

'How?'

'You'll see.' Miranda took another swig of vodka.

A passing woman frowned at her. 'You shouldn't be doing that,' she said. 'I'll tell your mother.'

'Yeah, tell her. Like she'll care,' said Miranda. She took a longer swig.

'Miranda! Come *on*!' I dragged her away down the street. 'Let's go to the park where no one can see us. I wish we'd bought that picnic – I'm starving.'

Miranda bought us large 99 ice creams from the van at the park gates. She sprinkled hers with vodka.

'Mmm, yummy! Maybe I'll start marketing my own alcoholic ice cream,' she said, licking enthusiastically.

'You're turning into an alcoholic,' I said. 'Do you drink like this on your own?'

'Sometimes. When I'm feeling fed up.'

'I don't get you. Why should *you* ever feel fed up? You've got everything.'

'Money,' said Miranda, walking towards the children's playground. 'Possessions. That's about it.'

'Looks. Personality.'

'Yeah. Well. Maybe.'

'So lucky lucky you! Don't start a poor-little-me rich girl rant, please.'

'Oh shut up, Titchy Face,' said Miranda, sprinkling more vodka on her ice cream. She licked again. 'Oh double yum. Mmm. No, more like double yuck, it's gone all *oily*. Maybe it's not such a good idea.'

She threw her ice cream into a rubbish bin and sat down on a swing, stuffing the vodka bottle into her blazer pocket. She started swinging violently, kicking hard with her mad boots, her skirt flying up, showing holes of white flesh in her black tights.

'I look like a Dalmatian,' she said, plucking at them. She put her head right back so that her hair nearly swept the ground. 'Hey, come and swing, Sylvie.'

'Carl and I used to come here when we were

little,' I said, standing on the swing beside her and jerking it into action. 'We'd pretend the swings were our magic horses. Mine was a black filly with a white star on her forehead and Carl's was a pure white stallion. We'd gallop for miles through the air, racing each other. Then when we were tired and dizzy we'd set up home on that twirly roundabout thing. We played that it had real rooms, one for each section, and we'd squash up between the metal bars pretending we were in the kitchen making our food, and then we'd climb over into the dining room and make out we were eating it, and we'd watch television in the living room, humming all our favourite theme tunes, then use the computer in the study, tapping our fingers in the air, then we'd go to the bathroom and wash, and finally we'd go to the bedroom and curl up together in our tiny bed.' I stopped swinging. 'It was so real. It was as if we were really doing it, even though we were making it all up. I thought it *would* all be real one day. Carl and I would be sweethearts all through school and then we'd go to art college together and we'd share a little flat, and it wouldn't matter even if it was as pokey as our roundabout house, just so long as we could be together. Then one day we'd get married. I even had my dress planned. Not a white meringue. I thought I'd have something soft and silky and simple with high-heeled glass slippers like Cinderella, only you can't really get glass shoes, can you? And I can't really marry Carl now, only

I still can't get my head around it because it's what I've been planning for so long and it's what I've always wanted and I always thought it was what he wanted too.' My voice cracked and I started crying.

'Sylvie?' Miranda sat up, groaning. 'Oh God, I feel sick. Don't cry. Look, maybe you still *will* marry him.'

'You mean he might just be going through a phase, like Jules said?'

'I don't know. I think we can all fall in love with anyone. And even if Carl stays gay he does love you, Sylvie.'

'Do you really think so?'

'*Yes!* You never know, you could still get married, and even if you don't have sex you could still have a lot of fun together. You'd probably be very happy together, unlike nearly all the other married couples in the world. Oh God, I seriously think I *am* going to puke.'

She heaved herself off the swing and staggered to the wastebin. I held her hair back for her while she was sick. She made a horrible retching noise and groaned and grunted. I'd have wanted to die with embarrassment, but once she'd finished she wiped her mouth and then grinned at me.

'Thanks, Sylvie. This is what best friends are for, eh? Stopping you getting sick all over your hair!'

'Any time,' I said.

She reached for the bottle of vodka.

'For God's sake, don't drink any more! That's *why* you were sick!'

'No, it was because I was swinging too much. I need to wash my mouth out with something.' She took a mouthful, but then shuddered and spat it out. 'Maybe *not* such a good idea. Have you got any gum? I really have to clean my teeth.' She checked her watch. 'I suppose we've just about got time to get back to my place. Though you're nearer the park. Can I clean my teeth at your place? Or do you think we'll discover *your* mother in bed with her boyfriend?'

'Oh God, I hope not.'

'No, I know! We'll walk in on little Miss Lodger Lady having it off with *her* boyfriend.'

'Oh, don't be so mean! Poor Miss Miles,' I said, but I couldn't help snorting with laughter.

It was even harder to keep a straight face when we got home and encountered Miss Miles peeping out of her room *in her kimono*!

'Oh, girls, you startled me,' she said. 'You've caught me out!'

We goggled at her.

'I was just having forty winks on my bed after lunch. Tut tut. You'll think me such a dozy old soul.'

'Not at all, Miss Miles,' I said warmly, pulling Miranda into my bedroom.

We collapsed inside, hands over our mouths, eyes streaming. When I stopped giggling I glanced round my bedroom anxiously. It looked even smaller and shabbier with Miranda sprawled all over the bed. She'd kicked off her witchy boots and they lay toes up on my grubby fake-fur rug. She wrapped herself in my old duvet cover. It had a faded pattern of fat teddy bears, all gurning with alarming cheeriness. Miranda imitated their expression and then sucked in her cheeks.

'Yuck, I *so* need to clean my teeth. Can I be really gross and borrow your toothbrush, Sylvie?'

She padded along the landing to the bathroom. I fussed around my bedroom, hiding old socks and underwear in my wardrobe, stashing a sheaf of Glassworld jottings in an ancient pink Barbie suitcase, and rearranging my bookshelves, tucking old Flower Fairy and Little Bear books behind all my teenage titles in case she thought me retarded.

Miranda smelled strongly of Colgate and my mum's best Boudoir perfume when she came back.

'Do I look a bit better?' she said, striking a pose. 'I couldn't find any make-up in the bathroom. Can I use some of yours, Sylvie?'

'Sure,' I said anxiously. I ferreted in my drawer for my make-up bag. It was embarrassingly frugal — natural foundation, two pale lipsticks and one waterproof mascara.

Miranda's lip curled. 'How am I meant to look beautiful, babes?'

She improvised, using my pinkest lipstick as rouge for her cheeks and commandeering my

301

deep-red felt pen for lipstick. She outlined her eyes with the black felt pen and gave her lashes three coats of mascara. Then she brushed out her hair and retied it into two little decorative plaits, the rest hanging loose and glossy down her back.

'You look lovely,' I said.

'Yes, I do,' she said, smiling at herself in my looking glass. 'OK, Sylvie, you get tarted up too.'

'Mmm, bit of a waste of effort for me,' I said.

'No, no, come here. Let me have a go,' said Miranda, sitting me down on the bed.

'Don't put too much on. I'll just end up looking like a clown,' I said.

'Have faith, little chum,' she said.

She did her best. She used my felt tips again, but the softer shades, peach for my lips and grey for my eyes. Then she restyled my hair, back-combing it on top so that it couldn't go into its little-girly parting.

I peered at myself in the mirror. 'I look . . . OK,' I said. I was secretly thrilled.

'You look flipping fantastic,' said Miranda. '*Almost* as gorgeous as me. Maybe I'll be one of those makeover women on television. I've improved you one hundred per cent. Now, get out of that manky uniform and put your jeans on. I'll need to change too. I'll have to borrow something of yours.'

'But it won't fit you.'

'Yes it *will*. Granted, you're a little matchstick

but I'm not Elephant Woman, you know. I'll squeeze into something.'

Squeeze was the operative word. Miranda tried on several T-shirts but could barely tug them over her breasts. Then she picked out the blue sleeveless vest top of my pyjamas. It always looked totally little-girly on me. It looked incredible on Miranda, the straps tight on her plump white shoulders, the lace edging straining over her cleavage, clinging to her curves.

'This will do,' she said complacently. 'Now, your jeans are going to be useless on me. What about a skirt?'

She wanted something short and tight. They were all *too* short and *way* too tight on Miranda. She couldn't even get them zipped up.

'Haven't you got anything with an elasticated waist?' she said crossly.

She flipped through the few clothes in my wardrobe, making disparaging remarks.

'Look, I'm not running a dress shop,' I said.

'Hey, what about this?'

She pulled out my old purple gypsy skirt. It came down almost to my ankles but it swayed round Miranda's knees, somehow looking just the right sexy length. The waistband stretched to its limit, just fitting.

'Tra-la!' said Miranda, wiggling her hips so that the lacy hem of the skirt flew out. '*Now* I'm looking good.'

'Yes, you are,' I said, sighing.

'Right, we're ready!' She looked at her watch. 'We'll have to get a move on.' She picked up the vodka again.

'Miranda!'

'Just one more weeny swig for courage!'

'Why? What are you going to do?'

'We're going to Kingsmere Grammar.'

'Oh no we're not!'

'Yes we *are*! Don't pull that silly face at me. We *have* to go, for Carl's sake. Don't you want to help him?'

'Yes, of course, but—'

'This will work. Trust me!'

I didn't trust her at all, but I went with her all the same. She wouldn't tell me what she was intending to do.

'I don't *know* yet. We'll just have to see how it goes. How they're all reacting to Carl. Maybe he was exaggerating a bit before.'

'Carl doesn't exaggerate,' I said.

We saw that for ourselves. We got to Kingsmere just as their bell went for the end of afternoon school. There was a pause for a minute, then boys started to stream out, a purple army, running, shouting, shoving, cheeky little Year Sevens with piping voices, great loping sixth formers, and all the years in between. The Year Nines came out last, when we were beginning to think we'd missed them. Carl was there at the front, his head up, whistling as if he was strolling down a deserted country lane, though all the boys were baying at his heels, shouting insults.

'Bender.'

'Queer.'

'Faggot.'

Paul was there, calling too.

'Glass boy.'

'*Ass* boy.'

They all guffawed. Carl strolled on, still whistling, though his face was bright red.

'*Glass boy, ass boy,*' Paul chanted, and they all chorused it.

'That bastard,' I said, trembling. 'We have to shut him up.'

'I know how,' said Miranda. 'Come on.'

We marched through the school gates into the playground.

'My God, it's that girl with the tits!' someone shouted.

'The tart on Paul's phone!'

'Paul's girl.'

'I'm not Paul's girl. Paul's an idiot,' said Miranda. 'I'm Carl's girl. Hey, Carl.'

She left me and went right up to him. Then she put her arms round his neck, snuggling up close, and kissed him on the lips in front of everyone. It was a long slow kiss, stunning everyone into silence.

'But he's *gay!*' someone muttered.

'Gay or straight, he's a better kisser than any of you lot,' Miranda said. 'Silly little boys. Come on, Carl.'

She gently took his bandaged hand. They

started walking. I thought they would walk straight past me, but Carl put his other hand out for me.

'Who's *that* girl?' someone said.

'She's Sylvie. She's my girl too,' said Carl, holding my hand as well.

We walked on, the three of us, out of the school gates. There was a stunned silence behind us.

'There you are!' said Miranda triumphantly. 'Was that not brilliant!'

'*Not* brilliant,' said Carl. 'But thank you, Miranda. Thank you, Sylvie.'

We were still holding hands.

'What do we do now?' I said. 'Walk off into the sunset?'

We walked back to Carl's house. Jules was waiting white-faced in the kitchen.

'Oh! Hello, Sylvie and Miranda,' she said. She paused. 'Hello, Carl. Good day?'

'Could have been better,' said Carl. He paused too. 'It caused a bit of a stir having the two girls come to meet me.'

'I'll bet,' said Jules, glancing at Miranda in my pyjama-vest. 'Coffee, girls? And I've made chocolate caramel shortbreads.'

They were Carl's favourites, usually kept for high days and holidays. The four of us sat round the table drinking coffee and eating shortbread. Miranda started showing off, but Jules had some inkling of what she'd done for Carl and indulged her now.

We heard the front door slam and then Jake

bounded into the kitchen. He did a classic double take when he saw us sitting there. A *triple* take for Miranda's chest. He gave me a little grin and then turned to Carl.

'Watcha, squirt,' he said. 'What's your secret, eh? How come you get *two* girls stalking you like crazy and I haven't got any?'

'My natural charm?' said Carl.

'Yeah, right.' Jake paused too. 'Good day?' he said.

'You're all starting to sound like spies in a James Bond film,' said Carl. 'I take it *Good day* is code for *Did the little shits beat you up now they know you're gay?*'

'Dad says you can't *know* you're gay at your age, squirt. Same-sex crushes are part of normal adolescent development, blah blah blah.'

'Yeah, whatever,' said Carl.

'Quite,' said Jake. 'Still, *did* they beat you up? Because if you tell me which ones I'll be round to sort them out.'

'You're too late, mate. *I've* sorted them out,' said Miranda.

'In her own inimitable way,' I said.

'Phew!' said Jake. 'Fancy sorting me out some time, Miranda?'

'I think maybe I'm going to start getting more choosy,' said Miranda. 'You guys don't seem able to cope with my physical charms. I'm not sure I like being called the Girl with the Tits. Maybe I'll bind them up and wear a modesty tent for a few years.'

'Spoilsport,' said Jake.

He aimed a mock punch at Carl's shoulder. 'Glad you've got your girl army, kiddo. Just pass them my way when you're done with them.' He sat down and started munching.

'I said, I'm afraid I'm no longer available,' said Miranda. 'I'm intending to lead the life of a nun.'

'OK, OK, I get the picture, Sister Miranda,' said Jake. 'But you're not the only girl, you know.'

He paused. He looked at me significantly.

I sighed, thinking he was sending me up. 'Yeah, right, ha ha,' I said sourly.

Jules nudged me. 'He's seriously got this big crush on you, Sylvie,' she whispered.

I blinked, astonished. Miranda raised her eyebrows. Jules smiled at me encouragingly. Carl looked hopeful.

Oh God. I could see them thinking this was the perfect solution. I could have Jake as a boyfriend and Carl as a best friend, a neat and cosy arrangement with the two boys next door. But it wasn't as simple as that. I didn't love Jake. I loved Carl.

Jake was looking at me, very red in the face, though he was trying to act cool, drumming his fingers in a syncopated rhythm on the table. He shook his head, tossing his wild fringe out of his eyes. I didn't want to hurt him.

'Oh gosh,' I said in a little-girly voice. 'Stop teasing me, Jake! And anyway, even if you were serious, you're like, so much older than me, practically grown up. Mum would never let me go out with you.'

I don't know whether I convinced him but he laughed shakily. 'Yeah, I'd be seriously cradle-snatching hanging out with you, Little Titch.'

Jules sighed and poured herself another cup of coffee. Miranda started talking about all the older guys she'd been out with, seventeen – and eighteen-year-olds, even some guy in his twenties. I couldn't tell if she was making it all up or not but it didn't really matter. Her voice went on and on, while we nodded and gasped and laughed, her captive audience.

Then Jake slouched off to do his homework. He ruffled my beautifully styled hair and made silly kiss-kiss noises at me, turning it all into a joke. He went to ruffle Miranda's too, but she caught his wrist and twisted it.

'Don't try that game on me, matie. No one messes with me.' She yawned and stretched. 'I suppose I'd better be sloping off home. Oh God, it's miles away. Maybe I'll get a taxi.'

'I'll drive you,' said Jules, getting her car keys out of her bag.

'You'll have to change back into your school uniform, Miranda,' I said.

'Can't be bothered. I'll come to school like this tomorrow, eh? That'll wind them up.'

'You're the biggest wind-up merchant I've ever met,' said Jules. 'But you're a great friend to my Carl and that's all that matters to me. Come on, sweetheart.'

'OK, OK. Thanks, Jules.' She looked at Carl and me. 'You guys are coming for the ride, yeah?'

'Sorry, Miranda, we've got things to do,' said Carl.

She moaned, but Jules led her away firmly.

Carl and I were left alone in the kitchen together.

'Things to do?' I said softly.

'I want you to come to the Glass Hut with me,' said Carl. 'I can't face it by myself.'

'OK,' I said, though my heart started racing. I took hold of his hand without thinking and he winced.

'Sorry! Are your hands still very sore?'

'It's my own fault. Sylvie, do you think I've smashed *everything*?'

'Pretty much,' I said.

'Maybe – maybe I can't stand to look just yet.'

'No, let's go now. We'll have one quick look, just to check.'

'OK. What are your shoes like? You be careful, you mustn't cut your feet. And put on Dad's gardening gloves, OK? Just in case you touch anything.'

We walked slowly down the garden. We came almost to a standstill as we approached the hut.

'I want to hold your hand, but look at us, we're like bloody boxers,' said Carl, tapping his big bandage against my leather gardening glove.

'Deep breath,' I said.

I reached forward and gently edged the door of the Glass Hut open. I sniffed the familiar

earthy smell, wondering just for a split second if
it had all been some mad and terrible dream. I'd
have given the whole world for Carl's collection
still to be there, carefully lined up and colour co-
ordinated. But my foot crunched on broken
glass as I stepped inside. I switched on the light.
We stood together, breathing heavily.

The Glass Boy was still shattered, only one
foot intact. All the little glass animals were
horribly maimed. The vases were smashed too,
great shards of colour creating crazy stained
glass on the shelf. But the paperweights were
mostly OK. I picked up Miranda's *Remember
Me.*

'Thank goodness.' I turned it round and
round, holding it up to the light. 'It's not even
got the tiniest scratch. How lucky, it's your most
valuable piece.'

'It's not the most valuable,' said Carl. His
voice was thick. I knew he was trying not to cry
again.

'You mean the poor Glass Boy,' I said, looking
at the little glass foot, five small perfect toes, a
graceful arch, a slimly turned heel and then an
ugly jagged edge of ankle.

'No, I mean my special champagne flute,' said
Carl. He nodded over at the shelf of glasses.
They were nearly all broken, snapped off at the
stem, but my champagne flute birthday present
seemed untouched.

'There!' I said. 'I'm so glad!'

I could see there was a little chip in the glass

at the top. I'm sure Carl could see it too, but we both pretended it was still perfect.

'You still have a collection,' I said. 'Small and select.'

'True.'

'And you can carry on collecting.'

'Maybe,' said Carl. 'Or maybe – I don't know . . .' He started very cautiously pushing bits of coloured glass around with his bandaged hand.

'Careful!'

'Yeah, yeah, I'm being careful. Look, you pick up that blue piece, and that one, and that darker bit. Look, if we put one piece here, the other there . . .' He nudged them into place. 'There!'

I looked. I didn't see what he was getting at. 'I don't think you can mend it,' I said gently.

'No, no, I'm not mending, I'm making. Pick me out some more blue bits.'

I didn't get it until Carl made me put a tiny chip of yellow against the top blue piece – and then I saw.

'It's a bird! A bluebird with a little beak!'

'Maybe I'll start glass appliqué? It might work, mightn't it?'

'You'd be brilliant at it. And maybe later on you could learn real stained-glass making, when you're at art school.'

'And you'll come to art school too.'

'And we'll rework all the Glassworld Chronicles and get them published and make a fortune,' I said, picking up the big book.

Little splinters of glass fell from it but it was safe too.

'And King Carlo and Queen Sylviana will always live together and love each other,' said Carl.

'Of course,' I swallowed. 'Even if we don't.'

'I'll always love you, Sylvie,' said Carl.

He took a step until we stood together, the Chronicles clasped between us. He leaned his head forward and gently, softly, sweetly, kissed me on the lips.

It wasn't the kiss I'd been hoping for. But it was the next best thing.